FABIOLA FRANCISCO

Copyright © 2021 by Fabiola Francisco
Publication Date: August 12, 2021
Perfect Mess
All rights reserved

This book is a work of fiction. The names, characters, places, and incidents are products of the writer's imagination or have been used fictitiously and are not to be construed as real. Any resemblance to persons, living or dead, actual events, locales, or organizations is entirely coincidental.

The author acknowledges the trademarked status and trademark owners of various products referenced in this work of fiction. Any trademarks, service marks, product names or names featured are assumed to be the property of their respective owners and are used only for reference. There is no implied endorsement.

This book is licensed for your personal enjoyment only and contains material protected under the International and Federal Copyright Laws and Treaties. Any unauthorized reprint or use of the material is prohibited. No part of this book may be reproduced, stored in a retrieval system, or transmitted in any form, or by any means, electronic, mechanical, photocopying, recording or otherwise, without prior permission of the author. This book may not be re-sold or given away to other people. If you would like to share this book with another person, please purchase an additional copy for each recipient. Thank you for respecting the hard work of this author.

Cover design by Opium House Creatives
Cover photo by Deposit Photo
Editing by Rebecca Kettner, The Polished Author
Interior formatting: Cary Hart

Dedication

For all the curvy, full-figured women. May we embrace our beauty, own it, and love ourselves.

Chapter 1

HALLIE

"Man! I feel like a woooman… Mhhm Mhhm…" My head bops back and forth as I drive down the country road, weaving through the mountains, and bring out my inner Shania Twain as I hit a high note. Or is it a low note? I wouldn't know the difference between high and low if it slapped me in the face with a permanent marker.

Listening to the rest of the song and focusing on the empowering lyrics belting through my speakers, I take in the beauty around me—tall fir trees, some lingering snow on either the side of the road that shimmers beneath the sunny day, and the rays that peek-a-boo through the branches.

Nothing feels freer than driving through unknown solitary roads on the way to a new adventure. And I need a change of scenery like yesterday. Not that I have much experience driving through country roads, but the hour drive from the airport has been liberating. New York City may be home, but lately, it's suffocating the life out of me. Coming to Mason Creek, Montana, is exactly what I need to get back in the right mindset.

And Uncle Sal needs me. I'd do anything to help him. As much as I hate that he's hurt, the timing couldn't be better for me.

I used to love visiting Mason Creek when I was a child and wander the small town full of kind people and a strong sense of community. It was such a contrast to walking the busy streets of New York, people cursing and shoving their way through the crowds. People opened doors and said hello instead of pushing you out of the subway door, so they can steal your seat. Mason Creek felt like it was on a different timeline altogether. It's where my mom is from, though she never moved back after college, and I feel a connection to the stories she always tells me about growing up in a small town.

I hope the same sense of community still exists. I could use some kindness in my life. Exhaling, I focus on the winding road and marvel at the snow-capped mountains in the distance. So much beauty surrounds me. *I wonder what it'd be like to live here.*

As the radio station begins to get staticky, I reach for the seek button, glancing at the radio in search of it. When a song I like comes through the speakers, I try to stop the search but pass it. I fumble with the buttons on the rental car to find the station again.

Thump.

What the... I slam on my breaks, and my eyes flash to the road in front of me when I feel something hit my car. My heart pounds in my chest as I lean over my dash and see a small rabbit lying on the ground. I gasp and cover my mouth with my hand before throwing the car in Park and swinging the door open to race out to see if it's okay.

"Oh my goodness!" I crouch in front of the rabbit and stare at it with squinted eyes, holding my breath as I watch to see if it's breathing or not.

I tentatively reach out, knowing I probably shouldn't touch it with my bare hands. My hand pauses midway, and I sigh, sitting back on the ground. I can't believe I hit a rabbit.

"Come on, little guy…uh, gal? Whatever you are, be alive. Please, please be alive. I'll never let the guilt go if you die because of me, especially because I was looking for a song."

Stupid country song and staticky radio in the middle of nowhere.

I stand with my hands on my hips and puff out a breath, blowing away wild strands of hair that have fallen to my face. I look around the side of the road where leaves and branches lay on the ground in hopes that I can find something to move this rabbit before it becomes real roadkill.

Tucking my lips between my teeth, and I grimace. I'm the reason it would be roadkill in the first place. I crouch down again, hesitantly reaching out. My hands snap up to my face when I hear screeching tires.

As if covering your face would save you. You're going to end up roadkill yourself.

An old pickup truck halts right behind my car, and I jolt when the door slams.

Please don't be a serial killer.

I've watched too many episodes of *CSI* where they find dead bodies in forests. I look around at the tall trees—so many great hiding places for my deceased body—as stomping boots approach.

I could run, but he'd probably catch me in two-point-five seconds. I could lie on the ground like the rabbit and pretend I'm dead. Or I could…

"Ma'am, do you need… What the hell?" His deep voice rises with his question.

I block out of the sun with my hand and look up at the man. He's standing with his hands on his hips, looking down at the poor rabbit.

"You shouldn't stop in the middle of the road without some warning sign," he chastises. Great, another person to tell me what I'm doing wrong.

"It's a lonely country road. You shouldn't be speeding." I arch a brow, putting on my tough face. By the way his car shrieked in protest at his abrupt stop, it's obvious he was going above the speed limit.

The man chuckles, and I stand to face him head-on. If I'm going down, it'll be with courage.

"Says the girl who hit a rabbit." He juts his chin toward the poor animal still lying there. I really need to move it or take it to a vet. I wonder if there's a vet in Mason Creek. There should be, considering there are a few ranches in the area.

I blow away the hair from my face and glare at him.

"It was an accident. It came out of nowhere, and I didn't have time to brake." I refuse to admit that I was looking down at the radio. "I'll move the rabbit to the curb. You can drive around my car and continue on your merry way."

"Just take it in your car. It'd make for a great dinner."

I whip my head toward him and gasp. "That's insensitive."

"Animals are food." He shrugs as if it were no big deal, but his blue eyes shine with mockery beneath his cowboy hat. I take a better look at him—bearded jaw, strong arms flexing across his chest, and full lips. He's ruggedly handsome, and something about him seems familiar.

"You can run off." I wave him off as I formulate a plan to save the rabbit, still unsure if this stranger is a threat or helpful.

He takes a step closer to me, and his voice drops. "And what if I don't?"

My heart leaps against my chest. Wasn't Ted Bundy known for his good looks and charm? He was also a serial killer.

"I'm sure you wouldn't want a bullet to your balls." I stand tall, rolling my shoulders back. I have no idea how to shoot a gun, but I can put on my poker face in the name of self-defense.

The stranger cringes briefly and then masks his reaction with a crooked smirk. "I'd like to see you shoot a gun." He cocks his head to the side.

"Just drive around my car. I need to save this rabbit, or I'll forever live with the guilt that I killed it."

"Again, one person's roadkill is another's dinner." This time he chuckles, and it's clear he's trying to get a rise out of me.

"I think I'm going to puke," I cringe. Rabbits are pets, not food.

"Come on," he sighs. The stranger gently grabs the small animal and places it on a grassy patch in the curb near some trees.

"Thank you. I would've done that. Don't wanna take up more of your time."

"My momma would kill me if I left a woman stranded on the side of the road, even if it's her choice."

"Huh… Well, I owe your momma a thank you." I smile.

He nods and points to my car. "Now you can go."

"Right. Thanks again."

"Still would've made a great dinner," he throws out before climbing in his truck.

I shudder and take a deep breath while he drives around my car. If I can't stand the idea of eating a rabbit, how in the world am I going to help Uncle Sal run his butcher shop for six weeks?

Chapter 2

WILDER

"What took you so long?" My younger brother, Levi, crosses his arms and raises his eyebrows.

I round my truck and drop the tailgate, tugging on a heavy bag. "It's a bit of a drive to and from Carson's place. I brought a bag of his new organic supplements for our horses."

"I see that. And, yeah, I know it's further away, but you've been gone for over two hours." He arches a brow, closing the tailgate.

The woman I came across in the middle of the road delayed my trip back to the ranch. I thought she was having car trouble, but then I saw the rabbit on the ground and couldn't help but tease her a bit. She looked distraught about having killed the little fella. She was hopeful it was still alive, and I couldn't bring myself to tell her it had gone to bunny heaven.

If she knew how many animals I kill a year, she'd probably think I was a monster. It comes with the job, though. No rancher would make a living without sacrificing his livestock.

"Anyway, what's going on?" It usually doesn't matter that I take a little longer when I visit ranches outside of our area.

"You mean besides Caleb and me being up to our elbows in chicken feathers, and you're out socializing?" Levi and Caleb, one of our ranch hands, were slaughtering chickens today. While we raise cattle to sell off to butchers, the chickens are for our home and to share with family and friends.

"I wouldn't exactly call going to Carson's ranch to do business socializing." While I get along with Carson, I don't have time to waste when I have a ton of work to do.

"Did you like the mare?" Levi asks as he grabs the bag.

"Yeah, she's a great horse." I close my tailgate and follow him to the tack room.

"I'm glad. Caleb is finishing up with the chickens. We still need to gut them." He drops the bag of supplements on top of the table in the tack room.

"I'll gut them." It's the least I can do. Levi hates plucking the birds, but I got caught up today to do it myself.

"You might want to check on Caleb. I'm not going back to plucking. Done with that shit," he grimaces.

"So much for being a rancher."

"Screw you. I'm as much a rancher as you are, but something about that process freaks me out. I'm gonna check on the herd and move them over to another pasture." He claps my shoulder.

"Check the fence line while you're out there," I call over my shoulder.

"Okay, Dad," he mocks.

"Dad's out of town with Mom, asshat," I throw back.

Levi chuckles as he walks out of the barn, and I go in search of Caleb. Ranching is what I was born to do. When I was a kid, my grandpa and dad ran this place. Levi and I knew it would soon be our turn to continue with our family legacy. I can't imagine doing anything else. Not that it hasn't caused some problems in my personal life.

Sighing, I shake that thought away and find Caleb out behind the barn. He's been working at our ranch for years, and there's no other ranch hand I trust more than him. We have two more guys who work for us, but Caleb has been here the longest.

"How can I help?"

"Hey, just finishing plucking the last bird."

"Thanks, I'll get ready to gut them."

"Yeah, doubt Levi will. He was looking a little green earlier," Caleb chuckles.

I laugh along with him and get to work, my mind wandering to the woman I met on the road. I don't know many people, if any, that will stop in the middle of the road to look after an animal they just hit. It's a pretty common occurrence in this area, though I've got a feeling that woman wasn't from 'round here. And the last thing I should be thinking about is a woman, especially one who is just passing by.

By the time I finish gutting chickens, the sun has set. After packaging them and storing them in the freezer, I go home to take a much-needed shower. I'm walking out of the bathroom with the towel wrapped around my waist when a loud knock startles me.

"Shit," I mumble, scrubbing another towel over my hair to dry the excess water.

"Wilder," Levi calls out.

Shaking my head, I walk to the door, not bothering to change first, and pull it open. "Can't a guy shower in peace?"

His eyebrows lift as he shrugs unapologetically. "Caleb and I are going to Pony Up for a few beers and gonna grab a bite to eat there. Wanna come?"

"Yeah, sure. Let me change, and I'll be at the house in ten." I throw on a pair of jeans and a flannel shirt. I finish getting ready and head to the main house where my parents and Levi live.

A few years ago, I invested in a side business. I built a few cabins on our acreage to rent either long-term or as vacation homes. People are always looking to escape their hectic lives, and where better than a secluded ranch nestled in the Montana mountains? It helps bring extra income during the slower months.

I took advantage and built a cabin for myself, so I could have my own space. As much as I love my family, I needed a place that was just mine. When my sister visits from college, it's five of us in the old ranch house. Besides, at thirty-two, I wanted to feel like I had some independence since I work with my family.

The fifteen-minute drive into town goes by quickly as Caleb and I rag on Levi for having a weak stomach when it comes to plucking chickens.

"Whatever, I'm not the only one who can't stomach that. Grandpa used to hate it, too," Levi defends.

"True," I nod as I pull into the bar's parking lot.

We wave at a few people littered around the lot as we walk toward the door.

Muddled chatter fills the space in a familiar way. Pony Up is our local watering hole and a place where everyone loves to get together. It's where we celebrate our wins and cry into our glasses when we have losses. People greet us, asking about the ranch as we pass their tables.

"Hey, guys, what can I get ya?" Emma, the owner, smiles at us as she places coasters in front of each of us once we're seated at the bar.

"I'll take a beer," I say.

"Same," Levi and Caleb say in unison.

When Emma drops our beers off, she lingers. "Did you guys hear about Sal?"

"No," I shake my head and lean forward in curiosity. "What happened?"

"He fractured his leg. He's gotta stay off it for a few weeks. Word around town is that his niece came to help him. Apparently, her mom's from here, and she'd visit over the summer when she was younger, but I don't remember her."

"Did you hear about this?" I look at Levi, who shakes his head.

"Well, shit. I've got a delivery for him this week."

Emma's eyebrows raise. "I hear she's from New York City."

"Great, this is gonna be fun." Sarcasm drips from my words, and I wash them down with a healthy drink of beer.

Chapter 3

HALLIE

I spent all night studying the charts Uncle Sal gave me so I'd be familiar with the product in the butcher shop and help customers without making a complete fool of myself. Complete being the operative word since I'm prone to some embarrassment no matter how hard I try. Like yesterday with that man, who still seems familiar, and it's bothering me that I can't figure out why. He was ruggedly gorgeous and definitely not the kind of guy you find roaming the streets of New York City.

"You ready?" Uncle Sal asks from his recliner. His leg is elevated per doctor's orders, but he's in good spirits. Although it's a hairline fracture on his ankle, he's been instructed not to put any weight on it.

"As ready as can be," I breathe out, drinking my coffee and walking into the living room where he's seated.

"You'll do great, kiddo. If you have any questions, call me. I've got the phone right here." He pats the small round table I placed next to the recliner so he could have everything he needs within reach.

"All the meats are displayed already, right?"

"Yup. I got Patty to help do that yesterday. She'll be around later to check up on you and make sure you're okay."

I nod, nervous butterflies flying in my belly and stealing my words. Uncle Sal's been talking a lot about Patty, and I wonder if she's more than just a friendly neighbor. I chug my coffee as I listen to a few last-minute tips he gives me before walking toward the front door.

I look over my shoulder, glaring. "Stay off your feet. If you need something, call."

"You'll be swamped," he calls back.

"Then call Patty."

I hear him mumble something that sounds like, "I plan to do more than call her," but I ignore it. I don't need to know about any extra-curricular activities my uncle has with any female.

Anxious, I walk to the butcher shop. The air has a bite to it, but the sun's out, which feels nice. I weave through the sidewalk, passing a few locals who smile with curiosity when I cross them. When I get to Town Square, where most of the businesses are, I see the town's already buzzing. A fountain sits in the center of the square, dividing Town Hall and the park. Some people are outside the bank. The beauty salon has a few customers already sitting in chairs.

I smile as I breathe in the fresh morning air. This is nothing like what I'm used to. Despite visiting when I was younger, I'm seeing Mason Creek with new eyes. I'm no longer that little girl, and I'm still deciding if that's a good or bad thing.

I hope that I'll have time to explore the town while I'm here. I have family in Mason Creek besides Uncle Sal, and it'd be nice to see them after so many years. Between working and helping Uncle Sal, it might be tricky to find the time but not impossible. I cross my fingers and hope that being here will inspire me to climb out of the rut I'm in and get over the damage my asshole ex did.

When I make it to the butcher shop a block away from Town Square, there's already a line of people outside the brick building. Panic makes my heartbeat speed. Checking the time on my phone, I note that I'm actually early, so I don't understand the crowd.

As I approach them, I smile tentatively. "Hello…" My voice wavers with uncertainty.

A collective hello rings around me while the people stare at me. My neck begins to itch, but I unlock the door and slip in. Before I completely disappear, I duck my head out and look at everyone.

"I'll be open in fifteen minutes." Uncle Sal made no mention about people waiting for him to open. On the contrary, he told me the first hour is usually slow.

As the door closes, I hear:

"She's pretty."

"She's grown up since she was a kid."

"I wonder if she's single. My son could use a nice girl."

My eyes widen as I lock the door and stare at the shop before me. Are all those people waiting in line because they're curious about *me*? *Small-town gossip is real.*

And as bad as I've seen on TV shows. I always thought that was a *Gilmore Girls* exaggeration.

I guess not.

I switch on the light and stare ahead at the huge glass display showcasing the different meats from poultry to pork to beef. As I step close, I exhale in relief, seeing that the parts are labeled and priced by the pound. That will help identify them faster.

The gray and white geometric vinyl flooring is dated yet looks like something a hipster in New York would choose for his upscale apartment. Or pretend he chose it to avoid admitting he can't afford to replace the flooring.

That's not the case here. Sal doesn't bother with details like that. He focuses on providing quality meat, putting all his investment in local products instead of decor people aren't interested in. He's always said, "They come in for my meats, not for my decorating ideas."

The shop could probably use a fresh coat of paint, though. Despite that, it smells clean, and natural light from the big windows illuminates the shop. I wander around, looking at the black and white photos hanging on the wall adjacent to the counter. My grandpa owned the butcher shop before Uncle Sal, who inherited it later on. The photos show my grandpa working it, a young Uncle Sal smiling, and even my grandma. I was too young to remember this place when my grandpa ran it, but I've seen lots of pictures. The memories I have are always with Uncle Sal owning it.

I shuffle around the display and behind the counter, stashing my purse in the office that's in the back of the storefront. Beyond that is refrigerated storage, where Sal keeps the meat he isn't displaying yet. It always gave me a bit of the creeps to walk in there as a child, so I'm not too familiar with that area.

I keep my cheat sheet with me and take a quick inventory of each item and where the different types of meats are located in the display—not that fifteen minutes is enough time to memorize an entire layout. Hopefully, as the days pass and I get into a routine, I'll start to remember where each item is.

For now, I breathe deeply, say a quick prayer, and put on an apron hanging on the hook near the door to the backroom. The shop area isn't too big, but it will fit at least ten people at a time. That's nine more than I can help at once, and I hope they're all patient.

I look behind the counter and see the white butcher paper I'll need to wrap the meats and the plastic bags to place it in afterward. Some of the meats are in bigger sections, which I'll have to cut for customers. Last night, Uncle Sal spent a couple hours showing me how to cut them while he sat at the kitchen table. I'm no butcher, but I like cooking and buy from my local butcher in New York, so I've seen enough to have some kind of idea how to chop the portions.

I run my hands across the laminate countertop, pieces of the material chipped. I assume they were caused by the knives Uncle Sal uses. I have a feeling I've naïvely volunteered to do this as a ticket out of New York, but I'm not one-hundred-percent aware of what this choice really entails.

With a deep breath, I figure I might as well find out, rip it off like a Band-Aid, and walk toward the door, turning the lock and flipping the We're Open sign. I'm not even back around the counter, and people are piling in. They talk quickly and loudly with each other, looking around the shop as if it magically got a makeover in twenty-four hours.

I plaster on a smile, smooth my hands down the apron to dry my damp palms and switch on the number display above on the wall, which I should've done when I arrived. People already hold number tickets in their hands, anxiously waiting and smiling. Geez, it's as if it were the Queen of England who decided to come help my uncle. I'm not that big on having attention on me.

As I call numbers and help customers—grateful most are patient with my lack of knowledge and slower-than-usual service—I overhear some conversations, shocked at all the information they know about me.

"She looks like her mother."

"She's from the city, you know."

"Oh, yeah… New York, right?"

"I hear she broke up with her boyfriend."

"Maybe she came here to get over her heartbreak."

"Mason Creek is peaceful, but I'm not sure she'll get used to life here. Not being from *New York*."

Goodness gracious, I can't help but eye the women talking as I slice a cutlet from a slab of meat.

"Oh," I call out when I almost nip my finger with the knife. Note to self: Don't multitask while cutting meat.

"Are you okay, dear?" One of the women who was talking about me asks.

I nod silently and ignore the rest of their commentary. It's for the best, especially if I want to keep all ten fingers by the end of my first day.

The morning passes in a blur. It's busier than I thought it'd be, which isn't a bad thing. It's forced me into action instead of overthinking about what it would actually be like.

By noon, Patty comes by with a wide smile.

"Hi, Hallie, how's it going here?"

"Good," I nod and use my forearm to push away the messy tendrils that have fallen from my ponytail.

"Great." She claps her hands excitedly and inspects the display case from the customers' point of view. Thankfully, it's slowed down. I assume it's because people are having lunch. Thank goodness for that.

I wash my hands in the sink behind the counter and rearrange my ponytail into a bun and tuck away all the loose strands sticking to my face.

"We'll need to restock this afterwards," she waves her hand toward the display.

I nod silently, wishing there was a seat back here so I could rest a few minutes.

"Don't worry about it. I'll help you. Go have lunch, and I'll keep an eye out here."

"Really?" My eyebrows lift hopefully.

"Of course, it's why I'm here. I told Sal I'd come by so you could have lunch."

"Thank you." I breathe out, and my shoulders slump, releasing tension. "Is there somewhere nearby I can grab a quick bite? A sandwich, maybe? Does the coffee shop sell anything? I could so use coffee, too." I'm rambling but can't seem to stop.

"Take a deep breath, sweetie. Head on over to Java Jitters and take a break. You also have a sub shop around the corner."

"Thank you, Patty." She waves me off with a no-big-deal face, and I grab my purse from the back room.

I stretch my back as I walk across the town square in the direction of some much-needed coffee. As soon as I walk in, the bitter and satisfying aroma of coffee hits me, and I instantly feel calmer. Mismatched furniture is spread around the space along with couches and armchairs, creating a boho feel. Paintings decorate the walls, and I wonder if they're from local artists.

This is definitely my kind of place. I can't wait to return when I have more time to take it all in and get lost in a book.

Some people sit at tables, but it's mostly quiet. I'm so grateful for that. I need a moment to just sit and gather myself after the rush of nosy people who came into the shop. I felt like I was on display instead of the meats, everyone watching and judging me. While their intentions weren't malevolent, it was still an uncomfortable situation for me.

"Hey! How can I help you?" A tall woman with auburn hair smiles at me.

"Hi," I bite my bottom lip and look around. "Can I have a latte and…" I glance at the display, noting there are only some baked goods. With the morning I've had, I could totally indulge in some sugar instead of a nutritional lunch. "A blueberry muffin?"

"Sure thing. Do you want whole milk, skim, soy…?" Her question trails off.

"Whole milk, please." Inwardly, I cringe at choosing the full-fat milk, but it's my comfort at the moment, and I no longer have douche-canoe telling me I'm too fat to drink whole milk. I shudder at the thought of my ex and push it away.

"Coming right up." She smiles again, eyeing me. "You're the new girl, right? Sal's niece?"

I can't hold in my eye roll, and the woman giggles. "Sorry, it's just habit," she apologizes. "I'm Jessie, the owner of this fine establishment," she holds her arms out.

"Hallie," I offer my name. "Nice to meet you. And it's totally okay. Sorry for rolling my eyes, but it's been an interesting morning already."

"Oh, I bet. I heard there was a line outside the butcher shop."

"I have a feeling people wanted first-row seats to the mess I'd create in there."

"I doubt it was a mess. From what I hear, you did okay."

"Well, that's good to know. At least I passed my first test." I lean forward, whispering conspiratorially, "How many tests will I need to pass before people leave me alone?"

"In Mason Creek? The tests are lifelong. If you're new, it begins when you first arrive. Dating someone brings a whole new level of gossip. And when that relationship fails?" She shivers. "Goodness, I don't want to be on that receiving end."

I can't help but laugh. "I'd say I can imagine, but I really can't."

She leans forward as well and drops her voice. "Especially if you're dating the newly single dad in town." Her eyes widen with meaning, and I grimace.

"That must be hard."

She shrugs. "I'm from here, so I already know what to expect. You'll get used to it. And hey, you're only here for a few weeks, right? Before you know it, it'll be time for you to go back home, and people here will stop gossiping about you."

I nod. She's got a point there. I'm so glad she's kind. After grabbing my coffee and muffin, I take a seat at a small table and pull out my creased book from my purse. I turn to the page I dog-eared and begin reading. If anything is symbolic of my life right now, it's this crumbled book and the folded pages inside.

Sighing, I focus on the story instead of my life and drink the warm latte.

Halfway through the chapter, I hear someone shriek, "Hallie?!"

My head snaps up." Oh my goodness, my grandma told me you were here, but I didn't believe it. You should've called me!" My cousin, Joy, bounces on her toes before taking a seat.

"Hey! Sorry, sorry," I grimace. "It's been a bit crazy. As soon as Uncle Sal called to tell us about his injury, I packed a bag and offered to come. I was gonna call you soon. Promise." Joy's grandma and mine were sisters. Although hers is still alive, mine passed when I was younger.

"How are you?" Her eyes shine with joy, perfect for her name.

"I'm good, and you?"

"Good, great. You know I took over Grandma's bakery, right? I sell some of my pastries to Jessie."

"Yeah, that's fantastic. I'll have to go see it soon."

"I'd love that," Joy smiles. "We should catch up after work one day. We can have coffee or go to Pony Up for a drink. Whatever you want."

"I could indulge in both coffee and a drink after this first day," I joke.

Joy laughs. "I get it. I'm so glad I saw you and that you're here. I gotta run, but we'll be in touch, okay?"

I nod, so happy to come across a familiar face. Joy and I would hang out together when I was younger and would visit my family. We've kept in touch throughout the years, thanks to social media. It's helped to maintain a close friendship even if we live across the country from each other and aren't first cousins.

I place my book back in my purse and finish my muffin before taking my coffee with me and heading back to the butcher shop. I don't want Patty to think I'm taking advantage of her help.

"I'm so glad you're here," she says when I walk back in. She's weighing ground beef while she talks. "Wilder is here to drop off a steer Sal ordered from him, but I can't go out there. Go on back, and I'll stay here."

"Wilder?" My voice cracks at the memory of that name. Patty furrows her eyebrows as she looks at me.

"Yeah, didn't Sal tell you about him?"

I shake my head. "He must've forgotten," I murmur as I walk around to the backroom and out the door that leads to the outside area behind the butcher shop. The name Wilder isn't very common, less so in a small town like Mason Creek. My heart beats furiously as I head outside to face my childhood crush…looking like the epitome of a hot mess.

As soon as I see the man holding a steer, a live one, I might add, I realize why the stranger I met on my way to Mason Creek looked familiar.

Wilder James. He never really paid attention to me. Being older, he was preoccupied with helping out on the ranch and hanging out with his friends, but I would daydream about those piercing blue eyes looking at me. And when they stare up to make contact with mine now, surprise recognition flashes in them before he scowls.

"Oh great, bunny girl is taking over our town's butcher's job."

Chapter 9

WILDER

You've got to be fucking kidding me. I stare at bunny girl, wondering what the hell is going on. She crosses her arms and furrows her eyebrows.

"You're Wilder? Wilder is you?" She's talking nonsense.

"Uh, yeah, I'm Wilder." I pat the side of the steer. "Sal ordered this steer. I heard he was injured and his niece was helping out but…" I eye her. How is someone who couldn't leave a bunny in the middle of the road going to run this place?

"Yup, that's me, Hallie." She's staring at the steer. "What am I-I s'posed to do with that?" She points at it.

I snort and shake my head. "Clearly, kill it." I lift a brow, taunting her. "I told you animals are people's food."

She blanches at my response, her body tensing. "Kill it? Me?" She points to herself.

I smile but remain silent, not denying or confirming it. She begins pacing, hands on her hips, and mumbles to herself.

"How am I gonna do that? I can't even get rid of the guilt of running over a damn rabbit. Kill a cow? With what? A gun?" Her voice gets progressively higher-pitched, and her arms begin to flail.

She looks like she's about to cry. Her chest heaves rapidly with each step she takes. Feeling sorry for her, I clear my throat. Her head snaps up, and she looks at me with bewilderment, almost like she forgot I was here.

"You're still here."

I lift my brows and nod slowly. The last thing I need is to deal with someone else's breakdown. Red creeps up her neck and cheeks.

"You can leave the cow here. I'll ask Sal what I'm supposed to do with it."

"It's a steer, and from past experience, you'll let it loose and encourage it to run away into the wilderness," I quip.

Her bottom lip gets lost behind her teeth, and she grimaces. "Guilty. Don't get me wrong, I like meat as much as the next person, but not while it's living, and I'm responsible for selfishly taking its life to satisfy a human desire." She pauses, her cheeks turning a darker shade of red. "That came out wrong," she quickly adds.

I hold back my laughter and shake my head. "I don't have time to waste. I gotta get back to my ranch. It doesn't run itself, you know. Let Sal know I dropped off the steer he ordered and have him set up the pick-up with Paul, his slaughterman."

"Slaughterman?" Her eyes narrow, finally catching up.

I smirk and nod. "I don't expect you to kill this big guy," I slap the side of the steer. "But lucky for you, Sal has a guy that takes care of the dirty work. You'll just have to butcher it once they return it dead and cleaned out. Think you can handle that?"

Her eyes flare with anger, but I don't wait for her response before I turn and walk away, leaving her with one of the best steers on my ranch. I pray she doesn't let that animal go the way she tried to save the rabbit. Something tells me that given the chance, she would.

As I drive back to the ranch, my thoughts run in circles. What are the odds that bunny girl is Sal's niece? She had the same deer-in-headlights look today as she did yesterday when I ran into her on the road. I have no idea how this is going to work. From the looks of it, she has no idea what she's doing. Sal is going to have to train her a bit better, so she at least knows that the steer will be slaughtered by Sal's guy and not her.

I have a feeling the next few weeks are going to be a challenge if I have to work with her on my deliveries. Sal knows the business—it's seamless with him. Now there's a city girl trying to run his business, and it's sure to be a disaster.

She may be beautiful, stressed and all, but I don't have time to waste talking someone off the ledge each time I need to see her.

Tightening my fingers around the steering wheel, I take a deep breath and release my frustration. I also shouldn't be thinking about her in any way but professionally. I'm not in the market for heartbreak.

I normally wouldn't go out this often during the week since I wake up at the ass crack of dawn every day, but after dealing with Hallie, I took up my brother's offer to come to Pony Up. I need a distraction, even if it comes in the form of amber-colored beer.

Levi shoves my shoulder as I'm going to take a drink, causing some of the beer to slosh over the rim. I glare at him, but he's too busy looking over my shoulder.

"Is that the new girl? Sal's niece?"

I frown, place my glass on the tabletop, and look behind me. Sure enough, Hallie is walking next to Joy with a tentative smile as she looks around the half-full bar.

"Yeah," I grunt in disinterest and turn back around.

Levi keeps staring at them, unnerving me.

"Stop," I growl lowly.

"What?" His wide eyes stare at me.

"You're being a creep by staring like that. They're gonna see you."

"So?" he shrugs and narrows his eyes in my direction.

"I didn't have a pleasant experience with her today."

Levi snorts. "When do you ever have pleasant experiences with people? Especially women."

I ignore his jab and take a chug of beer. He's not wrong, of course, but admitting that will open a whole can of worms I don't want to deal with. Some things are better left untouched and locked away in a fading memory box in your mind.

"They're coming our way," Levi whispers.

"What? Why?"

"How the hell would I know?" Levi furrows his brows, and then his head snaps up. His face transforms from a what-the-fuck look to all smiles.

"Hey, ladies." He leans back in his chair, looking relaxed and confident.

"Hey," Joy says. "What's up, guys? I heard Madelyn is coming next weekend."

"Yeah, she's got a couple extra days off school," Levi tells her.

"Awesome, I'm gonna call her so we can hang out." Although Joy is a couple years older than my sister, Madelyn, they're great friends.

"This is Hallie. Wilder, you met her earlier today. Levi, she's Sal's niece."

"Yup, hey," I offer a tight-lipped smirk and nod.

She shifts uncomfortably, avoiding my eyes as she nervously tugs her sweater by her ribs. It seems as if she wants to run in the opposite direction, and I blame the awkward encounter we had earlier today.

"Hi," Hallie gives me a fake smile before turning to my brother.

"Nice to meet you," Levi says, sitting straighter in his chair. "You wanna sit with us?"

"I'm gonna introduce Hallie to Emma, but thanks anyway." Joy waves at us before leading the way to the bar.

"Man, you really were unpleasant. Hallie looked like she wanted to run far, far away from you," Levi snickers. "What the hell did you do?"

"Nothing," I defend.

He scoffs. "Yeah, right."

"She has no idea what she's doing, and Sal didn't prepare her at all. She thought she had to kill the steer. Freaked the fuck out."

His eyes widen before he tilts his head and narrows them. "Did you tell her she *had* to kill the steer?"

"Do you think I'd do that?" I point to myself.

"Yeah," he doesn't hesitate. "I think that's exactly something you'd do to the poor woman."

I roll my eyes. "She assumed that's what she'd have to do."

"I'm calling bullshit. Don't torment her. She's only here temporarily and is trying to help. Jesus, you're an ass." Levi shakes his head, drinking his beer. It's probably to stop himself from saying anything else.

A few years ago, I kinda became a grump. The women in my age range don't bother with me anymore, instead preferring to hook my younger brother. He's funnier anyway, always has been more charismatic.

"It was a damn joke." I throw my hands up. "I eventually told her to call Sal and ask him to set up a pick-up with Paul." My lips quirk as I remember how relieved she looked when she realized she wouldn't have to do the dirty work.

"Whatever," Levi changes subjects. "Could you pick up Mom and Dad from the airport tomorrow?" He looks at me over the rim of his glass with raised eyebrows. Our parents went on a short trip to California. They always planned to travel more once my dad retired, and my mom's made sure he's kept his word. After years of sacrificing certain things in life for working the ranch, they finally get to do things they always dreamed of.

"No can do. I'm heading to Carson's ranch to pick up the mare."

"Why do I bother asking?" He shakes his head.

"Because you're naïvely hopeful," I shrug.

"Whatever," he grumbles.

I scan the bar, trying to resist the temptation to look in Hallie's direction. I wonder what she thinks about our little town. I'm sure it's nothing like she's used to in New York City.

"Hey, guys," Brayden, my best friend, says as he takes a seat at our table. I welcome his distraction. "What's going on?"

"Just met Sal's niece," Levi tilts his chin in her direction, sitting at the bar beside Joy, chatting with Emma.

"I heard about that. What's she like?" Brayden looks behind him. "Is she with Joy?" His lip curls.

"Yup," I smirk.

He turns around and shakes his head, jaw ticking. "Anyway, how's the ranch?"

"It's good. Cattle look great, and we've got a county fair coming up."

"That's great, happy to hear that. Good to see you're investing your money wisely." Brayden has been my best friend since we were kids. His family owns Bradford Bank, our local bank in Mason Creek. He's the CEO, part of a generation of Bradford men who have taken on that role.

"Definitely investing it wisely," I say. He's my go-to guy when I have a question about finances since he understands numbers better than I do.

He taps the table and looks over at the bar. "Service is slow or what?" He looks around. "It's not that full here tonight."

"Emma is short-staffed, so we have to grab our beers at the bar," Levi informs.

"Great," Brayden breathes out and stands.

Levi chuckles. "I'll bet you a beer he gets into it with Joy."

"He wouldn't bother going near her."

"You sure about that?" His eyes twinkle under the low lights.

I look toward the bar and watch Brayden glaring at Joy, who stares back with anger. Hallie looks between them with a raised eyebrow before turning her eyes to our table. As soon as our eyes lock, hers widen, and she bites her bottom lip. Brayden's confrontation is forgotten as I take in her round face, doe eyes, and plump lips.

"Who's the creep now?" My brother taunts.

I break eye contact with Hallie and scowl at him. His response is a resounding cackle that draws attention. I run a hand through my hair and finish my beer. The last thing I'm looking for is a complication.

Chapter 5

HALLIE

I turn and twist on my seat, trying to get comfortable. When Joy stopped by the butcher shop before closing time and asked if I wanted to get together for a drink, I desperately agreed. My first day working here was interesting, to say the least. The gossip continued throughout the day, and Patty left shortly after Wilder dropped off the steer so she could check in on Sal. Thankfully, Sal called his guy to pick up the steer.

I don't know if coming out was the best idea, though. I hate being the center of attention, and being the newcomer in town shines the brightest spotlight on me. It's obnoxious and makes me self-conscious. It doesn't help that I threw on the first sweater I found, and it marks my stomach, so I keep tugging it away from my body to stretch it out a bit.

"How's life in New York?" Joy smiles with fascination. When I was younger, we'd keep in touch through e-mail. Then, we had social media as a way to stay connected.

"Good," I shrug.

"That's not too convincing." She gives me a sideways glance, but her gaze snaps to her right when she hears a deep voice.

"Ever heard of personal space?" Joy snaps in a way that seems uncharacteristic.

The guy that was just sitting with Wilder glares at her and turns to the bartender, ordering a beer.

Once he leaves, I widen my eyes. "What was that?"

"Nothing," she waves me off. "Back to our convo. Don't you have a boyfriend in New York? I remember seeing that on social media."

I flatten my lips and shake my head. "Not anymore."

"Oh, I'm so sorry." Joy scrunches up her nose. "Darn, I'm the queen of bringing up awkward conversations."

"It's okay. It's definitely for the best. Tell me about your bakery?" I switch gears to a safer topic. Anything made of flour and sugar is my jam.

The way Joy smiles, I know she's proud. "I've been running it for a few years. After becoming a pastry chef, I inherited the bakery from my grandma. Although she always said I didn't need that kinda schooling, baking runs in my blood. Anyway, when I took over the bakery, I gave it a more modern spin with the decor. I almost changed the name to Joy's Sweet Spot instead of The Sweet Spot, but I read too many romance novels to ignore that innuendo," she giggles.

I can't help but laugh along with her. "I'd think the same thing. Although, Sal did name his butcher shop Sal's Meats. Knowing him, it was purposeful."

We both laugh as we take a drink of wine. The fruity white wine tickles my throat as I swallow.

"I guess if you're single, you might have a chance with a certain local," Joy's eyebrows waggle.

She knew about my silly crush on Wilder when we were younger. I wish I could say I'm unaffected, but as a grown woman seeing the type of man Wilder has grown up to be, I'm more curious about him. Even if he seems to have turned out to be a jerk by the way he treated me earlier.

"He has a…" Joy shakes her head to interrupt me.

"Really? I thought—"

"It didn't work out." She shrugs and sips her wine. I remember Joy telling me about Wilder and his girlfriend when we were younger. By the sounds of it, they were unbreakable. I guess everything can shatter if you don't take enough care of it.

Unable to stop myself, I glance over my shoulder toward his table. His tall, broad frame seems too big for the wooden chair he's sitting on. The way his muscles flex and relax as he grips his glass and runs a hand through his messy hair. It's not man-bun long, but it's long enough for him to slick back and that a few stubborn strands come over his eyes.

Basically, he's hot as hell with his strong body, rugged style, and broody energy. And me… Well, I'm nothing spectacular. Not to mention I've got more than a few pounds I need to shed. I doubt I'm anything like the kind of woman Wilder James would take a second glance at.

Unaware of my inner thoughts, Joy tells me more about Mason Creek.

"Alana manages the grocery store, and she's super sweet. We've been friends forever. Maybe I can introduce you this weekend. You already met Emma," she points to the bartender, who also owns Pony Up.

I nod. Emma's been really nice tonight.

"The bookstore is amazing if you like reading. Laken owns it. I'm a romance junkie, so I go in whenever I can and stock up. Besides, I love supporting our local businesses," she continues to tell me all about the different businesses before moving on to the locals.

"Lenora is Laken's sister, and she owns Squeaky Clean, a cleaning service. She's dating Malcolm, our mayor. He was a major playboy before he fell for the single mom. Olivia owns Queen's Unmentionables, a lingerie store. She comes from a wealthy family, but she's super down-to-earth."

I glance toward Wilder's table again, unable to talk myself out of it, and my face heats when he catches me. I quickly snap my head to the bar and pay attention to Joy.

"Mrs. Harley is a town gossip. She'll make sure to spread news before anyone else. She takes great pride in it. I try to avoid her because I don't like my personal life to be out in the open. However, she always manages to know what's going on. The running joke in town is that she's got all our houses tapped." Joy chuckles.

"Once, she gossiped about Mrs. Turner's daughter, so in turn, Mrs. Turner shared some insider info she had on Mrs. Harley. You know, giving her a taste of her own medicine. Well, Mrs. Harley didn't like that—such a hypocrite—and now the two women are sworn enemies. At the age of sixty. It's insane, but that's life in a small town."

"That sounds insane, but hat's off to Mrs. Turner for standing up to Mrs. Harley," I say.

"Yeah, a lot of people were happy about that. Mr. and Mrs. Bradford own the bank and are good people, even if their son is a pig." Joy rolls her eyes.

"Who's their son?" I furrow my eyebrows. The last name doesn't ring a bell.

"That hunk of a man sitting with Wilder and Levi," Emma sneaks up on us and giggles when Joy glares at her.

"I'm only kidding." She raises her hands. "I've got my own hunk."

Joy turns her head and glares at the same man who came up to the bar earlier. As if he could feel her death stare on him, his eyes find hers with as much fiery anger.

"Okay, I need to know what happened there." I point between them.

Joy grips my hand and lowers it. When I look back at the table, Wilder is clapping the guy's shoulder, and Levi is chuckling.

"Another day. I don't want to ruin our night out." She gives Emma a warning look. "Anyway…Mason Creek is a great town."

I nod.

"Do you want to order food?" Emma asks.

"Sure," Joy responds and looks at me. "Wanna share some nachos and wings?"

"Yea, that'd be great. All I had today was coffee and a muffin, so I should eat something if I'm going to drink another glass of wine."

"Sounds great. Do you want another glass, too?" She asks Joy.

"Yeah, definitely, thanks." She looks at me. "Emma's boyfriend's parents own Faulkner Farms. His name is Aiden." Joy giggles. "Maybe you remembered that. I'm talking to you as if you're totally unfamiliar with this place."

"I appreciate it. It's been way too long since I've been here, and the memories I have are from childhood. It's very different than being an adult here."

"True that. You're here for six weeks?"

I nod, swallowing a drink of wine. "Unless the doctor prolongs Uncle Sal's recovery time."

"Six weeks is better than none. I'm glad you're here." Joy's smile is genuine and contagious. It's been a long time since I've felt this welcome in any aspect of my life, which is a sad admission. When my eyes dart toward Wilder, he's staring at me with narrowed eyes. If only everyone was as welcoming as Joy.

Sighing, I ignore him the rest of the night. I don't need another man telling me how bad I am at everything I do. A shudder travels down my spine. I blink away tears at the memory of all the hateful things my ex said and focus on the fresh glass of wine in front of me.

Chapter 6

HALLIE

I survived my first week without any major mishap. I feel a bit more prepared working with the locals as well. Sal has given me a crash course in the evenings, and Patty comes by to give me a hand and relieve me for lunch. It's been such a welcome change from life in New York. The pace is slower. Everyone says hello and holds doors open for each other.

As far as helping Uncle Sal around the house, there's not much to do. Patty is there almost all the time, and I'm starting to believe they are definitely more than good friends but don't want to think too much about that.

I'm closing up shop when my phone buzzes in my back pocket. I press the finicky door with my knee so I can get the key turned while I fish my phone out of my back pocket.

"Hello?" I exhale.

"Hey, sweetie, how are you?"

I hold the phone between my ear and shoulder and turn the key.

"Good, Mom. How are you and Dad?"

"We're good. We miss you, though."

"I miss you, too." I straighten and hold the phone, walking to Uncle Sal's house.

"How's Sal? Is he resting? He better not be ignoring the doctor's suggestions. You know how stubborn he is."

"Breathe, Mom…" I roll my eyes. "He's good and resting."

"I'm happy to hear that. You're really okay?" Her voice drops.

"I am," I say with all the promise I can muster. For the first time in a while, I really think I'm doing okay.

"You sound good," she says softly.

"You see, I'm not lying to you." I move around a few people on the sidewalk who smile and say hello. I respond before listening to my mom again.

"Look at you, greeting people. Are you heading home? I assumed I'd called you at the right time."

"Yup, heading home now. I was locking up when you called."

"I wonder if it's changed a lot," she whispers wistfully. It's been years since my mom visited her hometown. Traveling across the country is expensive, and living in New York is already a hefty price tag to add in yearly trips to Montana when Uncle Sal could visit us in the city.

"I don't remember much about it, but it seems pretty much the same. There are new shops and stuff, but that's expected."

"Yeah," she sighs. "Anyway," her voice rises. "You received a letter today. It was from Jeff, so I took the liberty to open it."

My heart stops. Why the hell would my ex-boyfriend be sending me a letter? It's definitely not a love note with the way we left things.

"What does it say?" I hold my breath.

I don't realize I've stopped walking until someone says, "Excuse me," so I can let them pass.

"He's charging you for half the deposit of the apartment."

"What?!" I screech way louder than I mean to. I look around and see a few people whispering. Panicked, I start walking again. "That's impossible. I didn't even move in. I never even gave the okay for that apartment. He chose all that on his own and then added my name to the contract without fucking consulting me." I don't even apologize for cursing.

"I know. Your dad is going to look into it."

"Thanks," I say quietly. "I told him that apartment was way out of my budget, even if we were splitting the rent." Why must my biggest mistake continue to haunt me?

"I don't think he can really force you to pay since you didn't sign an agreement."

Thank God for that.

"I hope you're right. Jeff's a jerk, and he'll push it."

"Don't worry about that for now. I just wanted you to know what was going on." As always, Mom and Dad to the rescue. It's one of the things Jeff would always throw in my face.

"Thanks, Mom," I choke up and clear my throat. "I gotta go. I'll talk to you later, okay?"

"Okay, love you."

"Love you, too." I hang up and look at my surroundings. I'm still near the square, and when the neon lights that read Pony Up shine at me like a beacon, I grasp on, and my feet carry me over.

I walk through the Saturday evening crowd, people dressed casually, some men wearing their cowboy hats, excited chatter echoing off the walls. It's the total opposite of how I feel inside. I drag a stool back at the counter and take a seat.

"Oh, you do not look happy today." Emma frowns.

I shake my head. "Long day," I lie.

Although she narrows her eyes in disbelief, she doesn't press. "What can I get you?"

"Whiskey sour, please."

"Ouch," she teases.

I finally crack a smile.

"Coming right up."

She hands change to someone down the bar and then prepares my drink. It's barely hit the counter before I'm slurping a chug. Ignoring Emma's raised eyebrows, I grab a napkin and wipe my mouth.

As she goes off to serve other customers, I wallow. How can Jeff do this? I knew he was a jerk, but this is taking it to a whole different level of douchery. I had to deal with enough in our relationship. Not to mention, I get to become one of the cliché statistics that caught her boyfriend cheating on her…with a tall, stick-skinny modelesque woman. He always did say I wasn't skinny enough, so I guess he got someone who would better suit his fantasy. At least she had the decency to tell me when she found out. It seemed as if Jeff was two-timing the both of us.

Why not just break up with me?

It's like he got a sick pleasure for putting me down with his hurtful and cutting words. And I was the idiot that put up with them, too insecure to see it for what it was in that moment. He tore me down so much, I believed no one else would want me.

I swirl the thin straw around my drink, blending the water from the melting ice with the alcohol that will hopefully help me forget the conversation with my mom. The butcher shop is closed on Sundays and Mondays, so my weekend has officially begun, and I'm drinking to that.

I let Uncle Sal know I'll be home a little later and look back into my glass as if it holds the secrets of the world. Or at least, advice on how to finish dealing with my douche-cunt ex. With each drink I take, I hope it transforms Jeff into a faded memory I can hardly recall.

After I sway on the stool while ordering a second drink, Emma suggests I order some food to go with it. I nod, deciding on a burger because I know she's right. I've been in enough circles of gossip this week that I don't need to add a drunken scandal at the local watering hole.

Laughter catches my attention, and I look toward the entrance. My heart halts when I see Wilder and Levi walking in with a woman. By the resemblance, I'd guess she's the sister Joy told me about. I face forward again, curling my shoulders and ducking my head to hide inside of myself. I'd rather go unnoticed.

When Emma serves my second drink, I mumble a thank you and go back to staring at the whiskey, holding together my sanity. An excited voice a few spots down greets Emma, and I glance that way to see Wilder's sister. Both women talk so confidently. I can see it in the way they carry themselves. Then there's me, self-conscious and insecure. My relationship with Jeff didn't do anything to help that. On the contrary, he's responsible for it expanding and almost consuming me. I'm a work in progress, still searching for the elusive self-love everyone else seems to find.

I take a deep breath and blink away tears. I promised myself I'd be stronger than this. That I'd work on myself. Instead, I packed a bag and ran away the first chance I got. But New York was smothering me. I was stuck in the same loop, unable to break the repetitive cycle that was draining the life out of me. Not to mention the lack of funds from not finding a job in my career choice. I should've known being a financial advisor in the city would be competitive.

"Hey! I've been calling you." Joy's loud voice interrupts my thoughts.

"Oh, hi. Sorry, my phone's in my purse, and I haven't checked it."

"What's wrong?" Her nose scrunches.

"Nothing," I shake my head quickly.

She narrows her eyes and sweeps her gaze over me.

"I don't buy it." She sits next to me. "Talk to me."

"I'm okay, really. Just a long day." I force a smile.

"I don't believe you, but I'll drop it. I'm here to meet with Madelyn. Remember I told you about Wilder's sister. I was calling so you could join us. She's super sweet, and I think you'd get along."

I scrunch up my face and shake my head. "I appreciate it, but today's not a good day. Besides, I probably smell like a dead carcass since I came straight from work. Just gonna finish this and go home." Right on cue, Emma drops off my burger and fries.

"I'll sit with you a bit," Joy offers.

"You don't have to." I don't want her to feel obligated to babysit me.

"I want to," she assures me.

"Thanks. Want half of this burger? It's too much for me." I stare at the huge burger on my plate. It smells delicious, with gooey cheese melting off the sides and seasoned fries next to it on the plate.

"No, thanks." She eyes me as I pick up half of the burger and take a bite. "Are you sure you're okay? You can talk to me if you need someone to listen. I promise not to gossip after."

I finish chewing and nod. "I know you wouldn't. It doesn't have to do with that. I just want to forget about it for tonight."

I trust Joy, but I'd rather not rehash my conversation with my mom and get into my relationship with Jeff, especially in a public place.

"Okay." She nods and orders a beer while I take another bite.

"This is seriously the best burger I've ever had." I cover my mouth as I speak, forgetting my manners by talking with my mouth full, but this burger is so juicy.

"Thanks, we buy our beef from Sal. It's local," Emma calls out from a couple feet away after hearing my moan and compliment.

"Comes from Wilder's ranch," Joy whispers.

I swallow thickly as flashbacks of the steer he dropped off jump to the forefront of my mind. It's not the same steer, but it could be its brother or cousin. Great, now I feel guilty for eating this. How can he raise cattle and then eat it afterwards? Aren't they like pets?

"Now I'm picturing a poor cow," I confess.

Joy laughs loudly, holding her stomach.

"You'll get over that quickly. Besides, it's too good to pass up because our human minds are weird."

She's got a point. I take another bite and enjoy my dinner.

"Hey! Here you are." A female voice squeals as I'm taking a bite.

"I am! How are you?" Joy hugs Madelyn. "This is my cousin, Hallie. She's Sal's niece. This is Madelyn, Wilder and Levi's sister." She introduces me.

I finish swallowing my bite and run my tongue over my teeth before smiling. The last thing I want is to smile with food between my teeth.

"Hey, it's nice to meet you."

"You, too. Joy's told me you are in town for a few weeks."

"Yeah, I'm helping my uncle while he recovers from a fracture."

"So cool. You live in New York, right? It must be such an amazing city."

"Yeah," I nod noncommittally.

New York seems great to the outside world, but the day-to-day life loses its charm. I can admit it's different than anywhere I've visited, but it's also exhausting and catty.

"Do you guys wanna come sit with us?" Madelyn's blue eyes widen.

"Go ahead," I tell Joy.

"But…"

"I'm gonna finish this and leave. I appreciate it," I tell Madelyn. "It's been a long week, and I'm looking forward to taking a hot shower and reading." I smile, hoping it looks genuine.

"Oh, okay. I was looking forward to getting to know you. Maybe we can have coffee tomorrow?" Madelyn looks between Joy and me.

"Definitely," I answer. I don't want to seem rude.

"Awesome. It was great meeting you, Hallie."

"You, too." She seems really sweet. I glance toward their table to see Wilder and Levi talking.

"Call me if you need anything," Joy whispers as she hugs me.

"I will. Thanks."

As they walk away, I hear Joy ask Madelyn if Brayden is joining them. I assume that's the guy from earlier in the week that she clearly was uncomfortable around.

Sighing, I look down at my food, pick a few more fries and finish the half I was eating before paying and walking out. All I want to do is wash away the day.

Chapter 7

WILDER

Against my better judgment, I stop at the butcher shop while I'm in town. I admit I used my trip into town as an excuse to see Hallie, but I'd rather not share that bit of information with anyone.

She's been on my mind since I saw her at Pony Up on Saturday, sitting alone at the bar. She turned down Joy's invitation to sit with us, and I couldn't help but notice how sullen she looked. Even the likes of me could tell something was wrong, and I hate admitting it to myself. I shouldn't care, but guilt about how I treated her when I brought the steer has been sitting pretty heavy on my mind when Levi made it a point to call me out on it.

When I walk in, I'm surprised to see Patty tending the customers. She smiles my way and continues weighing the meat on the scale for Mrs. Wilkinson, one of our neighbors.

I should turn around and leave. I don't even know why I'm here. Before I can make a decision, Patty calls out, "If you're looking for Hallie, she's out back."

I nod once. "Thanks," I mumble and walk behind the counter and through the door that leads to the back of the butcher shop. I pass the small office, noting that she's not in there.

Before I reach the large refrigerated storage area, I hear mumbling. Pausing, I peek through the cracked door and find Hallie in the cutting room, staring at a large half pig carcass lying on the table. Her hair is wrapped in a bun with a hairnet over it. She's holding a paper in one hand and a cleaver in the other, which is covered in a metal mesh glove.

I tap the door with my knuckle and wait for her to say something.

"Sorry, Patty..." She pauses when I open the door. Her eyes widen, and her mouth opens and closes.

"Uhhh..."

"Patty told me you were back here." I put my hands in my pockets and rock back on my heels feeling like a fool for having no real excuse to see her.

"Oh. Well, yeah, here I am." She opens her arms wide and grimaces when she notices she's still holding the cleaver. "I'm just gonna put this down." She places the cutting tool on the table.

"Good idea." I walk closer to the table. "What are you doing?" I don't know why I ask if it's quite clear she's trying to cut this pig into parts.

"Besides avoiding losing a finger?" Her round eyes peek up at me.

I chuckle. "That's why you've got the metal gloves."

"Thank God. Anyway, I need to butcher this, cut it into pieces, the whole shebang."

I raise my eyebrows. "And you've never done this before."

"Not even in my dreams." She blows out a breath. "I thought you already established I was useless at this job." She raises an eyebrow.

"I never said useless," I shake my head. "But I was shocked to see you when our first meeting was centered around saving a rabbit."

"Well, I couldn't let it die."

"Ironic, huh? Considering what you're doing now." I chuckle and look at the paper in her hand. "That will help guide you where to make the cuts."

"That's what I'm looking at. I wish it was done to size so I could place it over the pig like a template and start cutting. Wouldn't that be a great invention?" Hopeful eyes meet mine.

"That'd be something." I nod slowly.

"Do you see these stamps?" I point to four stamps on the skin.

"Yeah, why are there so many?"

I smirk. "Those will help mark the four primal parts you'll need to cut." Helping her will clear my conscience.

"No shit," she breathes out, and I chuckle.

"Yes, shit." I look around the cutting room in search of what she'll need.

"Here," I say, holding up the saw, and her eyes bug out. "Have no fear," I assure her.

Then I grab a boning knife and a larger knife. "This is all you'll need. We can leave the cleaver to the side for now."

"Okay," she claps her hands and cringes when the metal mesh slaps her palm. "I'm assuming you know what you're doing, considering you kill animals for a living."

I look over at her but relax when I find her small smile.

"Comes with the job," I shrug. "Help me flip this over."

"But then, how will I see the stamp marks?"

"I'll teach you." Despite my initial reaction to her being some city girl, I feel bad for her. She's here to help her uncle and doesn't deserve my shitty attitude.

"Do you see this bone?" I point to the pelvic bone near the back end.

"Yeah."

"You're going to want to cut about an inch away from it. Cut straight through. When you reach the bone, you'll use the saw."

"Like this?" She holds the knife and begins cutting.

"Fluid cuts. You aren't cutting a cooked pork chop on your plate."

She side-eyes me but follows instructions.

"Hold the knife like this." I wrap my fist around it and Hallie giggles.

"Sorry," she rushes out when I look at her. "It's a bit of a serial killer hold."

"It's called the murder hold," I smirk.

"That's ironic." She presses her lips together.

"Why?"

She laughs again, her face covered in a blush. Shaking her head, she waves her hand. "Nothing."

"No, tell me," I insist.

"Really, I'd rather not. It's embarrassing." She looks over my shoulder.

"I won't teach you if you don't tell me." I risk sounding like a ten-year-old.

Sighing, she looks down at the pig. "When you stopped on the road behind me, I was afraid that the person would be a serial killer or something. I kept trying to come up with ways to get away. It's stupid."

A loud cackle makes my body shake.

"No serial killer here," I lift my hands. "You should be more careful, though." I arch a brow.

"I know, but I felt so guilty for hitting that bunny. Look at me now, cutting up a dead pig." She waves her hand over the carcass.

"This is your initiation into country living," I tease.

"Goodness, if this is the initiation, it's a wonder why people move here." It's meant as a joke, but her words kick me in the gut. A cold-bucket reminder that this lifestyle isn't for everyone.

Straightening, I hand her the knife. "Go on." I tilt my chin toward the pig, my face masked with indifference.

Her eyebrows slightly furrow, but she gets to work, continuing to listen to my guidance. After she's got the four main parts cut, she looks at me. Her face is red from the unfamiliar exertion she used during the cutting process.

"Thanks."

I nod once. "I should go. I've got another steer for Sal. He usually comes by the ranch to check them out and give his final approval. I don't think…"

"I'll ask him what I'm looking for and go myself. I don't want to give him any excuse to get out of the house. It's been less than two weeks, and he already has cabin fever."

"Right, so let me know."

"Thanks again, Wilder."

"You're welcome." I take in her green eyes and full lips.

Despite having just butchered a pig, she looks beautiful. There's an underlying emotion in her eyes, though, and I can't pinpoint it, nor do I have any business trying to discover what it is. Hallie is just another person passing through town, making it a temporary home before something new and shiny comes around.

Regardless of the warning bells ringing in my head, I'm curious about her. But you know what they say: curiosity killed the cat.

Chapter 8

HALLIE

I wrap my arms around myself, trying to keep warm. Just the other day, it felt like spring might be making an appearance. Today, it's colder than Jeff's heart. I sneak my hand in my tote and make sure I have the paper with all the details Sal told me to look for on the steer and questions to ask Wilder. I hope I don't screw this up. Surely, Wilder wouldn't sell Sal a less-than-perfect steer, considering it's his ranch's beef reputation.

Sal's old truck bounces down the dirt road leading into the ranch. Roman Wilde Ranch is proudly displayed on a metal sign, held up by huge tree trunks that frame the entrance. Snow-capped mountains stand tall as the backdrop of this stunning scenery. I was able to appreciate the view driving to Mason Creek from the airport, but this is on a whole other level.

The further in I drive, the more mountains appear, as if the ranch were hidden in a valley. Tall pine trees shroud parts of the land, which seems to be endless from this vantage point. Ranches need a lot of land, but this seems like the James family owns the entire outskirts of town. Geez, I can't find a fence enclosing the area.

As I round the path, I see a house on the right. My eyebrows shoot up when I realize it's a log cabin.

"Wow," I breathe out.

The ranch-style house has a long porch with rocking chairs and a stone chimney. I bet the views from that porch are gorgeous. The closer I get to parking the truck, the sweatier my palms grow. I am so out of my element.

I stop the truck and take a few deep breaths. I don't see anyone around, so there's no one to witness me trying to pull myself together. My eyes scan the paper with the notes one more time, remembering the weight range Uncle Sal told me the steer should fall under, how many months old it should be, and the price they already agreed upon.

Prepared to face Wilder, I step down from the truck and hear a splashing sound. Mud splatters on my boots, and I groan, looking up at the sky. I should've worn rubber boots, but my stubborn self chose my favorite brown suede ankle boots instead. They always make me feel confident, and I need all the confidence I can muster. But if this is any indication of how this meeting is going to go, then I'm in deep trouble.

I walk around to the back of the house, hoping to find Wilder nearby since he knows I'm coming. It's empty. However, I find a stone patio area with a fire pit and wooden chairs around it that looks inviting. I turn to see what the view would be from one of those chairs and gasp. The barn is a ways down, and beyond that, there are rolling hills that meet the mountains further away.

"Hello?"

"Oh!" I turn around, hand over my chest, and stare wide-eyed.

"Hi," I squeak. "I'm not an intruder, I promise. I'm here to meet with Wilder. My name is Hallie, Sal's niece." I look at the tall older man, who is clearly Mr. James by the resemblance between him and his children.

He chuckles and nods. "Hi, Hallie. I'm Benjamin, Wilder's dad."

"It's nice to meet you." I smile tentatively.

"Likewise. My son is out there somewhere. I'll give him a call. He probably lost track of time."

"Thanks." I look around, sneaking my hands into my puffy jacket pockets to keep them warm. I try not to listen to Benjamin's conversation, so I focus on the details of the surrounding area.

The rolling hills have some yellow blossoms on them. The pine trees near the house create a forest that seems like the perfect place to wander through.

"Wilder says you can meet him in the barn," Benjamin interrupts my observation.

"Thank you." I smile gratefully and trek toward the barn, careful to avoid any more puddles.

The door is open, so I sneak in and look around. The smell of hay instantly hits me, and it's oddly comforting. It's such a contrast from the toxic smell of exhaust in New York that I welcome the sweet aroma.

Rows of stables line both sides. Horses peek over the doors to see who the intruder in their safe space is. When I see a black head, I smile and walk straight over. The steer is gorgeous.

"Hey, there, buddy." I look at it in the eyes. "You're beautiful." I'm tempted to reach out and pet it, but I don't need it to try to bite me. It'd be my luck.

I lift on my toes to try to see over the stable door. He seems like a strong steer, but what do I know?

"Sorry I'm here to talk about your death. I really hate this, but I gotta do something right in my life before everyone gives up on me. Not that I think my parents would ever turn their backs on me, but I promised Uncle Sal I'd take care of his business so he wouldn't have to stress. Maybe it wasn't the best idea. Seeing you like this… I don't think I'll be able to butcher you once you're…you know." I nod my head, rambling to the animal, who probably can't understand jack shit of what I'm saying.

"Anyway, I wanna prove I can do this. Even if the douche-cunt who shall not be named won't be witness to it, I need to prove I am worth something." I lift my hand but think better of it and drop it by my side.

The steer, who I've decided could be named Midnight based on his dark coat, just stares at me. *Great, naming the steer isn't the right direction to butchering it.*

A throat clears, and I freeze. Heat rushes through me in embarrassment, and it lands on my cheeks, no doubt causing them to redden. Swallowing thickly, I turn around and find Wilder leaning against a post dividing two stalls a few feet away from me. I must've been so focused on dumping my emotional baggage that I didn't hear his steps.

The way he's looking at me, hard and distant, makes me want to grab Harry Potter's invisibility cloak and hide under it.

"Hi," I wave awkwardly. "Is this the steer?"

Wilder shakes his head. "That one is injured, which is why he's here."

"Oh." I look over at the animal. "You'll live another day, Midnight."

Wilder snorts. When I turn to look at him, he's covering his mouth with his gloved hand. I narrow my eyes but don't ask what's funny. His eyes scan the length of my body, stopping at my shoes with an eye roll. I shift on my feet, causing him to look back up at me.

"Those are the boots you wear to a ranch?" A hint of judgment laces his words.

Placing my hands on my hips, I defend myself. I'm tired of men putting me down and thinking they're better than me.

"What's it to you what boots I'm wearing?" I raise my eyebrows and glare at him.

Wilder's lips twitch, increasing my frustration.

"You got some mud there."

"I hadn't realized you were gonna clean 'em for me."

"Just don't wanna get blamed for ruining some expensive city boots that are just for looks."

"For your information, these cost me twenty bucks on clearance. Maybe you should check your stereotype thermometer. You don't see me calling all small-town people dense and cow-tipping folks." I cross my arms.

"Stereotype thermometer?" My blood boils even more when a hint of amusement lights his azure eyes.

"Yeah...a way to measure stereotypes. Ugh, whatever." I drop my arms. "Show me this steer so I can ask you the questions Sal told me to ask since, you know, this city girl has no idea, and I can leave."

Wilder takes a deep breath. "Okay, got it. Follow me." I give Midnight one more look before following Wilder.

After asking all the right questions, which Wilder seemed to be impressed by, we walk back to my car. Wilder stares at Sal's truck with a subtle smirk. "You're going all-in when it comes to living here, huh? What happened to that sedan you were driving?"

I tilt my head and raise a brow. "It was a rental, and I turned it in. Despite your skewed opinion, not everyone can afford weeks of car rental. Mason Creek is walkable enough I can get around on foot, and I use Sal's truck if I need to go somewhere further away."

"Maybe you'll change my opinion." He walks away before I can process his words. Shaking them away, I climb into the truck and turn the engine.

A full day of serving customers awaits me at the butcher shop. Hopefully, that will keep me busy enough to stop wondering why Wilder runs hot and cold.

"Honey, I'm home," I jokingly call out as I walk into Sal's house.

Mumbled words and a giggle makes me pause.

"Uncle Sal?" I squeeze my eyes shut.

"Hi, sweetie." Following his voice to the living room, I halt when I see Patty sitting beside him, rubbing the skin under her lip.

I stare at them for a second, and when Uncle Sal looks at me, I scrunch up my nose. "You've got a little…" I point to my lips. "You know what… I'm gonna go to the coffee shop for a bit. I'll be back later." My hand waves around before jutting my thumb toward the door.

"You don't have to go," Uncle Sal says.

"Oh, trust me, it's not for your benefit. I need to unsee this." I once again wave a hand in front of me as if that will magically erase whatever's going on. "You guys have fun, and next time put a sock outside the door or something." Patty's laugh echoes around the house.

"Sorry, sweetie. I got a little carried away kissing him, but that's all we were doing. Cross my heart," she giggles.

"Yeah, because he's got a broken leg," I mumble.

I wave over my shoulder and walk back out of the house. My uncle has his own life, and I'm not going to interrupt it by being in the way. Besides, I could always go for coffee.

As I walk back to the center of town, I remember the bookstore I saw one evening and make a detour. Comforting peace fills me as soon as I walk in. I could get lost in any bookstore for hours. Shelves bursting with books make me smile.

"Hello." A young woman with hazel eyes smiles at me from a crouched position in front of one of the shelves.

"Hi," I wave at her.

"Do you need any help?"

"Not at the moment, just gonna look around. Thanks."

"Great. If you need anything, let me know."

"Thanks." I begin to wander, taking in the shop and endless lines of titles. I pull out different books that call to me, reading the synopsis and keeping a few on hand while I search the romance section.

A reading nook is on the left toward the back of the store, which looks like the perfect spot to sit and read. There are also two leather loveseats that look cozy and welcoming.

"You're Sal's niece, right?" The woman breaks the silence, now standing behind the counter.

"I am," I nod. "I guess everyone's got me singled out already, huh?" I tease with a chuckle.

"Basically," she laughs as well. "I'm Laken, owner and book lover."

"It's nice to meet you. I'm Hallie."

"How are you liking Mason Creek?" She leans against the counter.

"It's great. Totally different than what I'm used to, but I would visit when I was younger, so it's not completely unfamiliar." I return a book to its spot on the shelf and keep browsing while making small-talk with Laken.

Another customer walks in, and I continue browsing the shelves until Laken calls me over.

"Hallie, this is Justine, a good friend of mine. She lived in New York until recently."

I smile at the woman, who must be about my age.

"Hey, it's nice to meet you." I wave awkwardly. "What a small world."

"It is," Justine returns my smile. "I've heard about you," she admits.

"Ah, yeah, so I've been told," I joke.

"Mason Creek is nothing like New York, huh?" Her brows lift knowingly, a hint of resentment in her tone that I'm too familiar with.

"Not at all, but I am loving this town. How long did you live in New York for?"

"Since college. I'm glad to be back, though."

"She works for a big-time magazine," Laken adds.

"Really?" I raise my eyebrows.

"Living Now," Justine adds with a nod.

"No way! I love their articles. This is so cool." I'm geeking out like a fool.

"Thanks." Her smile is proud. "I gotta go, but we should get together for coffee sometime."

"Sure," I nod. It's nice to meet more people from town, and it seems like Justine may understand me a little better since she lived in New York for so many years.

Deciding on a book I've been wanting to read for a while, I pay and head to Java Jitters. Coffee and reading are in my foreseeable future, and I'm so giddy about it—

nothing like fiction to make me forget my real-world problems and sexy, broody ranchers.

Chapter 9

HALLIE

I smile at Mr. Sullivan, the sweetest old man I've ever met, as I give him his change and wave goodbye.

"See you in a few days," he smiles with a wink that causes me to laugh.

I feel like I'm finally getting the hang of the shop and learning about the locals. So far, I've learned the names of most of our customers, and I love seeing their faces light up when I call them by name. I'm also starting to become more comfortable talking to strangers.

Butchering is another story altogether, but videos have helped guide me. So far, I haven't had to do too much of it. Uncle Sal offered to come in and do that part of the job, but Patty and I both vetoed it. He'd use it as an excuse to slowly ease back into his job, and according to the doctor, his fracture is taking longer to heal than originally believed.

With a few minutes left to closing time, I start to clean up behind the counter. I'll have two days off, and I plan to see more of Mason Creek. Uncle Sal assured me that Patty would visit him tomorrow so he'd be okay for a few hours. I'm not sure where to go, but part of the reason for me coming here was to get my life in order. I need to find a peaceful place to think clearly and gain perspective.

The door opens as I'm rinsing one of the knives, so I look over my shoulder to let the customer know I'll be ready in a second when my words get trapped. Standing before me with messy hair, worn jeans, and a white t-shirt under his open plaid shirt is Wilder in all his masculine, rugged glory. I've been dodging thoughts of him since I went to the ranch a couple days ago.

"Hi," I press my lips together in an awkward smile. "Give me a… Son of a biscuit," I cry out, dropping the knife with a loud clatter against the sink.

"Are you okay?" Wilder's question rushes out before he's around the counter and next to me, lifting my hand. Inspecting it, he grimaces. "That's a pretty nasty gash."

I nod, speechless, as I stare at the blood coming from the cut across the pad of my thumb. I'm gonna be sick. I reach out to hold on to the edge of the sink with my other hand, closing my eyes and breathing deeply. Wilder wraps his fingers tightly around my thumb in an attempt to slow the bleeding. He grabs a dishtowel, making sure it's clean, before wrapping it around my finger and lifting my arm over my head.

"Keep it like this for a sec. You think you can do that?" His voice is soft and soothing.

I nod, eyes still closed as I hear his footsteps get further away.

In and out. In and out.

I focus on my breathing instead of the pounding pain in my thumb. I've never dealt well with blood.

I should've been paying more attention, placed the knife down in the sink before turning to talk to the customer—especially when I saw that it was sexy Wilder with a crooked smirk.

I blink my eyes open, and nausea hits me when I see the blood in the sink. Quickly, I turn on the tap and rinse it out. I'm going to have to disinfect this as soon as my finger is bandaged. Wilder's heavy steps grow louder, and I turn to see him coming out of the back area.

"Here we go." He holds up the first-aid kit with a proud smile.

"Where was that?" I should've asked Uncle Sal where he kept the kit before I started working here.

"It's usually in one of a few places—the bathroom, the office of a business, or in the place you're most likely to get injured, which in this case is the cutting room. It was in a cabinet. How are you feeling?"

"Beside like I might throw up or pass out?" I lift my eyebrows.

"Yikes. I'll get it cleaned up and bandaged. It'll hurt for a while, but it'll get better. I've seen worse cuts than this." He gently holds my wrist and removes the bloodied towel.

"You can toss that there." I tilt my chin toward the garbage can.

After he tosses it away, he looks at my finger and begins disinfecting the cut. I turn my gaze away, cringing at the sting.

"Deep breaths," Wilder whispers.

I nod, heart in my throat.

"You must think I'm a wimp or something. I'm just not good with blood."

"I don't think that." He furrows his eyebrows. "Lots of people don't like blood. My brother gets queasy, too. We usually make fun of him at the ranch when we gotta gut animals. He doesn't stomach it."

I shiver, screwing my face. "Don't blame him," I say through clenched teeth.

Wilder chuckles softly, and it's such a nice sound. The few times I've seen him, he's reserved and serious. I can't imagine him being laid-back, laughing freely. It could be a misconstrued idea from my own interactions with him, though.

"Okay, this looks better."

I peek at my finger and nod. After cleaning up the injury, it doesn't look as bad. It's still a big cut, but I won't be losing any fingers.

"Maybe I should wear the metal mesh gloves to wash the knives," I joke.

There goes Wilder with another deep chuckle that moves through me. "I'd like to see that. Although considering this, it's probably a good idea." He places a wide Band-Aid over the cut and makes sure it's on securely before stepping back.

"You'll be good as new in no time."

"Thank you." I hold my thumb with my other hand.

"You're welcome. Painkillers will help with the pain."

"Yeah."

We stare at each other awkwardly. I shift on my feet, and Wilder scans my face with an expression I can't quite decipher.

Snapping out of it, I ask, "Why'd you come in before I almost sliced my finger off?"

He smiles, running his hand over his short beard. "I delivered that steer to Paul. He said he'd have it to you next week."

"Uh, okay, thanks. You didn't have to go out of your way and stop in."

"I was driving by, so it wasn't out of my way. Like that you can be prepared when he comes."

I nod, narrowing my eyes as I look at him.

"Why are you suddenly nice to me?" I tilt my head.

"Hey now, I was nice to you the other day. Even taught you to cut a pig carcass."

"Then, you weren't when I went to see the steer."

Wilder sighs. "Look, I'm sorry about that. Can we start over with a clean slate?"

"Sure," I shrug.

"I'm Wilder. I sell my cattle to Sal, but you won't have to kill any of the animals. He's got a guy to do that." He holds his hand out, and I can't help the giggle that bubbles out of me.

"You're so odd," I tease. "You're forgiven. Especially for making me think I'd have to kill the poor animal. By the way, how's Midnight?"

"Who?" He pulls his eyebrows down.

"Midnight, the steer that was injured? You know, the one that was in the barn when I went."

"Oh, we don't name our animals. He's better, though."

"Good." I clap my hands and jolt when I hit my thumb. "Crap," I mumble. "Anyway, I'm gonna clean up this mess."

"I'll help," he offers quickly.

I purse my lips and stare at him with furrowed eyebrows. "You don't have to."

"It's the least I can do after distracting you while you were cleaning the knife." He grabs another dishtowel and the spray bottle with diluted vinegar and begins cleaning down the counters while I disinfect the sink with Clorox. I keep my injured hand away from all the cleaning products while I scrub with my good hand.

We work in silence. I sneak glances at Wilder as he moves around the space. I never would've imagined him back here helping me, but I like the view.

"'Scuse me." His body glides against my back when he needs to move to the other side of the counter.

I suppress a shiver and look over my shoulder at him. His eyes catch mine, and for a brief moment, time stands still. Blazing blue eyes stare into my green ones, and the heat from his gaze consumes me. Clearing his throat, Wilder breaks contact and grabs a cutting board.

"I'll wash this," he says quietly, his voice husky. He could recite ancient history, and I'd find it exciting.

I move to the side and let him take care of it since washing the wooden cutting board with one hand would be challenging. While he does that, I take advantage by asking him about the town.

"So… I wanna see more of the town. Do you recommend any must-sees?"

Wilder turns his head and looks at me with a pensive expression, and I bite back a moan. He looks so sexy with his sleeves rolled up, hands soapy from doing dishes, and looking at me carefully. He oozes confidence as he lathers the board with the sponge.

"What did you have in mind? Outdoor places or stores in town?"

"Something exciting and different. Something that I can't find in New York."

Wilder smirks. "Ever climbed a water tower?"

My eyes widen. "What?"

"The water tower behind the butcher shop." I crane my head as if I have x-ray vision and can see through the walls in this place.

"Hell no." I step back as if I were facing the endless stairs in this moment.

Wilder laughs, drying his hands with a paper towel. "It's not scary at all." He reads my reaction. "It's actually amazing. You get the best view of town. Gives you a different perspective."

That catches my attention. "I could use that."

He regards me with curiosity. He opens his mouth but closes it without saying a word.

"What?" I ask.

He shakes his head. "Let me help you finish up here."

"No," I shake my finger at him. "What were you gonna say?" I press, crossing my arms, careful not to hurt my thumb.

"It's nothing. Let's finish here, and I'll show you something New York will never be able to provide."

Pretty sure that's you. I bite my tongue and nod before I say something embarrassing.

By the time we're done, the sun sits a little lower in the sky, creating a golden glow around town.

"Come on." Wilder's voice rises with excitement. I follow him around the side of the butcher shop, heart slamming when I see the tower.

He stops in front of the ladder and looks at me, squatting down, so we're eye-to-eye.

"I know I haven't been the nicest person in town to you, but trust me on this."

I nod, terrified, as I stare up the length of the water tower. It seems to go on forever.

He pauses and looks at my hand. "Maybe this isn't a good idea. You could hurt your finger even more."

"I didn't even think about that. I figured I could hold on without putting pressure on it, but it does seem as if I'll need a good grip on the ladder if my legs start to shake."

Wilder chuckles. I like that I've made him laugh more than once.

"And I'm on the heavier side, so I'll need more strength to carry myself." The words leave my mouth without a second thought. My face burns when I realize I said it aloud.

Wilder's face suddenly transforms from laughing to dead serious. He glares at me with hard eyes. "Who the fuck told you that?"

I look down at my body and back at him. "Uh, the mirror."

"Get a new mirror. You've got curves, and they're sexy."

My body reacts to his words in a way I've never experienced. He says it so naturally, as if he didn't compliment me in the most amazing way. Regardless, I shake my head.

"I wouldn't call them sexy; I just know how to dress for my body type."

"What the hell, Hallie?" He scrubs a hand down his face. "I don't know why you think that, but you're wrong."

"You don't have to make me feel better. I'm aware of what I look like." I glance away, arms hugging my body as if that will help hide me.

"I should go. Thanks for your help." I lift my hand and walk away, heading to Uncle Sal's house.

I don't look back to see if Wilder's still standing there. His words are on repeat the entire walk home, though. Sexy? Me? He must've gotten confused or felt bad for me. I never get sorted into the sexy category.

By the time I get home, my mind's reeling, and everything Jeff ever said to me has silenced Wilder's one compliment.

I should work out more, eat less sugar and desserts. If I lost at least ten pounds, my clothes would fit better. Adding whole milk to my coffee won't help me become skinnier.

Good thing I'm walking all around Mason Creek these days. Plenty of cardio.

Although, when I did lose some weight, I still wasn't good enough for that asshole. He didn't even notice. Instead, he found something else to put me down, slowly tearing me apart, thread by thread. He was so subtle about it, playing mind games, that I didn't realize it until it was too late, and I believed everything he said. Undoing that damage will take time.

Chapter 10

HALLIE

I stretch my arms over my head as a wide yawn takes over on my way to the kitchen.

"Morning, sunshine," my uncle chuckles.

"Morning," I say around my yawn and then cover my mouth.

"How's your finger?" He points to my bandaged thumb.

"It's okay. I just switched out the bandage, and it looks better than I thought. It should be healed in a couple of days." Seeing the blood yesterday made it seem like I cut half my finger, and while it is a deep cut, it's not nearly as bad as I imagined.

"That's good."

I nod, still not fully awake. I spent half the night tossing and turning.

"Patty left the latest edition of The MC Scoop by the door early this morning. Can you get it for me, please?"

"Of course and I'll make coffee and breakfast after."

I step out onto the front porch and breathe in the chilly morning air. Although Uncle Sal has neighbors, the houses have some distance between them, which is great for privacy. A bag next to the copy of The MC Scoop catches my eye. Maybe someone left a casserole for

Uncle Sal. I reach for the bag, noticing how light it is. *Definitely not a casserole.*

Peeking inside, I find a folded paper with my name on it placed over the back of a black hand mirror. I tuck the flyer under my arm and reach for the note in the bag.

Hallie,
Everyone needs a mirror that reflects the truth.

The messy print becomes blurry as my eyes water. I don't need him to write his name to know it's from Wilder. I grab the handle and turn it over. What I see on the mirror makes me lose my self-control.

Tears soak my cheeks as I read the words written in black marker on the mirror.

I'm sexy.
My curves are beautiful.
I'm worthy.

I sit back on the porch in awe. The words are spread over the mirror, so each phrase lands on a part of my face when I look at myself. I can't believe he did this.

I wipe my face dry with the top of my pajama shirt and stand, putting the mirror back in the bag and wrapping the plastic around it so, it's not obvious. I've always been open with Uncle Sal, but this is something I want to keep to myself. He'd just say how beautiful I am and that I'm a gem like he has many times. But he's my uncle, and he's supposed to love me unconditionally, just like my parents.

Perfect MESS

I sneak into my room, leaving the bag on my bed, and bring the paper out to Uncle Sal. While I prepare coffee, Uncle Sal comments on the news he reads about. Every time he does this, it's like a lesson on Mason Creek. It's helped me get to know the town in a different way.

"Whoa," Uncle Sal calls out as I pour coffee into our mugs.

"What happened?"

He laughs boastfully. "This couple got caught skinny dipping in the springs out in the Jackson property. Instead of making a run for it, they invited Deputy Murphy to join them for some fun."

"Oh, my goodness," I giggle. "Are they from Mason Creek?"

"It doesn't say. Lots of people tend to trespass into the springs, but they usually go quietly if they get caught."

"Guess this couple is a wild one." I pour creamer into the mugs.

"Yeah..." He's quiet as he scans the paper. "Aw, man."

"What happened?" His change from laughter to sadness catches my attention.

"Mrs. Graham passed."

"I'm assuming she's a local?" I don't think I ever met her.

"Yeah, she was ninety-nine and lived a good life, but it's always sad to see one of your own go. May her soul rest peacefully." He places the flyer on his lap and does the sign of the cross before gratefully taking the coffee mug I offer.

"I'll make some eggs and bacon."

While I cook, with the salty goodness hitting my nose and making my stomach growl, I update Uncle Sal on the butcher shop.

"Wilder told me Paul already has the steer you ordered. He'll deliver it once it's slaughtered."

"Sounds good. Are you sure you're doing okay with everything?" His question rings with uncertainty.

"Yeah." I smile, turning to look at him as the bacon cracks and sizzles in the pan. "Patty helps a lot, so I have a chance to butcher and cut down any meat we're running low on. I'm getting the hang of it, and YouTube videos help a ton."

He laughs, placing the coffee mug on the counter.

"Maybe you take after your uncle and granddad after all." His eyes shine with pride. My heart swells at the thought.

"Not sure about that," I shake my head. "You and Granddaddy were pros. Well, you still are." I smile sadly. I miss my grandparents. I had too little time with them, but I've always held the lessons they taught me close to my heart.

"That's because of years of practice and education. Patty told me you did a great job with that half-pig carcass."

"Yeah, because Wilder helped." My eyes widen as soon as the words slip out.

Uncle Sal seems to notice because he raises his eyebrows and tilts his head. "You don't say…" He draws out. A teasing smile mocks me.

"He came by, and I was in the middle of it, so he taught me the four main parts of where to cut." I shrug it off.

"Huh…" He takes a sip of coffee.

"What?" I ask defensively.

"Nothing." He smiles. "I'm glad you got help. How's that bacon coming along?"

"Almost done. Extra crispy for you."

I beat the eggs for the scramble before pouring it into another pan. We're quiet while I finish cooking breakfast and serve our plates. With a coffee refill, I sit next to Uncle Sal, the mirror Wilder dropped off fighting for my attention.

After breakfast, I take off with Sal's assurance that he'll be okay until Patty arrives and head into town. I love that Uncle Sal lives near the center. My walk has served as a kind of meditation where my mind clears.

Trees line the streets, reminding me that despite this being a town, nature rules in this area. I'm falling in love with Mason Creek. I haven't missed the concrete jungle I come from at all since I passed the covered wood bridge on the way in.

As I pass the front of the butcher shop, memories of yesterday hit me again. I hate that I reacted the way I did with Wilder. I've been working on my self-esteem since I broke up with Jeff, but it's been a struggle.

When I put on clothes, and they don't fit the same way they do on others, I get self-conscious. When I see everyone my age running businesses, having a secure job, and having their shit together, I remember all the rejections I've received and how my college degree is dying away the more time passes.

I keep going down the street the butcher shop is on instead of turning toward Town Square. A group of people is standing outside the church when I look in that direction. Hoping to avoid town gossip, I lower my head and walk toward One More Chapter in hopes it's open today. I'm not surprised when I see the Closed sign since it's Sunday, though.

Turning around with my hands in my jacket pocket, I spot a forested area across the street. I noticed it the other day as well. My feet guide me in that direction without a second thought.

I'm swallowed by tall pine trees and transported into a different world. Shrubs with small blossoms beginning to appear mark paths through the woods. Trees I wouldn't be able to name if they paid me are growing back leaves after a long and frigid winter. It's so peaceful here with birds chirping, the wind rustling, and colors from flowers blooming and fighting for attention against the green backdrop.

Now this is something New York City can't offer me—not even in Central Park.

I make my way around, listening for new sounds and searching for bright colors. With each step, I begin to relax. I forget all about Jeff and his stupid attempt to screw me over with the security deposit. I exhale all the nasty things he said behind a mask of genuine concern. He no longer has control over me.

Lapping water sounds nearby, and a beautiful old bridge opens up before me between shrubs and trees. "Wow," I breathe out, taking it in.

It arches upward, connecting two forested areas that are interrupted by a river. I walk on the bridge, the wood creaking beneath my feet but still sturdy and secure. When I reach the middle, I stop, looking out at the view before me. Ducks swim underneath, passing from one side of the river to another. I smile as I watch the baby ducks follow their mother like some game of Follow the Leader.

My gaze lifts to the trees overhead, covering most of the sky and creating a chilly shield. Wrapping my coat tighter around my body, I lean my elbows on the railing and sigh. This place is magical. It feels different, something swirling in the air that adjusts your perspective. Peace enters me in a slow flow, like the river passing beneath me.

I watch bubbles surface on the water and small fish swimming through. A bird bounces around on the end of the railing. I pull out my phone and take pictures of my surroundings so I can have keepsakes of the memories I make here. I turn around, leaning against the railing to take in the other side.

The sound of steps jolts me, and I search for the person. When I don't see anyone, my heart beats furiously. Maybe coming into the forest alone wasn't the best idea. I hold my breath and stand still, monitoring the area. I squawk when I see a man and then blow out my exhale.

"You scared the living bejesus out of me." My hand flies to my chest, over my pounding heart.

Wilder's deep laugh makes me smile. "Sorry about that." He stands at the end of the bridge, holding both sides of the railings. "How's your thumb?"

I lift my hand. "Much better, thanks. It barely hurts." I wiggle my thumb to prove my point.

"I'm happy to hear that." He takes slow steps on the bridge, and I watch him carefully. I need to bring up the mirror, but I'm afraid I'll choke up while I thank him.

Wilder stops in front of me. "I see you found something you wouldn't have in New York." He looks to his left, out onto the river.

"I did. This is a hidden gem."

"A gem, yes. It's not so hidden. Everyone in town knows about this place. It's quite popular."

"Really?" I smile. "How come?"

Wilder is quiet for a moment, running his hand over the railing. "This bridge has been here for years. It's a town treasure." He's pensive, but before I can ask him why he continues.

"Henry Davis created it for his wife when they were dating. She loved this part of the forest but was always frustrated she couldn't cross over to wander through the rest of it because of the river. He built the bridge for her so she could walk the forest without obstacles. It became their place. He later proposed to her here."

"Wow…" I whisper. "That's so romantic." I sometimes wish I was alive back then so I could experience that type of love story, more genuine and almost innocent to an extent.

Wilder stares into my eyes, searching for my secrets.

"Yeah," he finally looks away and sighs. "After that, it became a place where other men proposed, couples came on dates, all that jazz. It's on private property, so people sneak in."

He white-knuckles the railing and stares out into the water. I give him the space he clearly needs. After a few beats, he looks back at me.

"Anyway, did you receive the mirror?" His blue eyes look at me expectantly.

I nod and look down at my nails, lining up my fingertips on each hand. "I didn't know how to thank you without my voice cracking or choking up and embarrassing myself." I glance up at him from beneath my lashes.

"Thank you, Wilder," I whisper. "You didn't have to do that." I take a deep breath to control my emotions. No one has ever gone out of their way for something like this. I'm going to cherish that mirror for a long time.

His cold hand holds my chin and lifts my head. I shiver at the contact.

"Never look down or be embarrassed to say what you feel. I meant what I said yesterday and what I wrote on that mirror. I hope you start to believe it yourself."

Chapter 11

WILDER

Hearing Hallie talk about herself the way she did yesterday angered me. She's beautiful. Sure, she's curvy and voluptuous, but that makes her sexy as fuck. I haven't been able to get her out of my head, and I'm usually unaffected by women in this way. After getting your heart stomped on, you learn to be aloof. But Hallie is gorgeous, and she isn't even aware of it, which attracts me more.

My heart pounds as her green eyes look at me—her lips part as she breathes through them. I move my fingers from her chin to the side of her face, cupping her cheek. Hallie's eyes close as she takes a sharp inhale. Stepping closer, I brush my thumb over her cheek, feeling her smooth skin against my touch. If this is the only chance I get to touch her, I want to memorize the feel of her beneath my calloused hand.

I didn't expect to see her here. I usually come to this spot to clear my head, despite the memories that haunt me in this place, and I need major clarity after yesterday. Here she was, standing on this bridge like a goddamn dream. A dream I'm not sure I'm ready to chase.

"Never forget what that mirror says."

How can she think she's anything but beautiful? I've been fighting against it since I saw her again at Sal's butcher shop, even with the annoyance I felt of having to deal with a city girl.

She nods silently.

"Thank you," she finally whispers as her eyes search mine.

"You're welcome." I move my hand down the side of her neck, trailing a path along the curve that leads to her shoulder and drop my hand.

Hallie shivers and wraps her arms around her body. To anyone else, she'd seem like she's covering from the cool air, but now that I've had a peek into her thoughts, I'd say she's covering her body from the world.

I smirk, searching her face. "The forest leads to a lake." I point in the direction of it. "It's great for fishing and speed boating in the summers. Have you seen it?"

She shakes her head.

"Wanna go?"

"Sure." She smiles shyly, the hint of a dimple I never noticed before appearing on one cheek.

We walk side by side down the other side of the bridge in silence. Besides our ranch, I love this part of town, though it holds bittersweet memories.

Lisa loved coming here. I even considered proposing to her here after she returned from college—except she never did.

I shake away thoughts of my ex-girlfriend, even if she is part of the reason I came here today. After we broke up, I was never the same. Meeting Hallie has stirred up feelings I buried, and I need to reflect. But then she was here, looking as scared as the day I met her in the middle of the road. I've always lived in Mason Creek, so I can't imagine being so untrusting and cautious from living in a big city like New York.

"This area really is beautiful," she breaks the silence, her eyes glancing all over the place.

"Yeah, I love this town."

She looks at me out of the corner of her eyes. "Have you always lived here?"

"Born and raised," I nod proudly.

"Did you go away for college or anything?"

My jaw ticks and I shake my head. "Nope. I always knew I'd live here and take over the ranch. No college classes would provide real-life experience. The best way to learn more about running the ranch is working on it."

Hallie nods, pensive for a moment. "College degrees are overrated most of the time. Did you know about forty percent of college grads don't utilize their degree?"

"That many?" My brows lift.

"I'm not sure if that's the exact percentage, but I am one of them." She shrugs and rolls her eyes, looking straight ahead again. When the lake opens up, she gasps.

"Wow…this is beautiful." I take in her profile while she looks around the large lake. Her plump lips turn up in a smile, her cheeks pink, and her eyes alight with joy.

"It's a great lake." I nod. "Wanna sit?" I point to a trunk that's lying on the ground.

Hallie places her hands on her hips and narrows her eyes. "You mean, you're not gonna accuse me of being too city to sit on a dirty log?"

I chuckle, shaking my head. "I think you're proving to be different than I imagined."

Her breath hitches, and her eyes soften. The smile she gives me is enough to start crumbling my walls. We sit on the trunk, staring out at the pacific water, lapping softly.

"Why aren't you using your college degree?" I shift my body, so I'm turned toward her.

"New York is a competitive city, and I'm never the first pick at interviews."

"What did you study?"

"Finance."

"Oh…" I raise my eyebrows. "I can see how New York would be competitive in that field."

"Yeah," she nods, pursing her lips. "I figured it'd be a good option since it allows for many opportunities, but it seems everyone and their mother studied finance." I laugh at her expression.

"You must be able to find something."

She shakes her head with pressed lips. "I've gone to more interviews than I care to admit. They always go with someone more qualified, usually a man. Not to mention I probably don't have the look they want to represent their company."

"Hey, what'd I say about that?" I lock my jaw.

"Sorry," she frowns. "But it's true. These companies want tall, well-put-together people. I'm a bit of a hot mess, spill coffee on myself often, and stutter when I'm nervous. And dealing with high corporate people makes me nervous as fuck."

"It's their loss." I mean what I say, too. I may not know Hallie all that well, but she's worked hard to learn how to manage the butcher shop in a few short weeks, even daring to butcher carcasses. That says something about her character and work ethic.

"Thanks. Anyway, it worked out because I could come help Uncle Sal and get some much-needed time away from the city."

I wonder what she needs space from but don't ask. Maybe it's a person and not a thing. Her phone interrupts our conversation, and she looks at the screen.

I catch the word Mom before she says, "Sorry, I gotta get this."

"Of course." I press my hands into the sides of the log, watching her stand and walk a few feet away.

"Hey, Mom, how are you?" Hallie answers. She's quiet for a bit before hollering, "What? He's insane."

I try not to listen, giving her privacy, but she's a couple of feet away, pacing back and forth, so it's difficult not to hear her side of the conversation.

"I'm not paying jack shit. He signed that on his own. He's got no leg to stand on, except for the purpose of making my life miserable. What a—" She cuts herself off. Or maybe her mom did.

"Yeah, okay. I know... Thanks... Love you, too." Hallie shakes her head, fury in her eyes.

"Is everything okay?" I stretch my legs out in front of me, crossing them at the ankles.

"Yeah, it's fine." She waves her hand away.

Clearly, it's not, but I won't push since I'm basically a stranger. She drops beside me again, leaning her elbows on her thighs and scrubbing her face.

"Word to the wise—whenever you realize your boyfriend is a douche-cunt, leave him instead of thinking he'll change."

Surprised, I remain silent while she rubs her hands across her face. When she turns her head to face me, her eyes are rimmed red as if she's trying to hold back her tears.

"Douche-cunt… That's a new one," I smirk.

Hallie chuckles with a nod. "Yeah, I got creative with the nicknames after a while."

"What'd this guy do to deserve such a name?"

"Nothing worth boring you over this." She stands, walking toward the shore. "This really is beautiful."

I watch her from my spot. Her long blonde hair is in a ponytail, the end slightly curling. Her ass is round, emphasizing her curves, and fuck if I don't want to grab two handfuls and feel her against me.

Shit.

I blow out a breath and scrub a hand down my face. I need to get it together. Now's not the time for me to be thinking about her in that way. Not when she's clearly upset about some asshole ex.

And her stay is temporary.

"It is," I nod.

She turns to me, her eyes round and excited. "Does this lake freeze in the winter? Like, can people ice skate on it?"

"It does. People love coming here to skate. You'll find families, friends, couples, everyone."

"That's so cool. The only type of skating I've done is at Rockefeller with a ton of tourists, and it looks nothing like this." She spins around until she faces me again.

I stand, walking toward her. The desire to be close to her wins out.

"Your mom is from Mason Creek, right?"

"Yeah, she was born and raised. She left for college and never moved back after getting a job. She met my dad, and the rest is history." She opens her arms wide.

"So your dad is from New York?"

"He's from Philly. He got a job in New York, and they moved just after they got married."

"That's interesting. Most people around here haven't lived in so many different places." My mind wanders to Lisa. I'm not sure where she lives at the moment. If she moved from place to place or just stayed in one city after graduation. She barely visits, and I steer clear of her the few times she does.

"I guess," Hallie shrugs. "I've always lived in New York, so I don't know what it's like to experience different places. The most I've done is visit Mason Creek when I was younger to see my grandparents and Uncle Sal."

I tilt my head and narrow my eyes. "You'd come here?"

"Yeah," she nods with an awkward smile.

"Really? I don't remember you."

She waves me off, looking away as she says, "I was young, so it's been years. You're a few years older than me, so I doubt you'd remember."

"Huh…" I scratch my chin, trying to recall if I ever saw her around town.

Before I can ask more questions, she places her hand on her stomach and blushes. I lift my brows and laugh.

"Hungry?" Her stomach growls again.

"Yeah. I should walk back to town and get some coffee or something. I came this way in hopes the bookstore was open, but I figured it was a long shot since it's Sunday."

"Ah, yeah. Most places are closed today." I pause a moment, checking the time on my phone. It's already past noon.

Without overthinking, I ask, "Wanna grab lunch?" I'm not ready to go our separate ways yet.

Hallie's eyes bug out.

"Uh…"

"No pressure. I get wanting to be alone, so if that's the case, don't feel obligated." I chuckle awkwardly, running a hand through my hair.

Her smile is brilliant as she walks closer to me. Looking up at me, she says, "I'd love to."

My heart speeds as I take in her beautiful face, dimple on her right cheek in full display now. I want to hold the sides of it and brush my lips against hers, get a taste of her. It's been a long time since a woman's affected me this way. I don't know what it is about her, but I damn well want to find out despite my head warning me to stay away.

Chapter 12

HALLIE

Holy crapola. I'm going to have lunch with Wilder. Wilder James...the guy I secretly crushed on when I was younger but knew nothing would ever come from it since I was a silly girl and lived in a different state.

Spending time with him today has eclipsed the news my mom gave me about Jeff insisting I pay him half of the security deposit. Apparently, he got his lawyer friend to make up some bullshit story that we had a verbal agreement.

"We can go to the diner," Wilder interrupts my thoughts.

"Sounds good."

We walk side by side in silence. I inhale the fresh pine before we step out of the woods. I'm delighted the town has this area I can come and ground myself in. As we cross the bridge, I sigh at the romantic history behind it and smooth my hand over the railing. I'm definitely returning.

The town's buzzing with people as we make our way through Town Square. People look between us with curiosity and knowing smiles. I ignore their stares, keeping my head down. Wilder doesn't comment either. My guess is he's also ignoring them.

When he opens the door for me, I almost swoon. Then the bell over the door chimes, and people look our way with raised eyebrows and curiosity. The diner is crowded, loud chatter filling the space, children laughing, and families spending time together. It's the perfect place to draw attention and get the rumor mill spinning. Not that this is a date or anything.

"Do you mind sitting outside?" Wilder whispers.

"That's perfect. Seems as if every table here is taken. Besides, it's a nice day, so it'll feel good to sit in the sunshine."

"Perfect." He waves at a waitress and points to the back of the diner. She nods in understanding, and he guides me out the back to the outdoor seating.

Picnic tables and square bistro tables are placed throughout the space. The brick flooring is dark from people walking on it and adds to the rustic outdoor feel. Plants are potted in wooden crates, and some trees create shade.

We take a seat across from each other at a picnic table. Wilder grabs two menus held between the ketchup and mustard bottles and hands me one.

"What do you recommend?" I ask, scanning the options. My mouth waters and my stomach growls again, embarrassing me further.

He looks at me with raised eyebrows and a teasing smile. "Everything's good. It's your typical diner food, but it's better since a lot of the products are local."

"I think they buy some of their meats from the butcher shop. I know Uncle Sal has special pricing for local businesses."

"They do," Wilder nods. "Our beef is used locally." Pride fills his words.

"That's awesome. I know I had a burger at Pony Up that used your beef, and it was the best I've ever had."

His lips quirk with a smile, and he looks down at the menu. "Thanks."

I take the opportunity to observe him. His wavy hair is tousled, and his blue eyes are cast down toward the menu. His bearded jaw is sexy. Not to mention the roped muscles on his forearms from working with his hands. My confirmation about his calloused fingers came when he held my cheek on the bridge earlier. I shiver at the fantasy of him touching me with those hands and clear my throat.

"I'm gonna get the BLT," I announce.

"Good choice. Burger for me." He sets the menu on the table and clasps his hands. "So…did Mason Creek deliver something New York can't?"

"Yeah," I smile before pressing my lips together and biting down on them.

His gift alone this morning is enough to provide something New York hasn't in a long time—human kindness. "This town really is something," I add.

"It's special," Wilder nods, looking around. "It may not be for everyone, but I can't imagine living anywhere else." His body tenses and fingers tighten against each other as he says this, and I have to wonder if that's what happened with his ex-girlfriend.

"What else is there to see around here?" I change subjects, hoping to shift his mood to the happier version I've experienced today. I don't want grouchy Wilder. I want sexy and funny Wilder, who isn't as guarded as I've come to learn he is.

"Okay, spill," Joy demands as she sits down at a table in Java Jitters. I received a message earlier asking if I wanted to have coffee when she closed the bakery.

"I heard you had lunch with Wilder. What in the… How'd that come about?" Her hands flail, and her eyes widen.

I sigh and bite down my smile. I had fun talking to Wilder and getting to know him. When he refused to split the bill, I had to remind myself that it wasn't a date. He was just being a gentleman.

"Oh, my goodness. You're swooning!" Joy giggles.

I tell her how I went into the wooded area and found the bridge, how Wilder showed up shortly after, scaring the hell out of me, and our time together. My voice squeaks with excitement, and I tell myself to take it down a notch. My time with Wilder doesn't necessarily mean anything, but his words were so honest that the part of me that's fragile wanted to find strength in them.

"That's so sweet," Joy sighs. "Let's order coffee, and we'll discuss this further." She stands, getting my order, and heads to the counter.

I look around the coffee shop and find some people staring at me. I shake it off. If Joy heard about Wilder and me having lunch, I'm guessing others have as well. It's weird for people to know your business.

Joy returns, placing two coffee cups on the table and sliding mine over. "Alana is meeting us here. I hope it's okay. She asked if I wanted to grab a cup of coffee and told her I was here."

"That's fine." I met Alana briefly, and she was super sweet. She manages the market and offered to give me any tips on working with the Mason Creek crowd in the butcher shop.

"I'll drop the subject about Wilder when she arrives, but 'til then tell me what it was like. Did you get butterflies in our stomach?"

"Gah, I totally did. How stupid is that?" I drop my head and scrunch up my nose.

"Not stupid at all." Joy looks at me over the top of her cup. "I think it's sweet."

I roll my eyes. I haven't told her about Wilder showing up to the butcher shop yesterday or our conversation and the mirror he gave me. I'd rather keep that to myself since it will open an entirely different discussion I'm not in the mood for.

"Tell me it's true!" Alana says louder than I'd like as she sits down beside Joy, her hazel eyes shining with interest. She swipes her ponytail off her shoulder and smirks, leaning forward on her arms and lowering her voice, thankfully. "Did you or did you not have lunch with Wilder James today?"

"What the... Does *everyone* in town know this?" I drop my face onto my hands.

"Oh, yeah. I was working, and Hattie and Hazel were talking about it in the grocery line." She looks at Joy. "You know when they get wind of something, they make sure the entire town knows by sunset." Alana chuckles and then grimaces when she sees my face.

"Probably not what you want to hear?" Her eyebrows lift.

"Nope." I shake my head. Joy has told me about Hattie and Hazel, the older twins who own the ice scream stand in Town Square. They're the town's biggest gossips.

"It's part of being in Mason Creek," Joy assures me. "In three days, they'll be talking about something else. Right, Alana?"

"Oh, yeah, totally." She nods, but it's not very convincing.

I lift a brow and give them my best glare.

"They will," Joy promises.

"Yeah, everyone's already forgotten what happened with you and—"

Joy cuts Alana off with a death stare.

"Right," she nods. "No talking about it. I'm gonna grab a coffee."

I look at my cousin and tilt my head.

"Was she gonna mention Brayden?" I cross my arms and lean back in my chair.

Joy rolls her eyes and releases a deep breath. I haven't been able to get her to open up about whatever happened between them, but then again, I haven't told her about Jeff.

"Yes, and I'm not talking about it yet. But she does have a point. People move on from things here. It's new and fresh, so they're curious, especially since you aren't a local. They were already talking about you. Now you go and get yourself a lunch date with a guy who's been off the market—in more ways than one—for years."

"What do you mean?" I lean forward and twist my lips.

"Remember how Wilder had a girlfriend?" I nod. "Well, she broke up with him a few weeks before her college graduation. She was supposed to move back to Mason Creek but decided she wanted more from the world than this small town. He was heartbroken, never been the same since, actually."

"Wow." I breathe out the word and think back on our conversation. His shift in attitude when he mentioned this town isn't for everyone makes sense now.

"Yeah, I think he was planning on proposing to her when she graduated. He hasn't dated anyone. I mean, there are rumors he's slept with women, but never someone from Mason Creek. It's believed he does the deed when he's out of town for cattle fairs and auctions."

"Oh." I scrunch up my nose and sit back in my seat. I don't want to hear about him screwing some random woman.

"Who knows what's true, though?" Joy shrugs. "I've learned not to take everything that circulates this town to heart."

All this information is running through my mind. I'm unable to grasp it all. I roll my eyes when two women nearby whisper and look at me.

I hate being the center of attention, and I accidentally shone the spotlight on myself by agreeing to lunch with Wilder. After hearing what Joy said, I'm assuming he isn't very happy about that, either.

However, I couldn't resist spending more time with him. After the night I had and the mood I woke up in, today's events turned out to be exactly what I needed.

Mason Creek could be the place where I find healing from the crap I've grown to believe about myself. One step at a time, I hope to shed away the harming thoughts and see myself the way the mirror hiding in my room says. *Worthy, beautiful, sexy.*

I've never considered myself sexy. Not even if I lost twenty pounds. I see myself more as the girl next door and forever friend. Maybe that's why I stayed with Jeff for longer than I should have. I wasn't sure I'd ever find anyone else who'd want me. Until I realized he didn't really want me either.

Chapter 13

WILDER

Levi's got a shit-eating grin when I run into him at the ranch. We don't work on Sundays unless there's an emergency, so I tend to go on rides. It seems he has the same idea as he saddles up his mare, Juliet.

"Look who's back from town." His smile widens.

Ignoring him, I run a hand down Juliet's side. Her auburn coat glimmers. She's a great horse.

"You're going for a ride?"

"Yeah. Taking advantage of the sunshine."

"I had the same thing in mind. Gonna get Bro saddled."

"Want me to wait for you?" He buckles the saddle and turns toward me.

"Sure." I walk to the barn in search of my buddy. Some people say dogs are a man's best friend. I beg to differ. There's nothing like a horse.

As I enter the barn, I see the injured steer peeking out of his stall. Midnight. I smile to myself as I remember Hallie's name for him.

"Hey, there, buddy." I pet down the center of his face. "How're you doing? Soon you'll be completely healed and return with your family. Open pasture awaits you."

I walk to Bro's stall and find my quarter horse waiting for me. He's as patient and gentle as a horse comes. I've never had another like him.

"Ready for a ride?" I smile when he bobs his head as if he understands me. "Come on, then."

Sliding the lock on the door, I guide Bro, grabbing my saddle from the tack room on the way out. In no time, Levi and I are riding side by side in silence. I was expecting an interrogation by the smile on his face when I arrived.

People were looking at Hallie and me while we ate at the diner, but I let it go. I'm not going to feed into their gossip. It's Mason Creek; everyone is going to spin their own story about what they see.

We ride through the open field, miles and miles of land stretched before us. I look at the snow-capped mountains and smile. This is what I needed. If I was confused about Hallie before, today threw me for a loop.

I haven't considered taking a woman on a date since Lisa broke my heart. I've met women for the sole purpose of fulfilling a need, but they're never from town, and it's not nearly as often as the rumors around here say. I've never been one to jump from bed to bed. Maybe it's because I was with Lisa all through high school and most of her college years. Most of my young adult life consisted of a steady relationship.

"So…is it true what I heard?" Levi looks at me, finally breaking the silence.

"Depends. What'd you hear?" The rocking motion of riding Bro soothes me, my body bouncing with his steps. I know where he's going with this. Mitch, one of my best friends, called me earlier to ask if the rumors were true. Apparently, people are already talking about seeing me at lunch with Hallie.

"You were on a date with Hallie."

I roll my eyes and shake my head. "People talk without damn facts. I wasn't on a date with her."

"So you didn't have lunch with her?" His eyebrows pull together.

"I did, but it wasn't a date."

"How did that come about then? Sadie told me she saw you guys when she ran into town." Sadie is Levi's best friend. She lived in Los Angeles for some years before moving back to Mason Creek. Now she's married to Wyatt, one of our deputy sheriffs, and they recently had a little girl.

The soft sound of rushing water hits my ears as we get closer to the river that passes our land. I look a Levi, who's expectantly waiting for me to give him the truth.

"I ran into her by the Henry Davis bridge. We got to talking, and I showed her the lake. We were hungry, so I suggested we eat something." My tone reflects indifference, but seeing Hallie made me feel anything but.

"Just like that?" My brother's eyes are narrowed.

"Yeah." I shrug. "What else do you want me to say?"

"Nothing," he breathes out and focuses straight ahead.

After a few pensive beats, he adds, "It wouldn't be such a bad thing if you did wanna take her on a date. I see the way you look at her, the excuses you come up with to stop by the butcher shop. Don't let the past hold you back, Wilder. What Lisa did sucks, but at least she told you what she wanted before agreeing to marry you. People are allowed to change their minds. And you're allowed to date again."

He shakes his head. "Hell, maybe even fall in love."

"Levi," I warn. He knows this topic is off-limits.

"Nah, it's time you stopped being a fool. I get it. Being left behind after having all these plans together must be hard as fuck. I've never had someone like that, so I can only imagine it from the outside. But I know that not allowing yourself to feel anything isn't a way to live. It's been years, Wilder. Move on. You've got a woman catching your eye, and for some reason, she seems to like you when clearly I'm the better-looking brother," he jokes. It's his way of balancing out serious conversations.

But when I look at him, his face is serious. "Don't screw it up. Not over something you can't change. Learn from experiences and make the next one better."

"She's only here for a short while. I'd be a fool to get into anything with her. She'll leave once Sal's fracture is healed." If I do pursue Hallie, I'm setting myself up for another failed relationship.

"Maybe she'll stay," he shrugs. "From what I hear, she loves being here. If nothing is holding her back in New York, who's to say she won't give it a go here if things work out between you two?"

Perfect MESS

I toss his words in my mind. From the few things she's mentioned about New York, it does seem as if she's tired of the city. But a girl like her probably has bigger dreams than staying in a small town. If she couldn't find a job in the city, how would she find one here?

Too many thoughts bombard me at once. I came out here to think, not get more confused.

"We'll see," I end the conversation with my final words.

Levi doesn't push, but he's said enough to keep me busy thinking for days to come.

I have felt this need to check on Hallie. Hell, yesterday I went to the butcher shop for no reason. I'm running out of excuses, and it seems as if the town's watching.

No matter how hard I try to fight it, she's magnetic.

"I'll race you to the river." Levi wears a cocky smile.

"Do you want to embarrass yourself?" I lift a brow, gripping the reins.

He laughs boastfully. "Yeah, right." Without warning, he kicks his legs, and his horse sprints away.

"Mother fucker," I mumble, taking off after him.

I catch up with ease, my always loyal Bro taking the lead and winning the race to the river. When we get there, I dismount and let him drink some water.

"Damn it. I sometimes forget how fast Bro is." Levi dismounts, letting his horse wander to the river as well.

I clap his shoulder. "You never learn, little bro."

I roam the area, allowing my mind to clear from the messy thoughts. The cabins we rent aren't too far from here, and guests love the access to the river. Some parts of the river are nestled between pine trees like this area, but the section closer to the cabins is open, and the sun shines directly on it in the summers.

"We live in the best place in the world, don't we?" Levi says, staring off down the river.

"We sure do," I agree.

Mason Creek will always be home, and I can't imagine living anywhere else.

I walk into Pony Up with Levi, and the first thing I see is Hallie leaning against the bar and Danny Phillips, a guy a few years younger than me, standing way too close for comfort. His arm is resting on the bar, almost corralling her against it.

My fists clench and unclench as I watch her laugh. What the fuck? I didn't take her for a flirt.

A hard slap lands on my shoulder, followed by a deep chuckle. Levi shakes his head.

"And you say you don't like her."

"I don't," I shrug, looking away from Hallie.

Before I can step around Levi toward a booth, he says, "Looks like she does, too." He tilts his chin in her direction.

I look back at Hallie and find round, happy green eyes on me. A small smile lights her face before she takes a drink of her beer. Danny follows her gaze, frowning when he realizes she's looking at me.

He leans in and whispers something, way too fucking close to her for my liking. I narrow my eyes, my jaw ticking. Hallie breaks eye contact and looks at Danny, but her smile's not real. It's not the same dimpled smile I saw on her earlier today.

When she shakes her head at whatever he said, he steps closer with a grin I'd like to smack off his damn mouth.

"You gonna let him steal your girl?"

My eyes snap to Levi with a hard stare. "I have no claim on her." I go in search of a booth.

When he catches up and sits across from me, he slaps the top of the table. "Because you're being a pussy and doing nothing about it."

"I'm not a pussy. Hallie's temporary. In a few weeks, she'll go back to her life in New York, meet some asshole suit, and live her life. She'll want more than some uneducated rancher."

"Whoa now." Levi sits back and glares at me. "Check your damn attitude. You're not some uneducated rancher. Damn it, just because Lisa wanted to explore the world doesn't mean every woman will think Mason Creek's not good enough." He runs a hand through his hair. "Fuck," he murmurs.

"Sorry. Let's grab some drinks and change subjects." I wave down a waitress and order two beers, ignoring my brother's inquisitive stare.

"You're an idiot," is all he says before we talk about the spring festival happening next month.

I purposefully sat with my back to the bar so I wouldn't be staring at Hallie, but I'm fighting the urge to see if Danny is still talking to her.

"Hey, you're gonna let someone steal your girl?" Brayden drops down on the booth next to Levi. A few people sitting on the booth behind us look our way with knowing smiles.

"She's not his girl," Levi mocks me.

Brayden laughs, stretching his arm behind the back of the booth.

"Yeah, right. I heard you guys were out. It's all over The MC Scoop." He raises his eyebrows and looks at Levi. Damn small-town gossip blog.

"Hey, don't look at me. I heard the same, but he says it's nothing."

"I'm sitting right here," I interrupt them. "We went to lunch. That's all. She's free to do what she wants." I take a drink of my beer.

"Or who she wants," Brayden chuckles, elbowing Levi.

When they both look over my head with wide eyes, I can't fight it anymore and turn around. Hallie and Danny are dancing to the left of the bar, along with a few other locals. They're at a safe distance, but the idea of her dancing with anyone else spikes my jealousy. I can't ignore it any longer.

Levi's words from earlier take up residence in my mind, going over and over what he said. I drain my beer and slam the empty bottle on the table and stand. As if the gods were rooting for me, the current song ends, and

Perfect MESS

Hallie steps away from Danny with a polite smile. I get to her before she gets to the bar and smile.

"Hey, would you like to dance?" I reach my hand out and smile.

Hallie stares into my eyes before responding or taking my hand. "You know… People are already talking."

"So let's give them a reason to talk." I wink and grab her hand, leading back to the dance floor.

Tucker Simms, our local musician, is up on a small stage with his band. His smooth voice sings the beginning words to "Undone" by Joe Nichols, and I put my other hand around Hallie's waist, pulling her to me.

We move to the slow beat, Hallie's hand resting on my shoulder in a tight grip. Her body is stiff as she dances with me, so I lean down and whisper, "Relax." When she shivers, I smile to myself.

I keep my eyes on hers, not giving a damn who's staring at us or what they're whispering. The only thing I care about at this moment is the woman moving her body with mine, all curves and softness to my hard lines and guarded heart.

Hallie's fingers brush through the ends of my hair. I'm not sure if she's aware that she's doing it, but it feels so fucking good. I close my eyes and allow the sensation of her gentle touch to take over. I haven't felt soft touches like this in years. I haven't allowed myself to. Here comes this stunning blonde with pain written on her face despite attempting to hide it with her smile, and I begin to crumble.

It isn't until Hallie puts her hand on my chest and taps me that I realize the music has stopped.

"Wilder..." she whispers. "Song ended."

I nod slowly, looking back into her eyes with a smirk. "Sorry." I brush away a flyaway that's fallen from her ponytail.

"It's okay." Hallie tilts her head to look around me. She rolls her eyes, and I turn to see who she's looking at. Joy's making some motions with her hands, and her eyes widen when she realizes I'm watching her. She cringes and turns away to talk to Alana.

"Do you need to get back to your friends?"

"Uhh...maybe?" It comes out as a question, telling me everything I need to know as her eyes search mine.

"Or we could have a drink," I offer before I chicken out.

"Sure," she nods, her face lighting up with a smile that shoots straight to my chest, making my heart race. That was the right choice.

Whether I think it's a good idea to pursue her or not, I'm not keeping my distance from Hallie. I'll deal with the fallout later.

Chapter 19

HALLIE

"Are the rumors true?" Uncle Sal asks instead of his usual, "Good morning."

My heart stops, and my feet halt on the way to the kitchen for some much-needed coffee. If I thought I hadn't slept well the night before, I barely got shut-eye last night after spending the rest of the evening with Wilder.

When I saw him walk into Pony Up, I got excited but quickly deflated when I saw his glare. Maybe Grumpy Wilder was back after our lunch.

Danny had asked me if it was true that Wilder and I were dating when he noticed me staring at Wilder, which I had to deny since it isn't true. I saw the excitement in his eyes, though, and didn't know how to tell him that I'd only like to be his friend. It's awkward as hell when you've just met someone. I wasn't going to make an ass out of myself by assuming that's what he was thinking.

Then, Wilder asked me to dance right after I'd finish dancing with Danny, and I think he took the hint. After all, there is a foundation for the rumors going around. I do have a crush on Wilder.

By the time Joy, Alana, and I finished at Java Jitters, the story about Wilder and me having lunch together got so twisted that I couldn't believe it. I joked that I needed a drink, and Joy and Alana didn't hesitate to make plans to meet at Pony Up in the evening. It feels good to have genuine friends.

I was with Jeff for over two years, and in that time, I lost touch with acquaintances I had. Most of the people I spent time with were his friends. I never made real friendships in college, and the ones I had from high school dissolved into the pleasant and superficial chit-chat on social media after we all went our separate ways for college. It's sad when I think about it. I've been a loner for so long, relying just on Jeff.

My life is a mess. I have no real job. My ex-boyfriend is trying to get money from me that I don't have. And the future is so uncertain that I sometimes want to scream to the universe to shine a freaking light over which path to take. All I get is silence that amps my anxiety. I'm lost, but the past few weeks in Mason Creek have been a much-needed reprieve from real life.

"Hello? Is anyone in there?" Uncle Sal chuckles.

"Huh?" My head snaps toward him. "Sorry, I got distracted."

His deep laughter vibrates out of him. "Thinking about a certain someone?"

"Ugh, no." I head into the kitchen and serve some coffee. "Did you make this?" I lift the carafe.

"Yup, but before you say anything, I used the walker and didn't put weight on my leg."

"Good," I smile and prepare my coffee before looking at him in the eye.

"What rumors did you hear?" I look into my mug.

"Seems to be as you've caused quite the stir in town. I've heard everything from you going on a date with Wilder to being in a relationship with him to breaking his heart when you return to New York."

"Oh, my goodness." My eyes widen. "What the hell, Uncle Sal?" My voice rises.

"Hey," he lifts his hands. "I'm just tellin' you what I've heard."

"How did you even hear this when you're home all day?" I cross my arms and lift an eyebrow.

"Patty told me," he says with a head-shake as if it should be obvious where his source of gossip comes from.

"Of course she did. Well, I did not go on a date with Wilder. I ran into him, and we had lunch. That's all." I open the fridge and pull out the carton of eggs. "Want some?" I hold it up.

"Sure." Uncle Sal nods, eyes squinted. "So you didn't dance with him at Pony Up."

"Oh, my God!" I almost drop the carton of eggs on the floor. Not the kind of scramble I'm aiming for. Instead, I slam them on the counter.

"Are you freaking serious? You heard about that, too?"

He gives me a knowing smile. "I've got ears all over town." He chuckles, placing his arms on the counter.

"Are you asking people to update you on my whereabouts?" I arch a brow and press my lips together.

"No, sweetie." My uncle frowns, his thick eyebrows pulling together. "I wouldn't do that. I'm just teasing ya."

I sigh and drop my head.

"I know you wouldn't. It's just odd. There's nothing going on, at least not that I know of. We had lunch and danced." To the perfect song ever, but I keep that to myself. Slow dancing with Wilder was heaven. The way his strong arms held me close to his body made me feel safe.

"I think people are so curious about it because Wilder hasn't shown interest in anyone in years."

"So I've heard," I shrug. "Anyway, nothing's happened," I assure him and begin cracking eggs.

"If it does happen, it's okay. Your mom told me about that asshole ex of yours."

My eyes lift to his while I beat the eggs. "She did?"

Uncle Sal nods. "When you decided to come. She wanted me to keep an eye on you, make sure you're doing okay." His eyes harden. "If I get my hands on that little shit…"

I can't help but giggle. "What are you gonna do? He'd sue because he's that type of person. He isn't worth spending energy on." I look back down at the bowl.

I'm not sure how much my mom told him. I've never told my parents what Jeff would say to me, but maybe they picked up on things when they'd see him. He always spoke in a condescending tone.

"Anyway, do you need anything today? I can go to the market and stock up for the week."

Perfect MESS

"That'd be great. Thank you, Hallie. I appreciate you putting your life on hold to come help your old uncle."

I smile and shake my head. "You're not *that* old." I tease with a wink and finish cooking breakfast.

Uncle Sal's boisterous laughter makes my smile grow. "I'm young at heart."

"That you are." I plate the scrambled eggs and set one in front of him with a fork and toast.

Uncle Sal is a few years older than my mom, so he's reaching retirement age, but his attitude toward the world is filled with joy, which makes him seem younger.

"Any chance you can stop by Wilder's ranch and look at a few lambs for me? I'll give you the details of what to look for. I completely trust Wilder, but the old-school mentality creates a need to see the animal before it's slaughtered."

"Lambs?" I frown. "Those adorable little animals. Like, Mary had a little lamb?"

He laughs. "Yes. Many people in town buy them in the springtime. Not sure why they prefer it then, maybe because of Easter."

"Well, that's ironic considering the Lamb of God and all."

His laugh deepens. "Your sarcastic humor is on point today."

I scrunch up my nose. "I'll take that as a compliment, thankyouverymuch." I curtsy. "Yeah, I'll go look at poor innocent lambs and apologize beforehand," I deadpan.

"Thank you."

"You're welcome. It's why I'm here. If you need anything else besides help in the butcher shop, you know I'll do it."

"And that's why you're my favorite niece."

I roll my eyes. "Look who's funny now. I'm your only niece. Anyway, I'm gonna have lunch with Joy as well since the bakery is closed today. I can leave lunch cooked for you. Are you okay being alone for a few hours? If you need me to come home, just call."

"Go and have fun. It's what you're supposed to do at your age. Don't worry about me. I've got the TV and my recliner waiting for me. Patty may come by later, so she'll bring lunch."

"Okay." I nod. "Make the grocery list while I get ready, and I'll grab everything we need. before coming home."

"Thank you, sweetheart."

My nerves are amplified while I shower and get ready, knowing that each minute that passes will get me closer to facing Wilder after last night. We danced, talked, and drank a few more beers before he left since he wakes up at "the ass crack of dawn," as he said.

Dressed in jeans and *real* boots this time, I grab the grocery list from Uncle Sal and kiss his cheek before heading out on his old truck. I laugh to myself at Wilder's reaction when he saw me driving this truck the first time I visited the ranch. Maybe he's realized that I'm not the city snob he had assumed I was.

My palms sweat against the steering wheel as I make my way out of town and toward the ranch. Although it's a short drive away, the ranch is located in an area that feels like a different world with vast land, looming mountains, and fresh air.

More familiar with it this time, I park next to the house like I did last time. Instead of staring awkwardly at the patio, I trek to the barn in hopes that I'll find Wilder there. It's empty, but I spot my new favorite friend peeking out the stall.

Midnight is looking at me as if he recognizes me. I'm sure that's all in my wild imagination, but I walk toward him, letting him sniff my hand before petting the side of his face.

"You're still here, buddy." I'm relieved to see him. "How are you feeling?" He breathes heavily.

"I'm okay. Things have developed since I saw you, but I'm still working on my self-esteem. Your owner is helping with that, though. He gave me the perfect gift. Between you and me, it made me teary-eyed." I look into Midnight's black eyes and smile. He's such a gentle animal. Not what you'd expect from a steer.

"Anyway… Did I tell you about the douche-cunt? I don't think I did. He's my ex-boyfriend, and he's being extra douchey." I tell Midnight about Jeff's demands that I pay half the security deposit, among other things.

"He was always so condescending, making me feel inferior to him because I couldn't find a job or because I didn't look like a runway model." I blow out a breath, not letting the memories tackle me.

"You probably don't want to hear me complain all day, do you? How are you feeling? You seem to be in better spirits than the other day." I continue to pet the side of his face. I hadn't realized how therapeutic talking to an animal was. I never had a pet growing up, so I missed a lot of that connection with animals.

Midnight makes a huffing sound, and I chuckle. "What? I don't get a moo from you?" My laughter grows louder when I realize I rhymed.

"Thanks for the talk, Midnight. I hope you're one-hundred-percent better soon, but not well enough where they'll make you into burgers." I grimace. "Sorry. I'm gonna go search for your owner, so I can get this job done. Be grateful you're not a lamb."

A quiet laugh makes my eyes widen. My heart races as I turn around and find Wilder leaning against the entrance of the barn. *How much did he hear?*

He pushes away from the doorway and walks toward me with confident strides.

"Having fun with my cattle?" His eyes are lighter, like the clear sky.

"Uh…yeah?" I scrunch up my nose, embarrassed I've been caught talking to the steer yet again.

Wilder's smile is full of joy. "Looks like it."

He stops before me, his hands in his jean pockets. The washed denim fits him perfectly. The straight leg design accentuates his strong thighs, and if he turned around, I'd bet they show off his ass. *Cowboys are sexy as hell.*

Holding back my sigh, I smirk. "I'm here about some lambs."

Wilder tosses his head back and laughs. "So I hear. Follow me." He turns around, and I take a second to appreciate his backside. Oh, yeah, his ass looks great in jeans.

"Are you coming?" He looks over his shoulder. His blue eyes contrast against the black cowboy hat, and I'm about to melt into a puddle of lust.

"Yup." I quicken my steps and catch up to him.

I've got my list of things to look for from Uncle Sal in my hand. We step into a small pen with some lambs, and my heart instantly clenches. They're so adorable. They make me want to sit and pet them all day. I don't know how Wilder and Uncle Sal do this job.

"I can't stop reciting Mary Had a Little Lamb in my mind," I confess.

Wilder chuckles, covering his mouth. "Hey, boss man." A young guy lifts his chin in Wilder's direction. His dark hair is tucked beneath a cap. His shirt has dirt marks on it from working outside.

"Hey, Caleb. This is Hallie. Hallie, Caleb's our best ranch hand."

"It's nice to meet you. I'm here to sacrifice the lambs," I press my lips together, then mentally slap my forehead for my stupid comment.

"She feels a bit guilty," Wilder explains.

"Ah, Sal's niece," Caleb says with a smirk, looking between us. "I can see it," he mumbles, but I catch it.

"Huh?" I look between Wilder and Caleb.

"Nothing," Wilder glares at him. "Caleb, I need you to check the fence line on the west side of the ranch."

"You got it, boss." Wilder rolls his eyes, and Caleb laughs. "Only kidding," he tosses over his shoulder before climbing on a horse and riding out.

"He seems nice," I comment.

"He's great but loves to annoy me with the boss shit." Wilder opens the gate to the pen. "These are the lambs I separated for Sal. He wasn't sure how many he'd need, so I have a decent number. You don't need to take them all, but I wanted to make sure I covered his order."

I walk in, smiling at the adorable animals. Despite the guilt I feel, I've actually enjoyed learning the business. I don't think I'll be able to butcher these little guys, though.

After telling Wilder the specifics Uncle Sal's looking for, we agree on twenty lambs once I confirm with Uncle Sal.

I look up at Wilder and smirk.

"It's nice doin' business with ya," I joke, sticking my hand out.

Wilder doesn't hesitate to take it, and my body sparks to life at the rough touch of his calloused hands.

"Likewise." He gives me a crooked grin that makes my body heat.

"I'll, uh, let you get back to work. Don't tell anyone the crazy New Yorker likes talking to cows, okay?"

"Your secret's safe with me." He's still holding my hand.

I look down at our linked hands and back up. Before I say anything, he continues talking, "And you're no crazy New Yorker."

I roll my eyes.

"I can't make you believe what I do. I don't have that power, none of us do, but I can remind you that you're beautiful, funny, and a bit quirky."

A different smile appears on his lips when he says this. It's softer and full of meaning at the same time. It fills me with an array of feelings, the main one being wanted.

I smile, biting my lower lip. "Thank you."

"Don't thank me." He steps back, disconnecting our hands and placing his in his pockets. Wilder looks above my head, and unease fills me. Maybe I read our recent interactions wrong.

"But you could go out with me."

My eyes snap to his. "On a date?" I ask incredulously.

"Yeah," he chuckles. "Is that okay?" The fact that he asks squeezes my heart.

I nod as I say, "Yeah but…" I look away. "Is it a good idea? With my stay being temporary?"

Wilder sighs and shakes his head, rubbing a hand down his face. "I don't know, but we won't know if it's worth it until we give it a try, right?"

I chew on the inside of my cheek. Confusion and worry fill me. I like Wilder. I want nothing more than to get to know him better and see if there's more to this crush. Not to mention, he's sexy to look at and knows how to dance.

When I don't say anything, he whispers, "What would you like, Hallie?"

My eye bore into his. I'm not sure what I'm looking for, but what I find is an honest and vulnerable man. He's had his share of heartbreak, and yet he's daring to ask me out.

Biting down my smile, I say, "To give this town something else to talk about."

A deep laugh moves through him and washes over me, cementing my decision. Who knows, maybe this could work out.

"Then that's what we'll do. We've already caused quite the gossip." He winks, and I sigh. "Let's forget about the uncertainties of the future and the pain from the past. How about we focus on right now and enjoy it?" He steps closer. When his hand cradles my cheek, I lean into his touch.

"I think that's the most romantic thing anyone's said to me."

"Damn, you deserve so much more than that." His thumb caresses my lower lip. I'm starting to believe he's right.

Chapter 15

HALLIE

I've been a ball of nerves since Wilder asked me out on a date yesterday. *Me!* I still can't believe it, but I'm trying to. I don't want to be the insecure girl anymore. I want to inhale Wilder's words and let them sink into my heart so I could believe them as well.

I close the butcher shop right on time and rush to Uncle Sal's truck. I used it this morning, so I could get home quickly and cut my walking time in half. I don't want to be running late when Wilder picks me up.

I send pictures of my outfit choices to Joy. It's been so long since I've been on a date, and Mason Creek is definitely more casual than New York. I didn't pack a lot of "date" clothes with me since I came to help Uncle Sal, but I do have a couple of casual dresses and tops I can pair with jeans.

My phone rings, and I immediately answer when I see Joy's name on the screen.

"Hello?"

"Hey, are you excited?" she shrieks.

"More like nervous." I blow out a breath. I've spent time with Wilder, but none of those encounters were dates.

"Don't be. Have fun and relax."

"Yeah," I nod though she can't see me. "Anyway, which outfit did you like best?"

"I love the dresses, but the temperature will drop as the evening progresses. I recommend the jeans and pair them with the black off-the-shoulder top you have. The long-sleeved one."

I grab the top she's talking about and stare at it. "It's not too fitted?" I loved the top when I bought it, but I tend to get self-conscious every time I pull it out of my closet.

"Hell, no. It's sexy, and Wilder will love it. Plus, your jeans are high-waisted."

"Okay, thanks."

"Take your coat and wear your cute booties."

I chuckle to myself. I bet he won't mock my booties tonight.

"Hallie, enjoy yourself tonight. You have no reason to be nervous. If Wilder asked you out, it's because he likes you, so stop overthinking."

"Thanks, Joy." I smile, looking down at the outfit on my bed.

"You're welcome. I expect all the deets tomorrow."

I laugh and promise to let her know how it goes before hanging up. Sighing, I get dressed and stare at myself in the mirror. I try not to nitpick all my flaws. I'm more than what my body looks like, and from what Wilder's said, he likes what he sees. Holding on to that, I finish my makeup and curl the ends of my hair with my iron before swiping my lips with nude lipstick.

When I walk out of my room, Uncle Sal whistles, and Patty claps her hands.

"You look beautiful," she says with a huge grin.

"Thank you," my cheeks flush.

"You do look beautiful, darling. Have fun." Uncle Sal sits on his recliner.

"Thanks, Uncle Sal. Any chance I can take a shot?" I joke.

They laugh, and Patty stands from the couch and grabs my hand, patting it gently. "You don't need that. You look great. If you want me to open the butcher shop tomorrow, I can," she winks, causing my blush to deepen.

"No, no. I'm sure I won't be home too late." I shake my head, avoiding their eyes.

"Leave the girl alone, Patty," Uncle Sal chuckles.

"I'll be there anyway, just in case," she whispers conspiratorially.

I giggle and shake my head. I'm not planning on sleeping with Wilder. I mean, it's not like I haven't thought about it, but we've both been through a lot. Taking this slow sounds like a good plan.

Right on cue, a knock echoes through the house, and my heart leaps.

"Have fun," Patty and Uncle Sal call out at the same time.

I wave and grab my coat before heading for the door. When I open it, my eyebrows rise. Standing before me, in all his six-foot-plus glory, is the most handsome man I've ever seen. Dressed in dark jeans and a baby blue button-down that brings out his eyes, Wilder looks like a book boyfriend come to life. The sleeves are rolled up, showing off his toned arms. To think I've only ever read about guys that look like him. His hair is mussed as if he's been running his hand through it, and it looks sexy.

"Hey," one side of his lips lifts, and I hold back a sigh.

"Hi." I smile and hitch my purse higher on my shoulder.

"You look beautiful." He leans forward, brushing his lips against my cheek and inhaling. "And you smell like heaven."

My body tingles at his words. Heat rises up my spine. If this is how tonight will go, then the coat is unnecessary. Cold weather be damned. Around Wilder, I'm always on high heat.

His woodsy cologne hits me, and I inhale greedily.

"So do you," I whisper.

"Let's go." He places his hand on my lower back and leads me out of the house.

Wilder opens the passenger door for me and offers his hand to help me up into his truck. I smile as I settle in my seat and watch him round the truck with his confident strides.

"How was your day?" he asks as he pulls out of the driveway and makes his way into town.

"It was good. I cut down a pork shoulder with little help from YouTube," I brag a bit. Every day I get better at this job. While it may not be something I'll do forever,

I've enjoyed learning something new and pushing myself out of my comfort zone.

"That's great. You don't need my help anymore." He smiles over at me.

"Uh… Well, if you wanna butcher the lambs, I'll step away and let you do that," I half-tease because the idea of those guys makes me sad.

Wilder chuckles. "I'll see what I can do."

"I'm only kidding. I have to put on my big girl panties and do my job."

He arches a brow, glancing at me. "Big girl panties?" His eyes twinkle with mischief.

Heat rises up my neck and lands on my cheeks, causing me to look away. Wrong choice of words for a first date, I guess.

His deep laugh resounds in the truck. "I'm only teasing you." His hand pats my knee, and I tense, not with discomfort but with desire.

I look over at him, his eyes back on the road. I study his profile—his straight nose and short beard covering his strong jaw. Wilder's all man.

"Are you staring?" He mocks with a smirk.

"No," my voice rises, giving away my lie.

He laughs and never looks away from the road when he says, "Stare all you want. I won't be complaining about having your eyes on me."

Goodness, this man and his words. Is this the same man who was heartbroken? He may not have told me his story yet, but from what Joy's shared, it's a surprise to hear him speak to me as he does.

It doesn't take long for Wilder to park his truck by Town Square. He meets me by my door as I'm opening it and offers his hand to help me step down.

"You said you liked Italian, so I thought we could go to Sauce It Up. If we eat at Wren's Cafe two times in a week, people might lose it," he winks.

Giggling, I nod. "Yeah, soon they'll call it our place," I joke.

"Maybe they'll put a plaque on the table we sat on, and they won't let anyone else use it," he keeps the joke going.

I laugh more freely now, imagining that. It seems like something that would happen in a town like this. We walk toward the restaurant not far from the truck, and Wilder opens the door. His hand lands on my lower back again, guiding me inside the restaurant.

"Wow," I breathe out. "This place is adorable."

The restaurant is cozy. The tables are made of weathered wood, tying a rustic feel to the airy white walls and white subway tiles behind the bar. Dark wood beams are spaced out and line the white ceiling. Some people are sitting on stools at the bar. Others are at the tables. What's unanimous is when they all turn to look at us with wide eyes.

"I guess we couldn't go unnoticed, huh?" Wilder whispers. His breath tickles my neck.

"Nope." I turn to look at him, and my breath catches. The smile he's wearing is the same gentle one I saw yesterday at the ranch.

"We did agree to give them something else to talk about, right?"

All I can do is nod.

A waitress carrying a tray smiles and says, "You can take a seat at that table." She points at a table set for two. "I'll be back with menus."

"Thanks, Dana," Wilder says.

I smile as he holds the chair for me to sit and watch his easy strides around the table to the other side. My belly flips. The waitress brings the menus right away, making me break eye contact with Wilder.

I scan the menu before asking Wilder, "What do you recommend?" A few options stand out to me, and my mouth waters.

"All the pasta dishes are delicious. They use fresh products."

"That's great." I read the options. "I'm going to have the veal ravioli then. They're my weakness."

Wilder smirks. "Sounds good. The veal is local, too."

My eyebrows lift. "Are they yours?" He nods. "That's amazing. I love how everyone here supports one another. It's a true community."

"We are," he nods. "Sure, people gossip, and there are rivalries, but when it counts, everyone comes together to support you."

"That sounds lovely," I sigh.

"Honestly, it is."

Growing up in a place like Mason Creek must have provided so many life lessons. People here have a different mentality. In the short weeks I've been here,

I've noticed it in the manners, the way everyone says good morning or hello when they cross you on the street. It's incredible.

"Hey, I'm Dana," the waitress officially introduces herself to me. "What can I get you to drink?"

Wilder looks at me. "Would you like wine?"

"That'd be great." I haven't even looked at the drink menu, but before I can flip to it, Wilder orders.

"We'll have a bottle of the Cab." I raise my eyebrows—a man who drinks wine. Sign me up. "Is that okay?" He looks worried for a second.

"That's perfect. Cabernet is my favorite."

"Great." He smiles at Dana. "And we're ready to order."

After placing our order and Dana serves us each a glass of wine, Wilder and I relax into our seats as he tells me about his day on the ranch today.

"How's Midnight?"

"He's much better, even though you did see that for yourself yesterday." His lips quirk.

The reminder that he caught me talking to the steer causes embarrassment all over again. I nod silently.

"Are you gonna sell him for beef?" I'm not sure if I worded that question correctly since I'm still learning the correct lingo, but Wilder doesn't laugh at my attempt.

He nods. "Probably. It's why we raise them."

I frown. "But..." I look away. "Never mind, that's your job. He's just so cute. Don't sell him to me, okay?" My eyes widen. "Shit, don't tell Uncle Sal I said that, though."

Perfect MESS

He laughs quietly. "Your secret's safe with me."

"Phew," I swipe my forehead playfully, which makes his smile grow.

"Why haven't you found a job in New York? From what I've seen, you're capable of doing anything you set your mind to. That's evident considering you didn't know the difference between a heifer and a steer when you arrived."

"I think that's a compliment." I narrow my eyes.

"It is," he assures me.

"Honestly, New York is a competitive market. I sent resumes out before I graduated, thinking I was ahead of my game, but very few people actually scheduled an interview. None of them led to an opportunity. In the meantime, I worked odd jobs, so I had some income. It helped that I still lived with my parents because rent in New York is no freaking joke." I cross my leg over my knee and lean forward on the table.

"I can't even imagine," he shakes his head.

"Yeah," I nod. "Anyway, when I couldn't find a job after undergrad, I went back to school for my Master's in hopes that would help qualify me for more job opportunities."

"And it didn't?"

I shake my head. "The only thing I can think of is that I'm not five-eleven with a stick figure and take-charge attitude. It seems as if that's the type of person these CEOs want. What you look on the outside is as important as your brain when you need to impress clients." I roll my eyes.

"Or you need to have an in with someone at a company. It's how many people get jobs even if they aren't as qualified as other candidates. Their fathers are friends with the owner or with the CEO. Buddies always take precedence over everyone else. Like that, someone always owes you a favor. It's wrong, but it's the world we live in."

"Maybe it's the world *you* live in. That's not the case around here." His brows pull down, and Wilder's jaw is tight.

"I've noticed that. Living in a big city can make you cynical and untrusting. This town seems like one from a Hallmark movie or something."

"Sometimes it feels like it, but it's also got its problems. The good just outweighs the bad." His fingers stroke the stem of his wineglass.

I nod, taking a sip of the robust red. The flavors pop before I swallow. It's so good. There was no reason to be nervous about this date. Wilder puts me at ease. I feel like I can talk to him about anything, and he won't judge me. Well, at least now after he's gotten rid of the false idea he had of me as a useless city girl.

I laugh to myself.

"What's so funny?"

I shake my head. "Nothing."

He leans forward on the table and stares into my eyes. "Something's making you laugh."

"It's silly," I wave it off.

"Tell me," he demands, his eyes piercing into mine.

The way he looks at me makes my breath catch. "I was thinking about how you judged me when we first met. You thought I was some stupid city girl."

His lips press together in a frown. Damn it. This is why I didn't want to bring it up and ruin the good mood we had going on.

"I'm sorry about that." He reaches across the table and takes my hand. I suck in a breath when he squeezes it. "I was wrong to judge you the way I did. Don't take it personally. It was my own projection."

"Why?" I whisper.

He shakes his head. "I'll tell you another day. I don't want the past to ruin our night. Nothing is worth messing with this." He squeezes my hand again, and a boyish smile appears on his lips.

I nod, turning my hand over and curling my fingers over his palm. His eyes darken, urging me to repeat the action. His thumb strokes the back of my hand as we're caught in the moment, the mood shifting. He makes me feel things I haven't felt in a long time, maybe ever.

A throat clears, and we break contact, finding Dana smiling awkwardly with our plates.

"Sorry to interrupt."

I blush furiously, hiding my face from her with my hair while Wilder's body shakes with laughter. It's so easy to get lost in him, whether we're alone or in public with an audience.

"People are definitely gonna be talking about this all week," he jokes before refilling our wine glasses.

I'm still coming down from the feel of his touch on my freaking hand and just nod with a racing heart.

Chapter 16

WILDER

I haven't cared about spending time with a woman in years, at least not quality time where we get to know each other. I'm not sure what it is about Hallie, maybe the smile she always seems to wear despite her vulnerability and pain.

The ghost of her soft strokes on my palm continues to taunt me throughout dinner, my body reacting to her touch. Hallie has stirred something in me that I've been avoiding. Listening to her tell me about her life gives me insight into who she is outside of these few weeks I've known her. Her relationship with her parents is great, and I'm relieved she has their support.

"What's been the most challenging thing about working on a ranch?" I watch as she finishes her wine. Her lips smile around her glass as she eyes me.

I wish she saw how beautiful she is. After overhearing her talk to Midnight and the bits and pieces she's shared with me, I'm determined to make her see how amazing she is. Her curves are sexy like I told her. Any guy would kill to grab an ass like hers, but she's more than her body and should be reminded of that every damn day.

I clear my throat before responding. "How demanding it is. I love what I do, but it's a twenty-four-hour job. Sure, I get to go out for drinks, woo a beautiful woman," I wink, and her cheeks turn pink. "But I don't remember the last time I took a vacation. Being away for a week, even for a few days, is hard to do."

Hallie nods, spinning her empty glass. "That makes sense. But you have ranch hands, and Levi helps you."

I chuckle. "It'd seem like I had enough help, right?" She nods. "If I really wanted to, I know I could, but I don't want to add more work to their already demanding schedules. It takes all of us for things to run smoothly. Animals are unpredictable, and you've gotta be watching at all times."

"I can see that. Like Midnight's injury."

"Exactly. Or coyotes attacking our calves and chickens."

Hallie's eyes widen.

"Coyotes?" she whispers.

"Yeah," I chuckle. "Those bastards like to eat our animals."

She shivers and grimaces. "Aren't they super dangerous?"

"They could be," I nod. "But we're careful and keep our animals as safe as possible."

"That's good." Her eyes are still round with worry despite my reassurance.

"Are you ready to go?" I smirk when a flash of disappointment crosses her face.

"Oh, yeah. I guess we have been done eating for a while." Her hands wring around her napkin.

"I like talking to you, but I thought we could grab a coffee, and I'd take you somewhere else. Something I'm sure New York will never offer you."

Her eyes light up, and I promise myself to always make her this happy. Whatever it is about her that's driving me to make promises has forgotten about the fact that's she's temporary.

"Let's go." She claps her hands.

After we pay, we walk to Java Jitters for coffee. I link my fingers with hers, and Hallie looks up at me with a shy smile. Glancing back to the street in front of us, she takes her lip between her teeth. The few people around Town Square glance our way and point us out to their friends. We'll be the talk in town for a few more days, and then people will get over it.

Jessie's eyes sparkle when she sees us walk in, but she doesn't say a word. Instead, she greets us happily and takes our orders.

"It looks like she's bursting to ask what's going on," Hallie whispers and giggles.

"Yeah, did you see her face when we walked in?" I chuckle.

"Oh, yeah." Humor laces her words. "It's kinda fun keeping people on their toes."

"Look at you, getting the hang of small-town living." I wrap my arm around her waist and tug her closer to me.

"It's easy to fall in love with Mason Creek," she grins.

Her words pierce my chest. It's too soon to hope for a future with this woman, and yet I can't help but wonder if she'll love it enough to stay and give us a chance.

"Here you go," Jessie interrupts us, placing two coffee cups on the counter in front of us.

"Thanks," we both say, and Hallie chuckles.

We head back to my truck, her hand in mine. For the first time in years, my body feels lighter. I've been avoiding this situation with anyone for so long out of fear of getting hurt again that I'd forgotten how great it could be to have someone in your corner. While Hallie and I may not quite be there yet, she's reminding me that taking a risk on someone could be worth it.

"Where are we going?" She looks over at me as I drive away from Town Square.

"You'll see." I smile at her before focusing on the winding road that leads to the ranch. Hallie wants to see something she can't find in New York, and I'd bet all my money she'll never see a sky like the one we have here in Montana.

"This is the ranch." She leans forward on the console as I pass under the sign. "Are we gonna see Midnight?" Her eyes light up.

"Not today." She frowns, and I reach for her hand. "But I promise this will be better."

"Better than Midnight?" Her question is laced with incredulity.

"I promise."

I stop the truck when we reach an open field a few miles away from the houses. Turning off the lights, Hallie gasps.

"Wow," her hand covers her mouth. She cranes her head forward to look out the windshield.

"Come on," I say, opening my door.

Her face shines brighter than the stars overhead, and she jumps from the truck before I can make my way around to help her. When she turns to reach for her coffee in the cupholder, I can't help but groan. Without a second thought, I step closer to her, pressing my body against hers. She tenses briefly before a small gasp escapes her.

"I've got your cup," I whisper.

Hallie shivers, straightening up. It takes her a few seconds to turn around, and when she does, we're toe-to-toe. It's dark except the light in the cab softly illuminating her face. Her eyes are round as they search mine.

I give her her coffee cup and use my free hand to cup her face. Hallie's eyes flutter closed.

"You're so beautiful," I murmur, trying hard not to kiss her yet. Instead, I brush my lips against her forehead. When I step back, her eyes are on me again.

"Thank you." She looks down at her shoes.

"Hey," I lift her chin. "Remember what I told you. Never look down. Keep your eyes up and know how gorgeous you are." I step closer until our bodies are flush so she can feel my reaction to her.

Her eyebrows jump up on her forehead, and her lips part. Maybe I'm pushing too far on our first date, but I want her to know how desired she is, how she drives me crazy. Her eyes, her lips, her touch, all of it makes my heart race.

"Wilder," her voice is a soft moan.

"Yeah, babe?" I smile crookedly.

Her hand comes around my back, keeping me in place. I put my coffee cup on the roof of the truck and slide both of my hands into her hair, tilting her face to make sure she's staring into my eyes when I speak my next words.

"You are nothing like I imagined when I first ran into you. You're beautiful, gorgeous. The same curves you hate and judge drive me wild, but it's more than that. I haven't figured it out yet, but I damn well plan to."

We silently stare into each other's eyes in the quiet evening. My thumb strokes her cheek. Hallie's eyes move from my eyes to my lips. After the third time, I take the hint and brush my lips against hers. It's innocent at first. A few closed-mouth kisses. When she grips the back of my shirt and peeks her tongue out, all bets are off.

I grab her coffee, putting it on the roof of the truck next to mine, and grip her waist. I squat down, so our bodies are more aligned, and I deepen the kiss. My tongue seeks hers in her warm mouth. I angle her head to kiss her better and get lost in this woman. Her soft skin against mine, her hands roaming my body. Her touch lights me on fire, burning me—my heart slams.

It's been so long since I've fully surrendered to a woman.

Hallie doesn't miss a beat, her hands skimming up my chest. I wish her hands were under my shirt, but I'll take what I can get. She moans breathily into my mouth, our lips fused together.

"Babe," I groan, rubbing my lower body against hers. I'm tight all around, desire building.

"Shit," she mumbles. My chuckle turns into a growl when she grinds against me harder, causing my hard dick to twitch.

I grab her ass and lift her, her legs locking around my waist. We break apart for a moment, her wide eyes staring into mine. Lust and awe swim in her gaze. I wink and find her lips again, not wasting any time with tentative brushes.

I thrust my hips against hers, Hallie moaning and tightening her legs around me. It's wild and unplanned, yet I can't get enough of her. When her hands pull my hair, I growl, increasing my thrusts. Fuck wanting to take things slow. One taste of her, and I'm untamed. I wish I was balls deep inside of her.

"Wilder," she pants.

"Yeah? What do you want? Tell me, and I'll give it to you." My voice is gruff, my hands digging into her full ass the way I've been fantasizing.

"Everything. This feels like too much and not enough."

"I wanted to go slow, show you how special you are," I confess against her neck, sucking and biting her sweet skin.

"Hmmm…" is the only response I get from her.

"You're so sweet. So precious. But I can't think straight right now."

"That's the kindest thing any man has ever told me." Her arms lock behind me, but I slow down.

The reminder that she hasn't always been treated the way she should lands like a bucket of cold water over me. I've heard what she's told Midnight about that asshole ex of hers.

"W-what…" she trails off, leaning back to look at me with furrowed brows.

I kiss her lips and smile. "I want you to know that not all guys are assholes or douche-cunts." Her eyes soften, and she nods. "You deserve more than dry humping against my old truck."

"But it felt so good," she sighs.

I laugh gravelly. "Trust me. I'm struggling with keeping my self-control." I brush her wild hair away from her face. "But you are more than a body to get lost in. This isn't why I brought you out here. I swear I had a more romantic plan."

Hallie drops her legs from my body, and I hold her waist until I'm sure she's got her footing. I instantly miss her warmth wrapped around me, but it won't be the last time I feel it.

"I got carried away," she bites down her smile. "No one's ever grabbed me like that. I thought that was a move romance novels exaggerated, especially since..." Her eyes dart away, and she presses her lips together.

"Especially since what?" I narrow my eyes.

"Nothing," she waves me off.

"Nuh-uh. Tell me." I think I know where she's going with this, and I want her to voice it so we can move on from it. If she still thinks she's too fat, too plump, too curvy, I'm gonna squash that belief right here.

"Well, I'm not easy to lift."

Shaking my head, I grab her again, lifting her with ease. "Sweetheart, that's because you haven't been with a real man, then." I kiss her deeply before setting her back down.

"Uhh..." Her eyes are dazed as she blinks up at me. I smile triumphantly.

"Now, let's settle in the bed of my truck and look at the stars. New York may have celebrities that people consider stars, but they can't compete with this beauty. I tilt my head back.

I get my body under control and grab our coffees before leading her to the back, dropping the tailgate. I lift her, sitting her on it, so she can scoot back and settle beside her. Wrapping my arm around her, we're both quiet as we look up at the thousands of twinkling stars.

"This really is something. I've never seen so many stars at the same time."

"Perks of living in the country." I squeeze her shoulder and look at her.

She gives me a sexy as hell smile. "There are other perks," she winks and takes a sip of coffee.

Tossing my head back on a laugh, I nod. "Yeah," I whisper, kissing her cheek.

I may have fought against my feelings, but Hallie has wormed her way into my life, and I'm not quite ready to let her go.

"I hear things are going well with Hallie," Grady tells me before taking a drink of his beer. He and Levi came over tonight to hang out. We've always been close, grew up more like siblings than cousins. Our moms are twins. His wife, Charlee, is pregnant, so he's been at home more. We still try to get our family time in, though.

I look at him over the top of my bottle and nod. I can't deny it. We made it crystal clear last night when we were out at Sauce It Up.

"They're good."

Grady and Levi exchange a look.

"What?" I lean forward and stare at them

"Nothing," Levi smirks.

"Bullshit."

Grady chuckles and slaps Levi's shoulder. "I think it's great, honestly. It's about time."

"That's what I told him. He needs to move on, give himself a chance to be happy."

"He's right." Grady nods. "Look, I know it's not easy to open your heart after you've been hurt. I could say I regret my marriage to Courtney. Lord knows it was hard, but the truth is that I wouldn't have Jilly if it weren't for her. You gotta look at the silver lining. Things with Lisa didn't work out, but you're stronger now, more aware of the kind of person you want by your side, in your house and life."

I listen intently, soaking up what he's saying. I haven't felt like this in a long time. It's true I haven't given myself the chance to, but Hallie has a lot to do with that. It takes a special woman to get me to open up.

"I can see that. Life would be boring without our Jillybean." Our whole family loves that little girl. She's got us all wrapped around her finger.

"It would be," Levi agrees. "I just want to say that I told you a lot of what Grady said a while back, and you chose to scoff at me. Let it be observed that I also give good advice."

"The difference is that I've been in love and lost it, and you're still living the single life," Grady teases him.

"I could settle down." Levi crosses his arms and narrows his eyes at us. "I just haven't met a woman who has made me consider it." He picks up his beer and takes a sip.

"Assholes," he mumbles when we laugh at him.

Grady slaps my arm and nods. "Take the risk. I promise it'll be worth it. Look at me now with Charlee. I can't imagine missing out on that."

His words hit close to home. It's what I've been thinking about lately. I can't resist spending time with her. The more time I spend, the more I want of her. It's never enough, and I'm determined to learn as much about her as possible before she leaves.

Chapter 17

HALLIE

The sun warms me as I walk to the butcher shop with light steps. I've been in a dream the last couple of days. I feel like I'm floating through life with a permanent smile. My date with Wilder was great, but it's each day after that's made it much more special.

Wilder doesn't play by the same rules guys in New York do. Even though he dropped me off at night, he still sent me a goodnight text message that made the butterflies in my stomach flutter. He's contacted me every day since, even if we haven't gone on another date yet. Each time his name pops up on my screen, excitement bursts through me.

I never thought he'd want to go out with me. I actually thought he disliked me. However, he's been making it a point to show me how much he likes me since he dropped off that mirror outside Uncle Sal's house. Wilder makes me feel beautiful, sexy, and wanted. I still need to believe that when I look at myself, but the feeling I get when I'm around him helps to tear apart the ideas ingrained in me.

I unlock the door to the butcher shop and step inside, smiling at the display. A few weeks ago, I felt so lost. I'm no pro, but this place doesn't intimidate me as it used to. That's a point in my favor. I'm proud of that, especially since the rest of my life is a mess. Somehow my time in Mason Creek flows better than my life in New York. Who would've figured?

I prepare for my day, making sure the front is fully stocked. People have already started asking for lamb, and I've assured them we'll have some later this week as long as I get the courage to butcher them.

I blow out a deep breath, moving across the back of the counter, checking the knives I'll need, and keeping my cheat sheet hidden. It helps when I'm not one-hundred-percent sure how to cut a certain part. I've already made myself look like an amateur. I want people to think I've improved in this job and not watch me continuously stumble through it.

While I'm in the back checking inventory in the refrigerated storage, I hear a knock. Checking the time on my watch, I note it's still early. Whoever it is can wait until we open. The hours are on the door clear as day for everyone. I go back to counting the beef we have when a knock sounds on the back door, startling me.

"What in the…" I huff and walk toward it.

"Who is it?" I really wish this door had a peephole.

"Your favorite serial killer." His chuckle is muted through the door.

Opening, I smile at the sight of Wilder in his worn jeans, cowboy boots, and black hat. "Hey, what are you doing here?"

"Happy to see you, too," he teases.

"Sorry. Yeah, that." My hand waves in the air. "I just wasn't expecting to see you." I step aside so he can enter.

When he bends to pick up a box, I ask, "What's that?" My finger swings to the white foam box.

"Special delivery." He walks inside, heading toward the refrigerated storage.

I follow him, wondering what in the hell he brought. When he places the box on a shelf, he lifts the top.

My eyebrows pull together, unsure what animal I'm looking at until it dawns on me. "Did you cut the lambs for me?" I look up at him with wide eyes.

Wilder gives me that smile that makes my belly flip. "I know you were dreading it, so I picked them up from Paul and butchered them for you. They're ready to be sold, but some might want you to separate the racks, so they're individual pieces."

"I can do that," I nod, staring at him in disbelief. "Thank you." I tilt my head and look at him. I never thought butchering lamb would be romantic.

"I've got more boxes in the car. I'll bring them in here."

Before he walks away, I grab his wrist. Wilder turns to me with an arched brow. I smile and close the gap between us. "Thank you," I whisper. "That was really sweet of you."

That crooked smile that makes me swoon appears on his lips. "You don't need to thank me, sweetheart. I'm happy to help." His other hand holds the side of my face.

I squeeze his hand, pinching my lips together. "I appreciate it. More than you know. It's not just about butchering."

"I know," he winks, dropping a kiss on top of my head. "I'll be right back."

While he grabs the boxes, I organize them on the shelf. I'll ask Uncle Sal how he wants me to display them once Wilder leaves. After all the boxes are put away, I close the door to the cold storage and turn to Wilder. He's standing so close I can smell a mix of his cologne and slight sweat from already working hours outdoors. And it surprisingly turns me on.

"I've missed seeing you." I love that he doesn't hide what he feels.

"Yeah?" I smile, tucking my bottom lip between my teeth.

"Yup," he nods, stepping closer. "I like receiving messages from you, but I much prefer to see you in person." His hand reaches for mine. He lifts it, brushing his lips on the inside of my wrist, his eyes staring into mine.

It's intimate, and my body reacts with a shiver. A soft sigh leaves my lips, and I'm sure my face is displaying all of my emotions. I've never been good at hiding them.

"I have an auction two hours away on Saturday, but I want to see you on Sunday. We can grab lunch since you close that day or dinner. Anything you want." His deep voice blankets me.

"Dinner sounds great." I squeeze his fingers.

"Perfect." He steps closer, his other hand landing on my hip. "It's a date."

Hearing him say that makes my heart soar. Although Wilder has been vocal about his interest, my insecurities still take over, which causes me to internally sabotage what we have going on.

"Yeah," I breathe out, looking up at him.

When his lips meet mine, the world stops. I'm only aware of our locked lips and the way his beard simultaneously scratches and tickles my face. That feeling makes my core clench as I imagine it scratching other parts of my body. I've never been with a man who has a beard. I move my hands around his back, pulling him closer to me.

A tap on the front door breaks us apart, our chests heaving.

"Shit," Wilder mumbles. "Sorry, I got carried away."

I shake my head, rapidly blinking as I refocus on our surroundings. "Me too."

He picks up my hand and kisses the pad of my thumb. "Don't cut any fingers today. I won't be around to heal you," he winks. "I should go. It's opening time. We'll talk later."

He kisses my cheek and sneaks out the back door. Before I make my way to the front, I look at myself in the bathroom mirror. A few red marks cover my cheeks, which will hopefully disappear quickly.

Heading to the front, I open the door and apologize with the excuse that I was in the storage room and lost track of time.

The rest of the day passes with the memory of Wilder's kiss haunting me. As if I wasn't already daydreaming about him constantly, his actions today have only deepened my feelings.

I'm exhausted by the time I close the shop. My feet ache. I feel like everyone in town stopped by today. Word must've gotten around about the lamb arriving because I sold a ton.

I agreed to meet Joy at Java Jitters after work, so today is one of those days I wish I would've brought Uncle Sal's truck, but I feel ridiculous driving somewhere that's a ten-minute walk at most.

By the time I get to Java Jitters, Joy is sitting at a table. The adorable coffee shop has become our gathering place, and it already feels like home.

My feet stumble on the way to the table. That thought hit me hard. *Home.*

How can this place feel more like home than my actual home? I've been happy here. The people have been welcoming—gossip and all. I've been able to reconnect with Joy and my family here.

"Hey," Joy smiles.

"Hi." I take a seat, slumping back in my chair.

Joy's eyebrows fly up. "Are you okay?"

"Yeah, just tired." I hang my purse from the seatback and smile. "Today was crazy."

"The weather is nice, people are planning more outdoor meals on the weekends, so they stock up on meat."

"That makes sense."

"And the spring festival is coming up. We have some early planners in town."

"Spring festival? I think I read something about that."

"It's so fun. The entire town gets together. Tourists come as well. People set tables outside. There are games for kids. Local businesses set up booths. It's awesome." A nostalgic look passes her face.

"It sounds it. Will you have a booth for the bakery?"

"Yes," she nods excitedly. "I always make a special pastry for the festival. It's a surprise until I reveal it on the day of the event. Our neighbors love it, and some try to guess what it is in the weeks leading up to it. It's a way to keep customers excited about my products and making sure they stop by my booth when they can come into the bakery on any given day."

"That's a great idea. I can't wait to see what it is." I cross my arms. "Should we order coffee?"

"Are you too tired? We can totally call it a night and get together another day." She presses her lips together as she eyes me.

"No, I'm okay. Coffee will help. I feel like I haven't seen you in a week." Despite my eyes feeling heavy, I want to spend time with Joy.

"You were a little busy." She waggles her eyebrows and giggles when I slap her arm. A blush creeps up my cheeks.

Joy and I both got busy the past few days, and I haven't had a chance to see her in person. She made sure to call the day after my date, though, and demand details.

"Awww…look at you blushing and all," she teases.

"You're horrible. I'm gonna order coffee. Your usual?" I stand.

"Yeah, thanks."

After grabbing our drinks, I sit back down and tell Joy about Wilder's stop at the butcher shop this morning.

"It was so freaking sweet. He remembered I was nervous about cutting the lamb, so he did it for me and delivered it all."

"That is sweet. Romantic, even." She sighs with a smile.

"I know." My mouth splits in a smile. "Who would've thought butchering animal carcasses for someone would be romantic?"

"And they say chivalry is dead," Joy rolls her eyes playfully.

I laugh boastfully, nodding in agreement.

"I'm happy to hear things are going well."

"Thank you." I take a drink of my hot latte.

I finally feel myself relaxing after the hectic day. Hopefully, tomorrow will be better.

"Hey, ladies." I look up and see Canaan, Joy's older brother, standing by our table.

"Hey," I smile at him.

"Hi, big bro. What's brought you around?"

"Came for some coffee. I'm working the night shift at the fire station." He looks at me. "It's good to see you, Hallie."

"You, too." I haven't had a chance to catch up with Canaan, what with his busy schedule. Besides his regular job as a carpenter for a construction company in a nearby town, he volunteers at the fire station like some of the other locals. He's a few years older than us, so I was always closer to Joy growing up since we're the same age. He heads to the counter to order coffee and leaves with a wave in our direction.

"Grandma wants to invite you and Sal to dinner soon. I forgot to tell you. Do you think Sal will be able to go?" Joy looks at me over her coffee mug.

"I think so. He ordered a new walker where he rests his leg and rides it like a scooter. It's pretty funny watching him use it."

"Oh, my goodness. That's hilarious. I'd love to see that," Joy chuckles.

"I'll talk to him anyway, but I'm sure he'll be happy to get out of the house. Besides, he loves Aunt Ruth." My great aunt is a hoot, and she and Uncle Sal always love getting together. They're so much alike.

"Perfect. Talk to him first before I tell my grandma, and she starts cooking five days before." I laugh at her exaggeration.

"You think I'm kidding?" Joy's eyebrows shoot up. "The woman will use any excuse to make a feast."

"I bet. I'll talk to him tonight and let you know what he says."

"Awesome. Everyone is happy you're spending some time here." She smiles genuinely.

"Your mom told me when she came by the butcher shop. It feels good to be here and get to know the town as an adult." My eyes glance out the window and take in the square.

"Maybe you'll even wanna stay here," Joy's eyebrows waggle.

I smile. Wouldn't that be something? Me moving to my mom's hometown after she left all those years ago for greater opportunities. Somehow, that idea doesn't seem too far-off.

Chapter 18

HALLIE

I laugh at the story Aunt Ruth tells us about her run-in with Hazel and Hattie, the older twins who own the ice cream stand.

"Hazel was so flustered, huffing and puffing. You know she can be uptight," Aunt Ruth waves her hand. "Anyway, Hattie was adding to Leo's teasing until Hazel walked away with red cheeks."

I've seen Hattie and Hazel at the coffee shop a few times, and they're always gossiping and bickering. Hattie's blue hair shows her personality perfectly. It's comical to see these two opposites together. Even crazier that they're twins.

"They're a riot," Joy comments.

"They sure are," Uncle Sal adds.

When I told him Aunt Ruth wanted to invite us to dinner, he practically begged me to call Joy and tell her we would love to go. His cabin fever has gotten worse, but hopefully soon, he'll be able to move around some more. We're waiting for his next doctor's visit.

"Yeah, but don't get caught in their gossip because they'll make sure everyone knows your business," Canaan shakes his head.

It's been so nice to sit in Aunt Ruth's house with family I haven't seen in years. My mom always kept in touch with this side of the family, but it's still different than seeing them in person instead of random phone calls throughout the year.

Not only is the food delicious—Aunt Ruth made pork chops with a sweet and spicy gravy sauce and roasted potato wedges—but the conversation has been light and fun.

"You know a thing or two about that," Joy's dad, John, teases Canaan.

"Please, John," Becky, Joy's mom, lifts her hand. "The things I've heard in the form of rumors are more than I'd like to know."

"It's all lies, Mom," Canaan smirks with a wink.

Becky rolls her eyes before looking at me. "We're so happy you're here. I know Joy is ecstatic. Any chance your parents will come visit?" She smiles hopefully.

"I don't know," I shrug. "They're both busy with work, although I did bring it up before I came. I think it'd be nice if they take vacation time and come this way."

"I can't imagine how hectic New York is. I hope they follow your advice. It's been way too long." She smiles sadly.

"It has," I agree. Becky and my mom were close growing up since they're just a few years apart. Uncle Sal is older than both of them, so the girls were inseparable growing up. Becky has a brother that lives in Billings, so their family is also spread out in the state.

"It seems you've caused quite the gossip around town, too," Aunt Ruth says with a taunting smile.

My face heats, and I look away from her gaze.

"Leave the girl alone," John says.

"Oh, shush. Let your mother-in-law question her niece." Aunt Ruth arches an eyebrow. Her white hair is perfectly combed, looking like a white cotton ball.

"Yeah, seems like our girl here has caught someone's eye," Uncle Sal wraps his arm around me. I press my lips down, feeling my face burn in embarrassment.

"Hush or I'll never bring you out again," I elbow his rib.

He chuckles, squeezing my shoulder before releasing it.

"Wilder James is quite a catch," Aunt Ruth keeps going, not bothering to wait for my response. After a certain age, you can say what you want without a care in the world.

"He's a looker. In my day, a man like him would have all the ladies fighting for his attention. And you're gorgeous. You make a pretty couple," she nods in approval, and I bite back my nervous giggle. She's serious about approving this relationship.

"He comes from a wonderful family," Becky nods.

"Okay, let's change subjects before you guys start planning her wedding," Joy saves me.

I blow out a breath and smile gratefully.

"What's your secret pastry for the spring festival?" Becky asks Joy as she takes a bite of Aunt Ruth's huckleberry pie.

When I try it, I practically moan. Interrupting the conversation, I cover my mouth with my hand and say, "This is so good."

"I'm glad you like it," Aunt Ruth smiles with pride. "It's my specialty."

"I can tell," I nod. "I've never had it before, but I could eat this every day."

"Aunt Ruth is the pro when it comes to pies," Uncle Sal winks at her.

"You'd bribe me to make them for you when you were a kid." She points her fork at him and then looks at me. "He'd tell me he'd come mow my lawn, paint the house, fix anything that was broken if I made him pie. I'm pretty sure he purposefully broke a few things, so I'd accept his offer." Her eyes narrow in his direction.

Uncle Sal laughs. "Would I do that?" He raises his palms.

"Yes, you would," she nods with conviction.

"Don't think this is going to distract us," Becky looks at Joy.

Joy rolls her eyes and shakes her head. "You know I'm not telling." She crosses her arms and shrugs.

"Come on…" Canaan gives her a charming smile. "I need to know if I should stop by your booth or not."

Joy glares at him. "I'm your sister. You should support me no matter what."

"I know what it is," Aunt Ruth rubs in everyone's faces.

"Only because I had to ask you a question," Joy points out.

"So it's something you weren't completely sure how to make." Canaan taps his chin. "Cinnamon rolls."

"Asshole, you know I can make those with my eyes closed." Joy hits his chin with a leftover piece of bread.

Canaan laughs loudly, taking the bread and eating it. I watch their interaction with a smile. Being an only child makes it difficult to understand the dynamics of having siblings, but watching them makes me wish I had a brother or sister, someone to confide it.

It's later than I thought by the time we leave Aunt Ruth's house. Thankfully, I don't work tomorrow. I plan to sleep in, so I'm well-rested before my date with Wilder. Just thinking about seeing him tomorrow makes my belly flip. He's made sure I haven't forgotten about it, as if that would slip my mind.

"I had fun tonight." Uncle Sal sits on the sofa. "I feel like I've been a recluse, not being able to go out while resting. Doctor Carlson better give me the all-clear soon." He gently pats his injured leg.

I nod, swallowing thickly. I want him to get better, but that means my time here will be up. What will happen then? What will happen with Wilder? I don't want to think it's a mistake that he and I started dating, but it's going to hurt to leave him.

Why do you have to leave him?

I take a deep breath. That thought's been more and more present in my mind lately. Do I have to leave? I feel like I do, but…I'm not sure I want to. Blinking away tears, I head into the bathroom. I wash my face and stare at myself in the mirror.

Come on, Hallie. Get your damn life in order.

The past few years have weighed me down. Between not finding a job, the toxic relationship I was in with Jeff, and living with my parents longer than I wished, I feel like a failure. I love my parents, but I want independence. Just not at the price of staying with Jeff and moving in with him.

No, I deserve more than that. If I've learned anything recently, it's that. Stepping away from the place that built our relationship has allowed me to look at things from a different perspective.

My buzzing phone vibrates against my cheek. Groaning in my sleep, I press the side button to quiet it and tuck my arms under my pillow. My body relaxes as I fall back into a deep slumber, but my phone goes off again.

"Ugh," I groan, silencing it and tossing it to my side.

When the buzzing begins again, I cover my head with the extra pillow and squeeze my eyes. It's not even morning. I'm exhausted. What does a girl have to do to get some sleep around here?

I try to fall back asleep, but it's no use. My mind is already going. I check the time on my phone and am fully awake when I see Wilder was the person calling. Is he okay?

Sitting up in bed, I swipe my hair from my face. Before I can call him back, his name appears on my screen.

I jolt and answer.

"Hello?" I whisper. My voice is hoarse.

"Hey, sleepyhead, about time you answered."

"It's five in the morning."

"I know, but I have a surprise, so I need you up and ready in five minutes."

"What?" I ask in disbelief.

"Yeah, come on. Time's ticking."

"Ticking for what? We have a date tonight. As in P.M. not A.M."

His deep laughter serenades me. "I know, but I really wanna show you something. It'll be worth it, and we'll grab breakfast afterward."

I can't deny him when I hear the excitement in his voice. I also can't deny that I'd rather see him sooner than later in the day.

"Okay. Give me a few. What should I wear?"

"Something comfortable. Wear sneakers and bring a sweater."

"Okay." I stand and drag my feet to the bathroom. I look at myself in the mirror and cringe. My hair's a wild mess, my eyes are swollen, and I have sheet marks on my cheek.

"I'll pick you up in a few," Wilder interrupts my observation.

"I'll hurry."

We hang up, and I wash my face and brush my teeth, going through my routine. No way I'll have time to shower. I braid my hair, taming it as much as possible, and get dressed.

In the kitchen, I leave Uncle Sal a note, letting him know I'm out with Wilder. As I'm finishing it, my phone vibrates.

"On my way out," I say as I grab my purse and coat.

Wilder is standing by the passenger door with a wide smile.

"Good morning." He reaches for my waist, dropping a soft kiss on my lips.

"Hi," I whisper, loving the way his strong arms hold me.

"Let's go." He bounces on his toes.

"I have no idea what your plan is, but you're way too excited for five in the morning." I buckle myself.

Wilder shrugs with a smile. "I get to see you. That makes me happy." Every inch of me tingles at hearing his words.

"That makes me happy, too." I smile over at him.

He reaches for my hand as he drives toward Town Square. I always love the way his calloused touch feels.

"How was the auction?"

"Great. It was a successful one, which always helps the ranch." His fingers curl around mine.

"I'm happy to hear that." I trace his knuckles with my other hand.

"We're here," he whispers.

When I look up, my eyes widen.

"No," I shake my head. "I should've known," I laugh nervously.

He's parked on the side of the water tower, the looming giant taunting me.

"It's so worth it, and I'll be with you. The ladder is enclosed by a cage for protection."

I take a deep breath. I want to experience things I wouldn't normally be able to in my daily life. If anything yells small town, it's climbing a water tower.

"Okay," I nod. "Let's go before I regret it."

Wilder laughs and throws his door open. "Come on, Bunny Girl."

I meet him at the front of his truck, my nerves rattling. I have no idea what I've agreed to, but I want to take risks and try new things. I know Wilder would never take me somewhere dangerous. I just hope I'm capable of climbing this thing.

He grabs my hand and guides me. When we stand at the foot of the ladder, he asks, "Do you want to go first, and I'll be behind you in case you get nervous, or do you prefer I lead the way?" He looks warmly into my eyes.

"I'd rather go first. If you're behind me, I won't be able to look down as easily."

He chuckles. "Okay. If you want to stop at any time, we will," he promises and squeezes my hand.

"Let's do this." I clap my hands and walk to the ladder. The first few feet are uncovered, but then I see the cage Wilder mentioned. That will help me feel more like I'm climbing stairs indoors. I hope.

I begin to ascend, gripping the rungs tightly and taking my time, so I don't miss any steps. As I enter the protected part, I feel safer. I pause every so often to look around and catch my breath. Although the sun hasn't risen yet, there's already a glow in the sky, softly illuminating the town.

"You're doing great," Wilder praises from below me.

The higher we get, the more the view changes. It's fascinating to observe the transition. When I reach the top, I step onto the platform and move to the side to make room for Wilder. I hold on to the railing and stare ahead. Dawn is breaking, a myriad of colors painted in the sky. Some stars still twinkle, and it's the perfect scene.

Wilder stands behind me, caging me with his arms and kissing my neck. His hoodie sleeves are pushed up on his arms, showing off his roped muscles. I shiver against him, and my body reacts to him.

"Is it worth it?" He whispers in my ear.

I nod quietly.

"So worth the shaky legs and irrational fear," I joke, looking over my shoulder before staring at the view again.

The town lies below us—all the small businesses around Town Square, the apartment building, and houses beyond that. We have the perfect display of the town and the mountains surrounding it.

"I'm glad." He rests his chin on top of my head. "I love coming up here. Sunrise is the best time."

"I can see why." The town is slowly becoming more lit from the impending sunrise. The orange hues reflect off the buildings, adding a golden touch to the town.

"Just like the bridge in the forest, this place helps me clear my mind when I need to. It also inspires me." His breath tickles my cheek as he speaks.

"That bridge is beautiful," I sigh. I think that might be my favorite part of town so far, although this right here is special.

"Thank you for insisting I come." I turn around and smile at him.

"You're welcome. I knew you'd like it once you got over the initial fear." He brushes his lips with mine. "Turn around," he whispers against my lips.

I search his eyes for a moment before I do. I'm not sure what I'm hoping to find, but this moment feels a lot more intimate than two people just getting to know each other. Wilder draws me in from my core. It's not just his looks or his strong body; it's something beyond that physical part of us.

I turn and gasp. "Wow," I whisper.

The sun peeks from behind the mountains very low on the horizon, bringing with it a burning sky. The lingering night mixes with the sun's hues, creating purples and pinks. We have the perfect view from the top.

I watch silently. The only sound is our soft breathing. It is in this moment that I fall in love with this place. There aren't any concrete buildings blocking our view. The sounds of screeching tires, loud honks, and heavy bus engines don't interrupt the peaceful quiet. And the only thing I inhale is fresh air.

I'm amazed as the sun continues to climb in the sky, bringing about a new day. The fiery round star shines with all its might, majestic and sure. I'm almost envious of the sun's confidence.

Wilder moves one of his hands from the railing and places it around my middle, embracing me. I lean back into him. I've never felt more at peace than I do right now. Every inch of myself is calm. My heart feels light, and my mind is clear. It's like my personal meditation.

Once the sun is sitting in the sky, Wilder releases me. "Come this way. I wanna show you the ranch."

My eyes light up. "We can see it from here?"

"Yeah," he smiles.

I follow him around the platform and stop beside him.

"All of that land is part of the ranch." He points ahead to open space.

"All of it?" I look at him with wide eyes.

"Yeah. The house looks like a tiny speck from here. Do you see that roof there?" He points toward the right.

I squint my eyes, searching for it. When I see it, I yell, "Yes!"

Wilder laughs at my enthusiasm before explaining, "That's my parents' house."

It looks dwarfed in comparison to the land. I knew their ranch was big, but I had no idea exactly how huge it actually is.

"How much land do you have?" I tilt my head up at Wilder.

"A few thousand acres."

I cough. "Excuse me, what?" I'm sure my eyes are bugging out.

He laughs and runs a hand through his hair. "It was my grandfather's before it. The ranch was originally more land, but when he passed, my mom got the ranch and the few thousand acres we now have, and my aunt got the other half."

"How come your mom kept the ranch?"

"She and my dad always dreamed of running it. My dad already worked it with my grandfather. My aunt and uncle work in real estate, so they had other dreams. We had hot springs on the ranch, and it's now part of what my cousin, Grady, inherited from his parents when they retired."

"Wow, that sounds like a family web I'm not yet fully awake to comprehend."

He laughs at my joke, and I beam.

"Let's get you coffee then."

I look around the area one more time and nod. I'm torn between staying up here and coffee, but ultimately, coffee wins.

Chapter 19

WILDER

I didn't want to wait until tonight to see Hallie. I've constantly been thinking about her, so knowing today is one of her days off, I listened to my gut and woke her up. And I'm so fucking glad I did. Seeing her face of wonder as she stared at the view from the top of the water tower proved it was the right decision.

I grab her hand as we walk back to my truck. "How does Wren's Cafe sound for coffee and breakfast?"

"Like heaven. I feel deprived of caffeine."

Chuckling, I tug her arm in the direction of Town Square. "Caffeine deprived? When was the last time you had some?" I lift my brows.

"Pfff... Yesterday afternoon." She rolls her eyes playfully.

I smile at her. Being around her makes me feel lighter.

The town is pretty quiet as we walk toward the diner. Sundays are usually a slower day around here. It isn't until after church that the town gets busy, so Hallie and I should have the diner mostly to ourselves.

As soon as I open the door for Hallie, the salty and sweet combination of bacon and syrup makes my stomach growl. Hallie must hear it because she giggles.

"Guess you're feeling food-deprived," she pats my stomach.

I want to reach out, keep her hand on me, and feel her body over mine. I clear my throat as my body tenses and nod.

"Let's get you fed, then." Her eyes twinkle.

I want a different kind of meal, but I'm taking my time with her. She's been through a lot, and it's been a long time since I've been down this path with anyone. I want to make sure we do it right.

And she'll be leaving soon.

I close my eyes and take a deep breath, letting go of that thought. I'm living in the moment. We'll figure out where we stand once it's time for her to go.

We take a seat at a table, and Shorty's loud voice booms through the diner.

"Uhh…who is that?" Hallie stares at me with round eyes.

"That's Shorty, the morning cook."

"Does he know that those aren't the correct lyrics to that Carrie Underwood song?"

"Oh, yeah," I laugh. "It's his charming quality. He's constantly singing but messes up the lyrics or makes up his own." I lean forward on the table as I explain. "He's a character, but he makes the best pancakes and has a heart of gold."

"That's hilarious." Hallie giggles as Shorty's booming voice continues to serenade the diner.

"You know I like my bacon fried and hot coffee on a Sunday morniiiing... na-na na-na...hmmm..." Shorty changes the words to the popular Zac Brown Band song.

"He's a riot," Hallie laughs louder.

Shorty walks out of the kitchen carrying a plate, his stained white t-shirt stretched tightly over his large stomach, and Hallie's eyes widen.

"That's *Shorty*?" Her eyes widen.

"Yup," I chuckle. "We call him that because of his short stacks, not his size."

"No shit," Hallie breathes out, causing me to cackle.

"Shh... He's looking at us," she slaps my arm, but I don't give a shit. My laughter takes over.

"Ah, you're the new gal," Shorty says from behind the counter. "It's nice to meet ya."

"Nice to meet you." Hallie blushes, looking over at me.

Taking a deep breath, I smile at her. Her cheeks are tinged pink, and her lip is trapped between her teeth. She's fucking adorable.

"So, I guess I should try the pancakes?" Her eyebrows lift.

"Yeah," I chuckle. "I'd definitely recommend them."

Our food comes quickly after we order, and Hallie giggles at the different songs Shorty butchers throughout our meal.

"Okay, you were right," she says as she pushes her mostly empty plate away. "These pancakes are amazing. What the heck does he put in them?" She wipes her mouth with the napkin.

"I have no idea, but they're the best I've ever had."

Hallie nods, taking a drink of her coffee. I'm impressed, she's on her third cup, and she's not wired or hyper from the caffeine.

"Since you've proven to be a good tour guide, what else do I need to see in Mason Creek?" Her elbows rest on the table with clasped hands. She rests her chin on them.

"Mason Creek isn't big, but it's got a ton of nature surrounding it." I'm too distracted by her to think of a specific place for her to visit. I keep thinking of how I can get her alone after breakfast.

"The nature around here is gorgeous. I remember being in awe when I'd come visit as a child. I had forgotten exactly how beautiful it was until I returned. My memory didn't do it justice."

"Yeah," I nod. "How come you stopped visiting?"

"Life got hectic the older I got. After my grandparents died, there was less motivation for my mom to take time to plan a trip out here. Uncle Sal would usually visit us, so the years slipped by."

"Does your mom miss it?" I can't imagine living away from here and never visiting.

"Honestly, I don't know. I've been asking myself the same question now that I'm spending more time here. I can't imagine not missing this place, but she's made a life for herself outside of it. I think she's too caught up in the daily grind to truly think about it."

Perfect MESS

"That makes sense. I don't know if I could live away from all this." I look around the diner and out the window where people in town are already walking about.

"I don't blame you," she sighs, resting her chin on her hands again as she looks out another window with a wistful expression.

The way her face softens and the almost sad-like look reflecting in her eyes, I'd dare to guess she wants to stay in Mason Creek. I'm unsure if I'm part of the reason for that, but I hope she feels the same way I do. Spending time with Hallie isn't out of boredom. I've got enough in my life to keep me busy. I want her in so many damn ways, but the voice in my head keeps reminding me that she'll be leaving soon.

She focuses her attention back on me and smiles widely. Temporary or not, I want her by my side as much as possible.

"Sorry, I got distracted." She drops her arms and sits back in her chair.

"No need to apologize." I reach for her hand, lacing our fingers. "How about I pay, and we go?"

"Sure," she nods tensely.

"I want to show you something." Her eyes light up the same way they did after our dinner date when I told her the same thing. If I can help it, I'm going to keep that joy in her life. She deserves to be happy, not torn down.

After paying and walking back to my truck, I ask Hallie, "Have you ever been on a tractor before?"

Her eyebrows pull down, and she laughs, shaking her head. "I have not."

"Well, there's a first time for everything." I reach for her hand as I drive back to the ranch.

"Oh, my gosh! Can I see Midnight?" Her mouth splits into a huge grin as she sees the barn.

"He's back with the rest of the cattle, but we'll stop on the way."

Hallie claps her hands and unbuckles herself, jumping out of my truck. Her excitement is contagious, and soon I'm pulling her by the arm and rushing to start the tractor.

"So cool," she breathes out as I start driving the slow vehicle through the ranch. Hallie stares around, her right arm spread wide in the air.

We're both quiet as the loud roar of the tractor leads us toward the open pasture where the cattle are grazing. As soon as we approach them, some lift their head to look at us while others can't be bothered by our presence.

"Whoa," Hallie whispers. She looks between me and the cattle. "All of these are yours? How do you keep track of them all?"

"Yeah, they're all ours.

"Wilder, there are hundreds of cows here." Her eyes are glued to the animals.

"Five hundred, to be exact."

"Holy hell…" she gasps.

"Come on." I step off the tractor and walk around to offer Hallie a hand.

I lead her to the wooden fence that separates us from the animals and smile at Hallie's wonderment.

"This is amazing. I knew you had a large ranch, but this is just…incredible. How can you get rid of them?" She turns to me with raised eyebrows.

"It's my job," I shrug. "They aren't my pets. I was raised for this job. Ever since I was a small boy, I'd ride with my dad and help with the cattle. I'd learn all about them, soaking up every bit of information. They serve a purpose, not only on this ranch but in our community and those surrounding us. I'm grateful for them, and I respect them, but ultimately, they're raised to breed or feed." I look over at the work my family's done throughout the years.

"We've had our share of struggles. Ranching isn't an easy job, and it takes passion and drive to stick with this career, but I love it. I wake up each morning knowing I'm doing what I'm meant to."

"I wish I had that clarity." Her lips press together, staring out at the field.

"You will." I squeeze her hand.

Hallie shakes her head, avoiding my eyes.

"Hey," I whisper. "You'll find the right job."

"I don't know. I'm a mess. It's a miracle I haven't burned down the butcher shop."

"Considering you're not cooking in it, I think that's pretty normal," I chuckle.

"Well, with my luck, I'd probably accidentally figure out a way to burn it down," she shakes her head.

I look at her with confusion.

"Hey, that's not true." I cup her cheek.

"You're just being nice." Her eyes search mine.

"Nah," I shake my head. "If memory serves me, I'm not exactly the nicest person." I lift a brow, and she chuckles.

"True that." She pats my chest. "I just wish I knew where my life was going. It's all a mess. *I'm* a hot mess." She chuckles dryly.

"Nah." I step closer. "You're a perfect mess. Life isn't flawless. It can't be planned down to the minute detail. I don't give a shit if some people say they've got it all perfectly lined out. It's bullshit. Life is supposed to be messy and chaotic. It's tricky and mean at times. I won't let you put yourself down. You wanna call yourself a mess, then know you're a perfect mess. You're real and amazing. And, hell, we all need to get messy in life so we can learn. How will we know where we wanna go if we don't get lost on the way?" I stroke her cheek with my thumb while Hallie's lip trembles and her eyes water.

"Don't cry," I whisper.

"It's just…" her voice is shaky. A tear wets my thumb, and I swipe it away. "That was so beautiful." She sniffles.

"I mean it." I lean down and press my lips to hers.

I don't push. I don't force anything else. I want her to know how I feel without the expectation of having to give back. This feeling I have for her is utterly unconditional, and while it should scare me, it actually fills me with courage.

"Wilder," she mumbles my name against my lips.

"Yeah?"

Her eyes flutter closed, and she leans into me. Hallie doesn't say anything else. Instead, she wraps her arms around me in a tight hug. I hold her protectively, hoping that she's beginning to believe how special she is. Not just to the world but to me.

"Hey, look," I whisper in her ear, tapping her lower back.

"What?" she looks up at me with tear-soaked eyes.

I kiss her forehead, the tip of her nose, and her lips. Lifting my gaze over her head, I lift my chin in the direction of the cows. Hallie turns around slowly, and her eyes widen.

"Is that Midnight?" She looks at me with a full grin.

"Sure is. Looks like he recognized you."

Hallie steps closer to the fence and begins to reach out but hesitates. "Can I?" she asks.

"Of course." I whistle, calling Midnight over.

As soon as he sees Hallie step on the fence and lean forward, he comes to her. I watch their interaction in amazement. That steer holds her confessions, and it's clear that their love is mutual.

When Hallie turns to look at me over her shoulder with innocent happiness painted on her face, I know that this is one steer I won't be able to get rid of. Midnight will always be the tie I have to Hallie.

Chapter 20

HALLIE

Today has been unexpectedly perfect. When Wilder called me early this morning, I was unsure what he had planned. Now, riding his tractor after seeing Midnight, I feel freer than I ever have. Nothing is limiting me. Just like the vast land we're riding on, life has endless opportunities. Nothing blocks our path.

Turning to look at Wilder's profile, I want him to be an endless opportunity, too. I don't know if he wants the same or considers this a fling while I'm here, but the way he holds my face and stares into my eyes just before he kisses me feels like his heart and mine are connected.

The tractor slows as we reach a forested area. My eyes scan our surroundings with a smile. "This is beautiful."

"Yeah," Wilder nods. "We've got a river that runs along our property just a few feet away." He turns off the engine and turns to me. "Come on." He tilts his head.

I hop off the tractor and meet him in the front. Today's been full of new experiences. Wilder reaches for my hand, tangling our fingers. The way his calloused fingers feel against mine fills me with heat. He's strong and rough, while his touch is gentle and caring.

We walk along the river, the quiet rushing of water hums in my ears. The sun is blocked on this part of the river, making the air feel chillier.

"I love this land," Wilder breaks the silence, his eyes focused ahead.

"I can see why. It's so peaceful."

He tilts his head down to look at me with soft eyes, and the corners of his lips curve.

"Yeah." He squeezes my fingers.

My heart drums at the way he's looking at me. A combination of peace and sadness, almost like he misses me though I'm not gone yet. It makes my heart crack a bit. I don't have much time left here, and leaving this place is going to break me.

"You're beautiful."

I take a deep breath, my emotions all over the place. I swallow thickly, blinking back tears. "Thank you," I whisper.

"I mean it. I'm not just saying it because I'm trying to seduce you or anything. I want you to believe it." He stops, turning to face me. His hands land on my hips, and I tense, self-consciously tightening my muscles, so he doesn't feel the roundness on my body.

Wilder leans into my ear. "Relax," he whispers. His hands squeeze my hips.

"I love this." His hands skim up my waist and around my back before cupping my butt. "All woman." He pushes me into him, and I gasp at his hardness pressed into my lower stomach. My eyes fly up to his, wide with surprise.

"Wilder..." I sigh.

"You're perfect." His eyes burn into mine. "Never hide yourself from anyone. I hope you always show the world your beauty."

Tears sting my eyes, and I blink them away quickly. Shaking my head, I look away. It's as if he's preparing me to return to New York with a different mentality. He grabs my hand and kisses my palm, his beard tickling my skin.

"Look at me," he demands.

When I do, his eyes swim with sincerity. "Hallie, I love your body. Shit, if you read the thoughts that cross my mind when I see you. The way I envision you beneath me, over me, all around me."

"That's because you see me clothed."

His eyes darken and narrow, making me instantly regret my comment.

"If you want to strip for me, you'll see how I'll admire you." He steps back, and remorse runs through me. I've ruined the moment. We were having such a great day.

Wilder crosses his arms and arches an eyebrow. "Come on." He waves a hand at me.

"What?" I screech. My eyebrows pull down as my eyes widen.

"Show me." My mind is wild as heat burns my face. He's gotta be kidding.

Wilder chuckles, stepping closer again. "Naked, clothed, or in rags, I like what I see. But you need to like what you see. You need to forget the bullshit that asshole made you believe. If I ever meet him, I swear I'll kill him for treating a woman that way." His jaw ticks.

"You're too good for him. You're too good." He hugs me, dropping a kiss on top of my head.

"I've fought feeling anything for anyone for so long. Then, this city girl hits a rabbit and crosses my path, breaking away my walls." He speaks quietly over my head, his hold tightening around me.

"A city girl," he chuckles dryly. "The irony." I remain silent while he gathers his thoughts.

"I promised myself I wouldn't risk my heart again." He leans back, holding the side of my face. "But then you happened." He shakes his head as if he has no control over it.

"I get it," I whisper.

"I had a serious girlfriend, and she broke my heart." He opens himself up to me. "I want you to understand why I reacted to you the way I did in the beginning. I need you to know it had nothing to do with you and everything to do with my own experiences."

I nod silently, letting him express himself.

"We had plans. She was going to move back after college to be with me. I was ready to propose, live on the ranch with her. Then, she told me she wanted more than this small town. She wanted to explore the world, live in a city, and put her career to good use. This life wasn't good enough for her anymore. I always wonder if she met someone while in college that changed her mind about the life she and I had planned, but I never came out and asked her. I wouldn't have been able to handle the betrayal."

"Oh, Wilder..." I run a soothing hand up and down his back, kissing his chest.

"To say I'm closed off to outsiders is an understatement. She broke my trust, and I've been struggling to repair it. That's why I wasn't the kindest to you at first. I was projecting."

"It makes sense," I nod. Although Joy had mentioned something, my heart aches for him as I listen to him speak about it, the raw pain in his hoarse voice.

"With you, though, I see glimpses of my old self. Not the grumpy rancher I had become. Unknowingly, you've brought out a side of me I've hidden." His fingers skim my cheek and neck. "So whenever you think you're not good enough, remember that you're more than good enough for me. You've made a difference in my life. You've brought me out of my shell."

Tears well in my eyes and trail down my cheeks. Wilder leans down and kisses them.

"Don't cry," he whispers against my skin.

"It's just that..." I take a slow breath. "No one has ever made me feel so significant before."

"I hate hearing that." He rubs his nose against mine, his lips a whisper away. "You should always feel significant," his breath tickles my lips.

I lift my head, brushing our lips together. Wilder groans at the subtle touch. My hands grip the back of his hoodie as I press my body to his. One of his hands holds the back of my head, smashing my lips to his. Every ounce of emotion is poured into this kiss. This is more than a crush. What's brewing between us is deeper than I ever could've imagined—definitely more than what I thought about as a young girl with a silly summer crush.

I'm hungry for his touch and kisses. I want so much more than stolen kisses. I want more than impending deadlines and uncertainty. But if this is all I'll have with Wilder, I'm going to soak it up. I'm going to take all he'll give me and cherish it.

I finish cutting through the bone of a pork chop with a quick, confident hit of the cleaver. So much of myself has changed in the weeks I've been here. I'm no longer the nervous and insecure woman walking into a butcher shop wondering what the hell I'm doing.

I've learned the business, taken the time to study it. Learned about the cuts of meat, the knives to use for each, and how to butcher an animal carcass. I may not be a pro like Uncle Sal, but I can hold my own. Pride swells inside of me when I realize how far I've come.

"Thank you, Mrs. Hardy." I hand the customer her wrapped pork chops with a smile.

"It's my pleasure, sweetheart. When will Sal be back?" She doesn't make a move to go.

I frown. I'm sure they miss their butcher. As much as I've taken to the job, Sal has years of rapport built with the community.

"He'll be back soon," I assure her.

"Well, we're sure gonna miss you around here. It's nice to see the younger generation stepping up in the family business," she gives me a warm smile.

I nod, swallowing the lump in my throat. "Thank you," I whisper. I'm going to miss them, too, but I keep that to myself.

I spend the morning serving customers, chopping cuts of meat as if I've been doing it for years, and moving around with such ease that I don't realize it's lunchtime until Patty shows up to relieve me.

Instead of heading out, I grab the sandwich I wrapped up earlier and eat while I check the inventory in the refrigerated storage. Eyeing the half-steer, I finish my sandwich and laugh to myself. If anyone back home would see me eating while staring at dead animals, they'd probably puke.

I wash my hands and head back into storage, straining to bring down the heavy slab of beef from the hook it's hanging on and let it fall onto the huge metal cart, so I can wheel it to the cutting room. My heart races from the exertion while I catch my breath. Just one half of a steer is bigger than me.

One thing I've learned is that this job takes so much more effort than anything I've ever done. It's nothing like the finance jobs I've applied for, sitting at an office with fancy clothing. Here, I get down and dirty, literally, and it's shown me a different responsibility I've never had the opportunity to appreciate before.

Not only is the butcher shop a vital part of this community, I constantly have to be making sure I have the product necessary. Here, I can't call in an order and expect it to arrive overnight. When I call in an order, I need to get a living animal to Paul so he can slaughter it, let the meat process a bit before I can consider cutting it down and selling it. It's the definition of patience and planning, and it's exactly how life in this town is—slow-paced, natural, and honest.

After sliding the half carcass onto the cutting table, I look at the chart with the different cuts, preparing to get to work. I no longer need YouTube videos to guide me after doing this a few times. People love their beef here, which means I've had to butcher more halves like this than I thought possible.

I'm lost in my task, cutting down the huge piece into quarters. My muscles tense as I push the knife through layers of fat, muscle, and bone, but I keep going and use the knowledge I've acquired.

Once I've got my four main parts cut, I focus on the round, which is the back part of the steer. I've spent nights studying this process, asking Uncle Sal questions, and listening to all his tips and tricks. Using what he's taught me, I begin breaking the round down. I lose track of time, knowing Patty will stay for a few hours to help so I can do this part of the job.

When a throat clears, I jolt. Glancing up with the knife in my hand, I stare at a snickering Wilder.

"Are you insane? Sneaking up on me while I'm doing this?" I place the knife flat on the counter and press the heel of my hand to my chest. "Cheese on a cracker, you scared the living shit out of me."

He pushes off the door frame, chuckling. "Sorry, darling, I didn't mean to." He stops in front of me with a smile.

"What are you doing here?" I tip my head back to look at him.

"I had to come to the bank on some business, so I thought I'd stop by and see my favorite girl."

My heart pitter-patters hearing him call me that. I smile, knowing I don't mind one bit that he interrupted me.

"I'm glad you did." I bite down my smile.

It's been two days since we climbed the water tower and spent the day together before having dinner as he promised. Two days too long since he's kissed me. Each time I see him, I fall harder for the man I'm getting to know. After he opened up to me by the river, I haven't been able to stop thinking about the possibilities that could exist between us if I lived here.

"Yeah?" He smirks.

I nod.

Wilder tilts my chin up and kisses me softly. "I'm glad you're glad."

I giggle, bringing my arms around his shoulders, careful not to place my hands on him since the gloves are dirty, but I want to feel him around me.

"Come have dinner with me tonight," he whispers against my lips.

"Okay." I nod. "I just need to make sure Uncle Sal will be fine on his own."

"It's taken care of it. Patty will be with him." I raise my eyebrows, and he laughs. "I spoke to her on the way in," he winks.

"What exactly do you have planned?" I step back.

"Cooking for you, serving you wine…" he muses and waggles his eyebrows. "Kissing you."

"I like the sound of that. So…at your place?" I'm suddenly nervous and excited.

"Yeah."

"Okay, just tell me a time, and I'll be there."

"I was hoping you'd say that." He invades my personal space again, wrapping his arms around my waist and pulling me to him.

"I don't want to get you dirty," I whisper, heart racing as I feel him pressed against me.

"Dirty me all you want." He kisses me firmly. I sigh and lean into the kiss, my arms once again moving around his neck when his tongue slides against mine.

Heat and desire spike through my body as I get lost in the taste of him. Lost in all that is Wilder James, the man I'm starting to feel a lot more than attracted to. My heart thunders and splits at that thought, knowing I'll soon be heading back to where I came from, and he'll become a memory I'll always turn to when I feel lost. An anchor in the sea of life that always seems to attempt to drown me.

Chapter 21

HALLIE

"Things seem to be getting quite serious between you and Wilder." Uncle Sal's comment surprises me when I walk into the living room. He's not subtle.

"What do you mean?" I slip my arms through my military jacket. We haven't really talked about Wilder besides him knowing that we've gone out.

"Just sayin'. You're seeing him again tonight, and you were out together two days ago. Spent the whole day with him." He smirks.

"I like him," I shrug. "Is that such a bad thing?" My eyebrows dip as I play with the drawstrings on the waist of my jacket.

"Not at all," he shakes his head. "Come." He pats the sofa next to him.

I carefully walk around his elevated leg, so I don't bump into it and sit beside my uncle.

"I just want to make sure you're okay. I know you've had a rough couple of years, what with your career not going as planned and that jerk you were dating." His jaw ticks.

Uncle Sal may have only met Jeff once when he visited us in New York, but it seems as if that first impression and whatever my parents have told him is enough for him to hate the man. I can't blame him. I despise him now, too.

"Wilder is a good man, but you're a sensitive soul. I don't want you to get hurt when…"

"When I leave," I finish for him.

He nods, reaching for my hand and squeezing gently. I look down, attempting to hide my emotions. It's no use, though. I've always been told I wear my heart on my sleeve.

"I like him a lot, and I know that we may not have a future with what me living so far away, but…" I shrug. "I don't know."

"I get it." He pats my hand, shifting on the couch. His face screws and I instantly lean forward to help him, placing a pillow behind his back.

"Are you okay?"

"Yeah," he huffs. "I'm not a young kid anymore, though," he chuckles. "Anyway, go have fun. Patty will be here soon." He waves me off.

"I can wait for her to arrive."

"No," he shakes his head firmly. "I'm okay. There just isn't a way to get comfortable with this thing." He pats the boot on his leg. "Go and enjoy your evening." Our conversation about Wilder is forgotten.

"If you're sure…" I eye him with concern.

"I—You see." The doorbell rings right on cue.

"Okay," I sigh, grabbing my purse. "If you need anything, call." I lift my cell phone.

"Sure," he placates me. I can tell by his expression that he has no plans to call if he needs something.

I open the door to let Patty in and head out in Uncle Sal's old truck, taking the road to Wilder's ranch. While I've been to the ranch a few times, I have no idea where exactly his house is. When you own thousands of acres, I guess you can live on the same property as your family and be far away.

Nerves ricochet inside of me the closer I get to the ranch. While Wilder and I have gone out, it'll be the first time we're in the privacy of his home. Different thoughts cross my mind, a few leading to the two of us ending up in his bed, naked. My heart beats furiously at the idea of him seeing me. I've never had a man speak to me the way he does, but it's still scary for someone to see you in your birthday suit for the first time—especially when I sure as hell don't look like a model or athlete.

He likes you just as you are. You have to accept yourself.

Breathing away any negative thoughts, I focus on the dirt road and follow Wilder's directions. I never noticed that the road that leads to the barn actually forks. Taking the path he instructed, the truck bounces as I drive away from the main house in the direction I hope is Wilder's.

I sigh in relief when I see a cabin appear, and Wilder is standing on the porch.

"You made it." He smiles when I step out of the truck.

"I did." My eyes glance around the area. The two-story cabin sits in a wooded area. It's secluded and beautiful—nature at your fingertips.

"This is gorgeous," I say as I approach him.

"Thanks," his smile grows. "I built it a few years ago when we added the cabin rentals. It's nothing special, but it's home."

"It looks special to me." I spin around. "You live in a magical place."

Wilder laughs at my comment, wrapping an arm around me when I'm facing him again. I gaze up into his blue eyes, my breath hitching. He's so handsome.

"Having you here is magical," he says quietly before his lips land on mine in a passionate kiss.

My arms move around his body so I can hold on, feeling as if my legs might give out at any moment. The way his tongue slides against mine and his hard body presses into me, I feel like tonight may go a lot like I fantasized. And for a beat, I don't care about my soft and round body.

"Hi," he breathes out when he pulls away.

"Hi," I mimic.

"Come on, let's go inside."

Wilder keeps an arm around my shoulder as he leads us into his home. It's cozy and simple. It's a guy's house, which makes me smile. A dark brown leather sofa faces a television mounted on the wall, and stools line the peninsula counter that opens from the living room. The entire house is open concept, and I assume the bedrooms are upstairs.

"It smells delicious."

"Thanks. It's not much yet, potatoes roasting, but I'll start cooking soon."

"Can I help?" I look around the kitchen, but nothing gives away what he's making.

"You relax and drink wine." He gives me a lopsided smile that makes my body tingle.

Wilder serves two glasses of wine, and we toast before he pulls seasoned steaks out of the fridge and places a cast iron pan on his gas stove.

"How do you like your steak? Medium?"

"Yeah," I nod. "Are those from your cattle?" I can't help but ask now that I understand better how the business works.

"Yup, best of the best."

Chuckling, I take a drink of wine. "Would you ever think anyone else's beef is better than yours?" I eye him over the rim of my glass.

"Nope. Mine's the best. I know what I feed them, how they're raised and treated. Nothing beats that." He washes his hands before oiling the cast iron and letting it heat.

"How was the rest of your day?" His hip rests against the counter, the glass of wine in one hand.

"It was good. It went by so fast." Between butchering one quarter of that half-steer and serving customers, the day passed in a blur, which is good since I've been excited about tonight ever since Wilder stopped by to invite me.

"I'm glad. Mine was slow."

"Really?" I scrunch up my nose.

"Yup," he nods, setting his glass down on the counter and making his way around to where I'm sitting on one of his stools. Wilder stops before me and grabs my glass, placing it on the counter as well.

"The anticipation for tonight was driving me crazy. No matter how hard I worked, I couldn't stop thinking about seeing you." His hands cradle my face, and I swoon. My body feels light, and I sway as if I were drunk—more like drunk on Wilder and his words.

He brushes his lips against mine, ever so softly, and I whimper in complaint. His laughter tickles my cheek.

"If I could spend the rest of my life kissing you, I'd die a happy man."

I blink my eyes open, staring into the sincerity swimming in his blue orbs. My words get caught in my throat, but he doesn't seem to need a response. With a final kiss, he moves back to the stove.

When he places the steaks in the pan, loud sizzling pops around us, and the savory aroma of garlic hits me. My mouth waters—both at the smell of the food and at watching Wilder's strong frame move around the kitchen with ease.

A man who cooks is sexy as hell. His arms flex beneath the rolled-up sleeves of his plaid shirt. His back shifts as he grabs oven mitts and lifts the pan from the fire. Wilder looks at me over his shoulder and winks. He knows exactly what he's doing. He's working the kitchen like his own stage.

Each time I'm with him, it seems as if a piece of my heart gets set back in place. A piece of myself gets rearranged so that the past pain can no longer seep into my soul.

How am I going to leave him?

Uncle Sal's concern hits me, and I understand why he voiced it. I've never been the type of girl to have a fling. I don't think that's a part of my DNA. When it comes to being with someone, I'm all in, which is why I'm so easily hurt. Jeff knew my weaknesses, and he played them in his favor. Wilder seems to do the opposite. He sees my weaknesses and nurtures them into strengths.

The idea of not seeing Wilder daily, whether it's a date or crossing each other in town, makes my heart splinter. When I packed my bags to come help Uncle Sal, I didn't expect my heart to get tangled in the process. And untangling it will hurt like hell.

Shaking away those thoughts, I focus on right now. I'm with Wilder in his home while he cooks dinner for us. I'm happy for the first time in a long time. It's not the superficial happiness where you laugh at a meme. It's the kind of happiness that pierces your soul, restores your heart, and overshadows all the bad you've endured in the past.

I'm going to soak up that kind of happiness and keep stock, store it away for a day when I'll need a boost of it. Wilder will never understand what knowing him has done for me. He says I've opened him up again, but he's stitched me back together, made me whole again.

After a delicious meal, we're sitting on his couch with our almost empty glasses of wine. Wilder's fingers gently trace a trail up and down the back of my neck while he tells me about the upcoming auction. I'm too distracted by his touch to fully hear what he's saying.

His fingers stop, his hand holding my neck as his thumb massages the muscles there. I sigh and will myself to relax. His touch is exactly what I need after a long day of work. Butchering isn't for the weak, and I've used muscles in the last weeks that I'm sure I've never used before or knew existed. My eyes flutter closed as a shiver runs through me, and Wilder's chuckle sounds close to my ear.

"Are you even listening to me?" His breath tickles my cheek.

I shake my head, unashamed. "I'm thoroughly enjoying this massage." I relax further, my body letting go of any tension stored in my back and muscles. I've always held my stress there, creating back pain and tightness. His hands move over them skillfully.

"Hallie…" His whisper is gruff.

"Hmm…" I hum.

Instead of responding, his lips skim my jaw up to my ear. My eyes snap open when his teeth nip my earlobe. I turn my head to find him with a cocky smirk. His ocean blue eyes have turned stormy as his gaze moves from my eyes to my lips to my neck. I shift, causing his hand to fall from my neck, but he doesn't seem to mind since both hands instantly move to my hips.

"Hi," I whisper self-consciously. Now that I'm facing him, I'm not sure what to do.

"Hi," he smiles, brushing away my hair over my shoulder. His thumb strokes the side of my neck down to the base of my throat, feeling my pulse point. I'm sure he can feel my racing heart. Nerves rush through me, knowing that this moment can lead to so much more.

We stare at each other for what feels like hours, no words necessary in this moment. I can see it in his eyes, the need and desire, but also the emotion swimming in them that tells me this is more than a hook-up.

"You're beautiful. Perfect." He traces the bridge of my nose, my lips, my eyebrows. His other hand tightens around my hip.

I inch closer to him when his hand moves to the back of my head, fingers tangling in my hair. His breath tickles my nose right before his lips land on mine, soft and gentle at first. I kiss him back, slow and lazy, memorizing the way his lips move over mine.

Moaning, I loop my arms around his neck, scooting closer. Wilder nips my lower lip, and I shiver. My nipples tighten, and my core clenches at that intimate action. Heat fills my veins, turning the kiss from measured movements to desperate. I angle my head, Wilder's fingers tightening around my hair, pulling it to the point of pain. It rolls and blends with the pleasure he's causing my body, creating this hazy combination that pushes me forward.

My tongue swipes against his. They tangle as if they need each other as an anchor, the kiss deepening. Wilder groans, and I feel the vibrations down to my toes. It sparks my desire further.

"Babe…" he mumbles against my lips.

His other hand roams the side of my body. His touch sears me. It feels private and possessive. Like he's the only one who knows my body.

A shaky breath leaves my lips when he kisses down my neck, his tongue swirling over my heated skin. My hands claw at his back, pulling him closer but the awkward sitting position on the couch makes it difficult. It doesn't stop Wilder from sucking the spot where my neck and shoulder meet, raising goosebumps all over my skin. I need his touch in other places. I don't think I can handle just kissing with the way he's doing it tonight.

As if reading my mind, Wilder grips my backside and tugs me until I'm straddling him. He releases a hiss, eyes closed and head tipped back on the couch. It gives me a moment to observe him. His face is etched in longing, almost as if pained. His thick neck is exposed to me, luring me in like a bull to a red flag.

I drop my head, peeking my tongue out to taste his skin. I swirl the tip of my tongue around the base of his throat and them up his neck. Wilder growls, hands tightening on my hips.

"Hallie…" My name comes out on a guttural groan. The bulge behind his fly presses into me, causing me to rock my hips against him. I need more.

I don't respond. I keep going. His tense body encourages me to move around to the side of his neck, leaving sucking kisses until I reach the spot behind his ear. I kiss him there, nipping the sensitive skin before taking his earlobe between my teeth and sucking.

"Fuck," he groans.

His hands are wild on my body, sneaking under my shirt so his calloused hands can burn the memory of his touch to my back. I'll never be the same after him.

I lean back to stare into his eyes, and they're wild. In this moment, his name matches his mood. The usually measured man is lost in desire, wild with lust.

"Wilder." My voice is hoarse to my own ears.

He doesn't let me speak. He doesn't speak. He slams his mouth on mine, kissing me as if it were the last time we'd have the chance to. It's passionate, hot, and intense. The slowness from before has dissipated as our lips meld and hands desperately touch any part of each other we can reach. My hips rock over his, needing to feel any part of him against me, even if through our clothed bodies.

"I need you," he says after a while. "So damn much." His eyes search mine. "If that's okay. If you're ready."

His thoughtfulness chokes me up, so I swallow back my emotions and nod silently. He's proven time and again how considerate he is, how important I am to him.

"Need you to say it, Hallie." His thumb strokes my cheek as a crooked smile tilts his lips.

"I do, too. I want you. I want this." My fingernails gently scrape down his neck. Wilder closes his eyes and hums. When I glide my hips over his, they snap open, fire burning in them.

"You keep doing that, and we won't make it to my bedroom. Hell, I won't even have time to undress." He stills my hips, but I continue to feel his hard length pressing into my core, taunting me.

"You make me so fucking hard. So desperate for your body." His fingers indent my skin, and I whimper at his words.

"You're so damn sexy." He smooths his hands up the sides of my body, where I never thought I'd be sexy. He glides over my curves, my bumps, and to my stomach.

Wilder leans up to kiss me. I take it with greed, wanting to steal all his kisses, wishing he'd never kiss anyone else after me.

His hands move to the hem of my shirt and lift a few inches. "Is this okay?" I nod silently, staring at him intensely.

As he lifts my shirt, he drops kisses up my body. When he removes it, he leans back, admiring me. He palms my heavy breasts through my bra, his thumb sliding over my peaked nipples. He touches my exposed skin slowly and delicately before moving his hands around and gripping my ass through my jeans.

I yelp when he stands with me still straddling him, and my hands slam down on his shoulders to hold on. Wilder chuckles as he effortlessly moves us through the house and up the stairs to his bedroom. I don't have time to see what it looks like because he places me on the bed and crawls over me.

Who cares what his bedroom looks like when this man is staring at me as if I were his greatest prize?

My body prickles.

Wilder's lips trail kisses down my body. His fingers unsnap my bra, and a hint of uncertainty causes me to tense until I catch his stare right as his tongue peeks out and swirls around the pebbled point. My back arches when his teeth scrape over my sensitive skin, and my hands move to his head, holding him in place.

His free hand moves down my body and unsnap the button on my jeans. The purr of the zipper barely registers when I have the stinging pleasure of his beard scratching my skin as his tongue repeatedly flicks my nipple.

When his warm hand sneaks into my jeans, I wriggle. Wilder smiles against my skin and looks up at me. No questions asked. He removes my jeans and underwear until I'm naked before him. The most vulnerable I could be with a person, and he's looking at me hungrily. There's no trace of judgment or disgust. There's no hiding my body so that he's not distracted by the extra pounds I wear around my middle. Tears sting behind my eyes, and I close them, blowing out a breath.

"Are you okay?" Wilder's soft concern warms me.

"Yeah," I whisper, blindly reaching out to him.

I lace our fingers together and tug him toward me. His body presses into mine deliciously, his weight reminding me of the man he is, the work he does, the strength he owns.

"I'm gonna make you feel so damn good," he promises.

Wilder reaches between us, fingers stroking my clit. He growls, pressing harder into me.

"You're so wet, babe," he whispers into my ear before taking my mouth in his.

Lost in pleasure, all insecurities wash away. I don't think about what I look like to him, what he's thinking about my body. He's making me feel as good as he promised, his fingers working magic between my legs and his mouth kissing all over, enhancing the pleasure building between in my core.

"So gorgeous," he murmurs against my chest on his way to my breasts. When his teeth tug my nipple, I cry out.

"That's it, squeeze my fingers again." He fucks me with his long fingers as his teeth continue to torture my sensitive body.

Soon, I'm calling out his name and so fucking glad we're in the middle of nowhere on his ranch so that neighbors aren't witnessing the way I'm spiraling. Wilder continues to rub my sensitive core, his thumb flicking my clit until I'm thrashing, gripping the sheets, and begging for him to stop.

"It's too much," I moan.

Ignoring me, he continues his torment until I spiral out of control, blackness taking over, so all I can sense is the pleasure rolling through me.

Wilder leans up on an elbow once my breathing has slowed, smiling down at me as he licks his fingers. "Another day, I'm gonna taste you for real. Right now, I need inside of you."

He kisses up my body, gentle and slow as if we had all the time in the world. As if I deserved to be worshipped. And worshipping me is exactly what he is doing. He makes everything else fade away until all that's left are the two of us in this moment. Nothing more, nothing less, and it's perfect.

Chapter 22

WILDER

I haven't felt a connection like this to someone in a long time. Hallie makes me feel alive. She lights a fire in me. To have her laid beneath me like this, not just physically naked but exposing her heart to me, I've never witnessed such beauty. And having her surrender to me, to us, it's magic.

I kiss my way up her body. I need to feel her tightness around my dick, but I'm not rushing this. I'm not sure how or when we'll be able to be like this again, so I want to make sure we take our time. She deserves more than a quick fuck to find release. She deserves to be shown how special she is, how important she is to me.

Her creamy skin begs to be kissed, and I smile with pride as I see the red marks my beard leaves on her. She hasn't complained about it, so I'm guessing she likes the sensation.

Hallie's arms try to pull me up, but I shake my head before flicking my tongue over her nipple and then moving to the other one, giving them both the same attention.

When I finally reach her lips, I kiss her hard before looking into her sea-green eyes. I smile and brush away her wild hair.

"I can't get enough of you." I brush my nose with hers.

"Me either," she says quietly as her hands move to the buttons on my shirt.

I lean back and help her finish removing it. My eyes close as her hands brush my chest. Her touch is soothing and fiery at the same time. It's a heady combination I've never felt before.

"Your jeans." She eyes my covered body, and I smirk.

"You want me naked?" I waggle my eyebrows.

"Yes." She doesn't hesitate, sitting up to undo the button. I grab her tits, thumbing her nipples, while she gets to work removing my jeans. A tremble shakes her body. She's so sensitive to my touch, reacting immediately. I love it.

"Stand," she demands.

I follow orders and wait for her to take control. Hallie crawls over to the end of the bed, lowering the zipper. Before she pushes my jeans down my legs, she cups my hard dick through them. A hiss moves through my teeth. I've been dying for her touch, but I needed to make sure she went first. That I showed her how much I like and desire her.

"Impressive," she murmurs, and I laugh at her abrupt honesty.

She bites her lower lip, and her cheeks turn rosy.

"I told you that you needed to be with a real man," I say, removing her lip from between her teeth.

"So confident," she shakes her head.

Her fingers sneak into the sides of my jeans, and she pushes them down my body along with my boxer briefs, freeing my hard length on a bounce. Her eyes widen as they snap up to mine.

"You make me this way," I assure her.

Silently, Hallie wraps her hand around my dick and strokes a few times. I groan, holding on to her shoulder for support. She licks her lips, and I know if she wraps those pretty lips around me, I'll be a goner before the count of five.

"Not now," I warn her, placing my hand over hers and taking over the measured strokes as I lean her back on the bed. "I want to come inside of you, not in your mouth. Not tonight."

"I want that, too." Her doe eyes stare at me.

"Good." I kiss her, my hand moving down her body until I find her wet folds.

Hallie arches up and moans.

"No," she bites. "I wanna come with you." Her hand lands on mine, stopping my movements.

"I can't get enough of you, though. I need to touch you. Make you feel good. Damn it, I want to spend the rest of my life on this bed with you." My confession comes out more vulnerable than I intended.

"I know the feeling," she smiles, stroking my cheek. I close my eyes and lean into her soft touch.

Her other hand reaches for my cock and brushes the tip against her soaked pussy. I fight the urge to slam into her and squeeze my eyes shut.

"Hallie…" I warn gruffly.

"Come on." She urges me on, lifting her hips, so her pussy glides along my length.

"Shit," I groan with a deep breath. "Give me a sec." I control my breathing, blindly reaching for my nightstand.

When I don't find the box of condoms, I lean up and look into the drawer, keeping my hand on her. Fishing out a foil packet, I cover myself quickly and angle my body over hers. I pause and stare into her eyes.

"I want you to know this means something to me."

She nods silently.

No more words are necessary. I grab one of her thighs, lifting it on my hip as I line up and push into her, her tight pussy consuming me. I moan in pleasure, holding myself inside of her for a beat.

Hallie's arms are wrapped around me, holding me to her. We're silent except for our heavy breathing. I hold her gaze, hoping she can see everything I feel that I can't quite verbalize yet.

Her legs squeeze around me, and that's my cue to begin moving. I kiss her as my body moves over hers. We meet thrust for thrust as if we were made for each other. It's effortless and sensual. I move my lips to her neck and increase my speed, fucking her hard and fast, hitting every pleasure point.

"Wilder…" she moans, tightening her hold on me.

"Give it to me, babe," I say through clenched teeth. My body is tense, but I'm holding off until she's coming.

"You feel so amazing. So thick and big," she whispers as her fingers brush the ends of my hair. I growl at her words.

"Look at who's a dirty talker," I tease, twisting my hips and lifting one of her legs so I can thrust deeper.

"You bring it out in me. The way you feel… Oh, God," she moans, back arching. "So right," she kisses my chin.

"That's because you're right for me. Perfect. I can't get enough of you." I pinch her nipple with my free hand, and she cries out.

My orgasm begins to build in my spine, and I reach down to rub her clit. "Need you with me," I grit out.

"Don't stop," she begs, fingers clawing at my back with desperation. She can mark me all she wants. I'll never belong to anyone else. I need her here, to stay, permanently.

Hallie tenses and calls out my name, her pussy milking me, and I can't hold off any longer. With a deep thrust, I lose myself in her, giving her everything I've got. I bury my face in her neck, nipping her skin as I climax.

We stay like this for a bit, her holding me and me breathing her in, connected in the most intimate way two people can be. Our beating hearts slam in time.

"Wow…" Hallie breathes out eventually, and I chuckle.

Lifting my body, I look at her. Her lips are swollen, and her face shines with that freshly fucked glow. Thanks to me. Just the thought makes me want to do it again.

I drop a quick kiss on her lips and slide out of her, removing the condom.

"Be right back." I walk into the bathroom, taking care of business, and return with a damp towel.

Her eyes narrow briefly, but she doesn't argue when I clean her up.

"I really thought guys only did that in romance novels," she chuckles a bit awkwardly.

"Nah," I wink.

After discarding the towel in my hamper and she goes to the bathroom, we climb into bed, and I wrap my arms around her, turning her into me. I kiss the top of her head and close my eyes for a moment, allowing myself to feel without walls or pained past limiting me. Hallie's breath tickles my shoulder, and I relax.

Her fingers trail aimlessly along my skin as we both lay silently in bed. This woman has pushed me out of my safe zone, making me feel things I swore I never would again.

"Stay the night," I whisper against her forehead.

"I have work tomorrow." She lifts her head to look at me.

"I do, too. You'll have plenty of time to go home and get ready."

Doubt crosses her face.

"If you want," I quickly add. I don't want her to feel like she has to.

"I want to, but…" Her lips press together.

"What?" I lean up on my elbow.

"I'm not sure Uncle Sal will be okay by himself."

I nod. I almost forgot about Sal and his broken leg. Instead of moving away, though, Hallie cuddles closer into me. I hold her protectively, not letting go until she tells me to.

"Just give me a few," she says quietly.

"Take all the time you need."

"What the…" A loud voice rings in my ears, and the bed shifts.

I blink my eyes open and find Hallie sitting up in bed, looking around in confusion. She rubs her eyes to clear away the sleep, her naked body calling to me when the sheet drapes around her waist.

Her eyes find mine, and her eyebrows lift.

"Oh…" She rubs a hand down her face. Her hair is disheveled, and she looks like she's still half asleep.

"I didn't know where I was. Sorry for waking you up." She leans back in bed, covering herself up again with the blanket. I'm tempted to remove it but hold off.

"Hmm… It's okay. You can wake me up any time you want if you're lying in my bed naked." My voice is hoarse.

I turn toward her, bringing my arm around her body and pulling her closer to me. I'm not quite ready to let her go.

"So much for going home, huh?" Round eyes find mine as she chews her bottom lip.

I chuckle. "Well, it worked out for me." I squeeze my arm around her waist. "I'm glad you stayed." I brush my lips against hers.

She begins to relax, sinking into the mattress and my embrace.

"It'll be awkward to face Uncle Sal, but I'm glad I stayed, too." Her legs wind with mine, and I feel her heat against my hip. My body reacts, and I'm sure she'll be aware of it any second.

"Hmm... Is that right?"

"Yeah," she sighs.

Her body presses into mine, and I groan.

"Uh, Wilder?" She looks up at me and then down to where the blanket is covering our bodies.

"Yeah?" I shift closer.

"You're, uh..."

"Yeah," I breathe out. "You make me this way." My erection rubs against her, and she moans.

"What time is it?"

"I don't know, but my alarm clock hasn't gone off, so it's not time to get up just yet." I roll her over, landing above her and kissing her neck. I've learned she loves that. When she pulls my head closer to her skin, I bite her and suck, pulling a moan from her.

"Hmm..." she sighs. "That feels good."

"You feel good. So fucking amazing. I want to bury myself inside of you." I bite her jaw on my way up to her lips.

"That'd be heaven," she moans, rubbing her body against mine. Desire coats her words, and her body takes over, grinding against mine.

"Yeah," I agree, searching for a condom.

Morning sex is my favorite, and I don't need foreplay with the way her slick pussy is coating me with her wetness. We're both ready.

Wordlessly, I thrust into her, feeling like I'm sliding home after a long day of strenuous work.

"Fucking heaven," I murmur against her lips before taking them in a deep kiss.

We both moan as we move together. She's my missing piece. She's what I never thought I needed. She's heaven on earth. My kryptonite.

I get lost in her body and moans long after my alarm clock goes off. I'll deal with the consequences later. Right now, all that matters is having Hallie.

When we're both satiated, we take showers, and I kiss her goodbye, already forming a plan to get her back in my bed.

I'm going to soak up all the opportunities I can get before she has to leave for New York again. I'm a selfish masochist. I want all her time and attention despite knowing it'll kill me when she's gone. Another woman who'll leave me, but this time I'm making the choice to break my own heart.

Chapter 23

HALLIE

I hum to myself during some downtime while I clean the counter at the butcher shop and see kids leaving the school across the street. Many times, the middle schoolers will walk out with friends instead of adults and head toward the center of town. I can't imagine living in a town like this where it's safe for a fourteen-year-old to walk alone with friends.

Lately, I've been wondering what would happen if I did live here. After sleeping with Wilder a few days ago, things have changed. My feelings for him have intensified. The way he treated me, the way he made me feel. No other man has brought out those emotions, that sense of security.

And I'm afraid that it'll all be over soon. Uncle Sal is seeing his doctor today, and depending on what he says, I'll know when my time in Mason Creek is up. The doctor has already extended my uncle's recovery, but it won't be long before he gives him the all-clear.

My heart aches at the thought, which should be telling. However, I feel like I don't really have a choice to stay. What would I do in Mason Creek? Soon, Uncle Sal will be working the butcher shop again, and while he's successful, I'm not sure it's enough to pay me to work alongside him. I don't exactly see a future here when it comes to my career, though the same has happened back home.

Inhaling deeply, I focus on my task and get ready for the last two hours of work. I'm meeting Joy for coffee, and I'm excited to spend time with her. I've been spending so much time with Wilder that I've missed seeing her. I want to soak up everything Mason Creek has to offer at once.

After the last-minute rush before closing time, people grabbing things for dinner or on their way home from work, I clean up and get ready to end my workday. The wave of people is routine, and I've learned to calculate how it flows. It doesn't take long for me to lock up and walk toward Java Jitters to meet Joy. I'm looking forward to some girl time, and maybe she can help me gain some perspective.

I smile as I walk around town, waving at some people on my way. This town makes me feel different. I *am* different since I arrived. My stress level is almost nonexistent now that I know what I'm doing around the butcher shop. I'm happier and more at peace than I've been in years. Mason Creek gives me a sense of belonging.

I smile sadly to myself as I see Joy waving just outside Java Jitters. As soon as I reach her, I wrap my arms around her.

"Hey," I say when I lean back.

"Hi." She tilts her head. "What's going on?"

Shaking my head, I open the door to the coffee shop.

"I don't buy it," Joy pushes.

"I was just walking around town now, thinking about things." I take my spot in line and wait for her to comment. I wish she were a mind reader so I wouldn't have to verbalize the mess in my head.

"What kind of things? About Wilder?" She leans in and whispers.

"Among other things." I step forward in line.

"Okay, we'll talk once we're seated," she decides with a firm nod.

Joy keeps her promise as soon as we take our seats and leans forward on her elbows while her coffee cools. "Tell me what's on your mind." She smiles tentatively.

I attempt to collect my thoughts, but they're all jumbled in my brain like a junk drawer. "I'm confused. I feel lost about where my life is going. It's been like that for a while, and I hoped that coming to Mason Creek would give me a different perspective."

"And it hasn't?" She draws out slowly.

"I think I'm more confused than before," I chuckle dryly. It'd be just like me to get dragged into the lost and found of life when seeking guidance.

"Start from the beginning," Joy suggests, taking a drink of her coffee and cringing while sticking her tongue out. "Damn it. I was hoping it'd be colder than it is."

I laugh at her reaction, feeling myself relax. She stares at me with raised eyebrows, and I tell her everything.

"I've had a hard time finding a job in New York. I haven't found anything in finance that makes my college degree worth it. It's tough there, super competitive, and

I'm always overlooked. Not to mention my whole relationship with Jeff was a disaster. I put up with a lot when I should've ended things a long time ago. In reality, I probably shouldn't have even started dating him, but it was rare for a guy like him to notice a girl like me."

"Whoa, whoa whoa…" Joy lifts a hand, eyes narrowed. "What the hell do you mean a guy like him noticing a girl like you?"

"He was…is a suit guy, put together and successful. I always felt inferior to him, so the fact that he noticed me—short and chunky—instead of some tall, skinny model-type always made me feel better. I don't know," I shake my head. "Now, I realize that wasn't the case. But a year ago, I thought Jeff was the best I could do."

Joy shakes her head, lips pressed together. "There is so much I could say about this, but let's focus on how you could definitely do better than some stuck-up asshole from New York. Mainly, a rugged, sexy rancher from Mason Creek," she waggles her eyebrows.

I sigh, looking down at my cup.

"What's that face for? You do like Wilder?" Although she means it as a statement, her voice rings with a question.

"Of course I do." I snap my eyes back to hers. "A lot." I clasp my hands together. "Wilder has been amazing. He's helped me open my eyes to things I was overlooking."

"That's good, then," she nods.

"Yeah, but instead of gaining clarity, I'm so freaking confused." I drop my chin and close my eyes. The muscles in my neck are tight from the building stress.

"Being here is amazing, and I'm going to be sad to leave. Not to mention, I'm no closer to knowing what I'll do when I get back to New York. I guess start dropping off more resumes and cross my fingers I'll get a job."

"What about Wilder?" Her eyebrows pull together.

I frown, eyes misting over. "I don't know what will happen. We go our separate ways? We both knew I'd be leaving eventually, so it's pointless to ask him if he sees a future for us. It's probably just a fling for him." My words get clogged in my throat.

"I don't think it is. I've already told you Wilder hasn't shown interest in anyone since he and Lisa broke up, at least not anyone in town." I nod, and Joy leans forward, lowering her voice.

"Some people are speculating what will happen after you leave. The MC Scoop has a post about it. There's talk that you'll end up staying. Others think you'll try to drag Wilder out to New York with you."

"What?" My eyebrows bunch. "That's ridiculous. I'd never try to take him away from this place. I know how much he loves this town. I'm not selfish."

"I know you aren't. People are just talking shit," Joy lifts a shoulder.

I drop my head in my hands, taking a deep breath. The aroma of my coffee hits me, but I'm too torn to bother drinking it.

I want to read the post. I reach out my hand for her phone. The MC Scoop is the local gossip blog run by a girl in her twenties. It's the place to read all about the town's happenings.

"No." She shakes her head.

"Fine." I fish my phone out and start googling the website since I don't know the exact link.

I take a deep breath before opening the site and searching for the post that talks about Wilder and me.

Heading to Brokenheartsville?

We've all been witness to the blooming romance between our favorite rancher and the new city girl. I don't think anyone thought he'd let himself find love again, but it seems all it took was an outsider to rope his heart.

Time's ticking, though…and soon she'll be gone. Will he pack his bags and leave for the Big Apple (something he refused to do with his first love). Will we have a new resident in Mason Creek?

Surely he won't make the same mistake twice. Or is there a third choice? Seeing him nurse his broken heart at the local bar once again?

"This is insane," my eyes widen as I drop the phone on the table.

"Ignore it. It's the best advice I can give you." Joy shakes her head. "It's gossip, nothing more."

I'm speechless, the words replaying in my head. I refuse to be the reason Wilder hurts again.

"Why can't you stay here? You said you hadn't had luck in New York, so it's not like much is waiting for you. Your parents will understand." My eyes snap to Joy's.

This is the same question I've been tossing around for a few days. The idea of staying in Mason Creek makes me so damn happy, but…is it really a part of my reality? It's not supposed to be.

"I don't know. There's so much to think about, and I can't make that decision based solely on a guy, no matter how much I like him." I spin my coffee cup around.

"It wouldn't be only because of him. Look at me." Joy tugs at my arm, and I hesitantly lift my gaze. "You look so much happier than when you arrived. Well, not right at this moment," she jokes, and I snort.

"Thanks," I deadpan.

"You know what I mean. You got here looking a bit…disoriented. Now, you're a pro butcher, you know the people in town, and you've got friends." Everything she says is what I'm feeling on the inside. That sense of belonging from earlier expands, and something inside of me is whispering to stay, to take a risk, and see what will happen.

"Where would I even work? Sal won't be able to hire me once he's back on his feet."

I'll be back to square one if I stay here, same as back home, unemployed with no real prospects. That'll just prove Jeff right. I won't have made anything of myself. Instead, moving from my parents' house to where? My uncle's house? No. I won't get in the way of his life. I already feel like I've disrupted his privacy by being here, even if it is to help him.

"We'll figure something out if that's what you really want." Joy's optimism is appreciated, but without a real plan, I don't see how staying here is a good idea.

I feel no better than when I arrived. I thought talking it out with Joy would give me that aha moment I keep waiting for. Instead, I'm sad and craving sugar.

"Can we change the subject? How's the preparation for the spring festival coming along?"

Joy's face lights up, and she claps excitedly. "So good. I finally perfected my secret pastry. I mean, I knew how to do it, but something felt like it was missing, and yesterday it came to me. *Now,* it's perfect. So freaking amazing." Her voice rises with each word, and I laugh at her enthusiasm.

"That's great. It's in two weeks, right?"

"Yeah. You'll be here?" Her eyes round as it dawns on her that I may be gone by then.

"I'm not sure, but I hope so. Maybe I can stay 'til then, even if Uncle Sal is already working. I'd have to make sure it'd be okay with him."

"I'm sure it will be. He's so happy to have you here." She smiles genuinely.

I nod silently, finally drinking my now cold coffee. I've got a lot to consider, although it feels like I don't really have a choice but to return to New York.

My funk doesn't dissipate as Joy and I talk about the spring festival and local gossip. By the time I walk home, I feel like a weight is crushing me. It doesn't help that I haven't heard from Wilder all day. I don't want to seem clingy by sending him a text message, but I'd give anything for one of his hugs right now.

When I walk through the door, I'm surprised to see Uncle Sal standing in the living room…sans boot. His arms are spread wide, and his smile is blinding.

"Hello!" he sings out, wiggling his leg in front of me

My eyebrows lift, and I swallow thickly. I knew this was a real possibility when he went to the doctor today. My heart squeezes at the realization that my time here will be shorter than I thought.

"Wow…" I whisper when he stares at me expectantly.

Great, now I'm Eeyore. I blink away tears and hug Uncle Sal.

"This is great." I attempt to keep my voice steady, but it trembles at the end.

"Are you okay?" Uncle Sal leans back, keeping his arms on my shoulders.

I nod and force a smile.

"You aren't," he states matter-of-factly.

"I am," I wave a hand. "It's just been a long day. I'm going to shower, and then I'll prep dinner." I move around him, but he stops me.

"Let's go out to dinner. I haven't been out of this house in weeks."

"Sure," I nod. "Do you want to go to the diner?"

"Yeah, that's perfect." He watches me with narrowed eyes but releases me this time.

I shake off my mood and allow the hot water to drain it down the shower. I should be happy for Uncle Sal, but my mood is just worsening with each passing minute. More so now that I am going to talk to him about staying for the spring festival in two weeks.

When I head back into the living room, Uncle Sal crosses his arms and arches a brow. "Tell me what's going on."

"Nothing. I'm moody, is all. Come on, let's go get dinner." I lead Uncle Sal out and help him step up to the truck.

"Are you okay?" I ask when he grimaces.

"Yeah, but my leg's still sensitive. Doc said it'd be this way for a few months, so it's nothing to worry about." He takes a seat, smiling proudly at his accomplishment.

The drive to the diner is quiet, but my mind's screaming all different thoughts at me. I park as close to Wren's Cafe as possible and help Uncle Sal step down from the vehicle. He's got a small limp, but besides that, he seems okay.

"Do you need to go to therapy?" He's been off his leg for weeks, and I remember when a friend's mom in middle school broke her leg and had to go to therapy to fortify her muscles again.

"Yeah, a couple times a week. It won't be too bad."

We walk toward the door, and my feet halt when it opens. Wilder steps out with Levi. He laughs at something his brother says then looks forward. His eyes connect with mine and widen in surprise before a slow smile spreads across his lips.

"Hey." He turns to see who I'm with, and his smile drops.

Wilder looks from Uncle Sal's healed leg to me.

"Hey, son," Uncle Sal says, seemingly oblivious to Wilder's expression.

"Hey," Wilder shakes his hand, Levi following.

"How are you feeling?" Wilder asks.

"Better than ever. Actually, that's not true. I don't recommend breaking any bones in your sixties." Uncle Sal laughs.

"You look good," Levi comments.

I look between the three of them and notice the moment Levi stills, realizing what this means.

"I'll wait for you in the truck." He claps his brother's shoulder and walks away.

"I'll go grab a table," Uncle Sal comments, limping into the diner.

Wilder and I stand by the outside entrance, looking at each other wordlessly.

"Hi," he says again.

"Hi." My hands sneak into my back pockets, and I shift my weight.

"How are you? How was your day?" He inches closer.

"Good. How about yours?" I hate that the conversation is stilted after everything we've been through and how close we've become.

"Shitty," he shakes his head. "Sorry I haven't called today. We've had issues with coyotes, so I've been dealing with that all day and setting traps. Levi and I decided to grab a bite to eat since we skipped lunch, and I was hoping to call you tonight."

"Coyotes?" My eyebrows furrow.

"Yeah, they got onto our property and attacked our herd." He rubs a hand across his bearded jaw.

"Oh, no." My hand covers my mouth. The way Wilder looks at me makes my heart crack—concern and guilt shine in his eyes. "Is Midnight okay?"

His lips press together. "I wasn't sure how to tell you. He's badly injured. We're caring for him, but…" his voice trails off.

I blink away the tears. Today's been a crap day. I want to wake up to yesterday and change the direction today took.

"I promise I'm gonna take extra good care of him and make sure he makes it." He reaches for my hand and squeezes.

I shake my head, a few stubborn tears trailing down my cheek. "It doesn't matter. Everything's meant to end anyway." It's like the universe is showing me a clear sign.

"What?" His face screws.

"Can we talk later? I don't really want an audience watching me cry." I swipe away my tears and look down at my sneakers.

"Sure," he nods.

"Thanks," I murmur.

Wilder's fingers tilt my chin up, forcing me to look into the cloudy expression in his eyes. "Are you okay?"

I shake my head. "Please, let's talk later."

His hand slides along my jaw, cupping my face, and he steps closer, so we're toe to toe. His warm lips press against my forehead, and it takes everything in me not to wrap my arms around him in a tight embrace and steal his comfort.

"I'll call you tonight, okay?" He gazes down at me.

"Yeah."

This feels an awful lot like goodbye. As I stare into his eyes, confusion and worry swimming in them, my heart crumbles. What I feel for this man is a lot more than a crush or lust. It's reminiscent of love, a kind of love I haven't felt before—pure, honest, and comforting. It's all-consuming and unconditional, which is why it hurts more knowing that it's temporary.

I step around him, walking into the diner. I'm sure people are looking at me, some of them having witnessed my exchange with Wilder through the big windows. When I sit across from Uncle Sal, his face tells me he isn't buying my bullshit story anymore. I'm anything but fine.

Chapter 29

WILDER

I stare at the time on my phone for the hundredth time, and Levi slaps my arm. "Man, give it a rest."

I glare at him and pocket my phone. "I need to talk to Hallie. Something was off with her today."

"It's only been thirty minutes since we left the diner. You can to call her later. Now, let's look at these damn tracks before we lose daylight and have wandering coyotes."

I push away any negative thoughts and get to work with Levi. We've had two coyote attacks in two days, which makes me uncomfortable. It's not the norm for us, and it messes with our livestock.

Some of the cattle are injured but thankfully survived. Coyotes tend to attack calves, and they got one of ours along with some sheep. The stress of it all didn't allow me to write to Hallie during the day, and I don't like what I saw earlier.

Forget about the shock of seeing Sal walking on his own. It's the reminder I've been trying to avoid—she'll be leaving sooner than I'm prepared for. Not that I'll ever be ready for her to leave.

"Look." Levi points a few feet in front of us. I stop Bro and climb off, looking at the fresh tracks.

"Shit," I breathe out.

"Yeah." Levi inspects the surrounding area. The tracks are too close to our herd, and we need to prevent another attack. This is our livelihood.

"Do you think it's a pack?" I voice my concern.

"It might be. Two attacks back-to-back is a lot for just one coyote, in my opinion."

"I agree. Let's set a trap here and go." Dusk is approaching, and these animals tend to come out at night. I don't want to get stuck in a face-off with one of them unarmed.

"Let's hope the traps help," I clap Levi's shoulder and hop on Bro, ready to ride home and hopefully talk to Hallie.

"Fingers crossed," he says, guiding his horse back toward the barn.

Once I've put Bro in his stall and fed him, I go home and shower to kill some time before calling Hallie. I don't want to push, but I hated seeing the tears in her eyes today. I'm not sure what's happened between yesterday and today. I need answers.

As soon as I throw on shorts and a t-shirt, I grab my phone and call Hallie. She answers after a few rings, and I breathe out.

"Hey." I sit on the couch, dropping my head back on the headrest.

"Hi," she whispers.

"How are you?"

"Good, sorry about earlier. I'm just a little emotional."

"Why? What's going on?" I rub my forehead.

Hallie sighs, and I hear rustling on the line. "Uncle Sal is better, as you saw. The doctor gave him the all-clear to go back to work without overdoing it. He'll have to go to therapy at first, but…he doesn't need me anymore." Her voice cracks and I wish we were talking in person.

"Babe… I'm sure he still needs you."

"No, Wilder, that's the thing. My being here is temporary, and the clock rang with the deadline. I did talk to him and asked if it were okay to stay until after the spring festival. I promised Joy I'd try to be here."

I squeeze my eyes. I knew what I was getting into, but hearing it out loud hurts.

"So you have two weeks left?"

"Yeah," she whispers. "If you don't wanna keep seeing each other, I understand. I wouldn't blame you." Her voice is watery, and it punches my heart.

"Listen to me, Hallie. I haven't felt this way about anyone in a long time. If I get two more weeks with you, I'm going to make them the best damn weeks we've ever lived. I promise you that. I'm here 'til the end." I stand, grabbing a beer from the fridge and taking a deep pull.

"Are you sure?" She sounds uncertain.

"Positive. If it were up to me, I'd keep you at my place until you leave, memorizing every inch of your body and the moans you make while I pleasure you."

"Wilder…" she sighs.

"Wouldn't you like that?" I drop on the couch again, my dick getting hard.

"Yeah. A lot."

"I wish you were here now. I couldn't even kiss you earlier. All I've been thinking about is getting you alone again, feasting on you. Shit, I'm hard just thinking about it."

She whimpers, and I ask, "Are you wet?"

"Probably." Her word is clipped, almost embarrassed.

"Nah, I need a certain answer. Touch yourself and tell me. You should feel how hard my dick is thinking about your naked body—all luscious curves and smooth skin." My hand sneaks in my shorts, squeezing the head of my cock to alleviate some of the pain.

"I'm wet," she says after a beat.

"Good, I want you to feel the same as me, to know I affect you just as much."

"*God*," she quietly moans. "You've got a dirty mouth."

"And you love it. I witnessed how your pussy tightened around my fingers when I'd talk to you like this. You were practically begging for more." Her reaction to my touch was heaven.

I run my hand up and down my cock, unable to stop myself. "I wish it was your hand wrapped around me. Better yet, your pretty lips. Fuck, what I'd give to see that right now." I hiss as my dick jerks.

"Wilder," Hallie pleads. "Stop talking like that…"

"Or what?" I push.

"I'm gonna have to take care of this, and I don't live alone like you do." The idea of her masturbating pushes me, and I'm desperate to make it happen.

"Bite a pillow. I wanna know you're getting off listening to me." She moans. "Come on, babe. It'll be practice for when you're away. Don't think I'm gonna let you go that easily, not when I've just found you." I have no idea how we'll make it work, but I'm determined to give this a chance, see if we've got more to go on than just a few weeks.

"Tell me what you feel," I demand.

"Wet, so wet…" Her words come out breathy. "Fuck, my clit…"

"Are you rubbing your clit? Feels good, right?" My hand keeps a steady pace on my dick so I don't blow my load before it's time.

"Mmhmm…" I imagine her lying in bed, legs wide open… *Fuck,* I want to see that for myself.

"My dick is begging for your pussy. Slide home. You feel that way, like home. Fuck yourself with your fingers. I want you to make yourself come." I rub my thumb over the head of my dick, squeezing tightly to fight off my orgasm.

Her breathing is heavy on the line. I can hear her trying to hold back, groaning quietly.

"I wish I were eating your pussy right now. I want to do it all at once—hands, lips, cock. I'll never get enough of you."

"I want that, too. The idea of you…there…" She's struggling to speak through her moans.

"I know, so damn good. I bet you taste delicious. Then, I'd fuck you so hard and so good, you'll never forget about me." Possessiveness takes over. I want to make sure that regardless of what happens, she'll always remember me because I sure as hell won't forget her.

She holds back a cry, probably muffling it with a pillow. My hand speeds up, pumping myself to the image of Hallie's naked body, her warm pussy, her pouty lips sucking me. The visions consume me until I'm grunting. My dick jerks and I cum hard and fast. Too fast, but it's better this way since I'm alone and not with the woman I want in my bed tonight.

"Wilder?" Her soft voice breaks through the cloud in my head.

"Yeah?" I answer gruffly.

"That was hot as hell."

I smirk at her admission, standing to clean myself up.

"Yeah, babe, but it'd be hotter if you were here, and I'd've been watching you finger yourself."

"Goodness gracious, man, stop talking like that. I may have orgasmed, but it wasn't as satisfying as it is with you." I hear water splashing and assume she's also cleaning herself up.

"Ditto, babe, but I'll get you to myself tomorrow. I don't care if I'm exhausted the next day." I pause a moment, heading back into the living room. "Are you feeling better?"

"Kinda. I'm just sad, so ignore me."

"I'm not gonna ignore you. I like you a lot, Bunny Girl. If I didn't, I wouldn't waste my time with you. Trust me. I'm not that nice." She snorts at that.

"Oh, I know you're not that nice," she chuckles.

"I want you to know you can talk to me, turn to me for comfort."

"I don't want to make you uncomfortable." I pause at her comment, repeating it in my head.

"Why the hell would you make me uncomfortable?" A deep sigh comes through the line, but I get silence for a few beats. I patiently wait for her to explain.

"Because it's about us, and I don't really know what exactly this is between us. We both knew I'd be leaving soon, but…" She blows out a breath. "I don't want to lose you. This is definitely more than a fling to me. However, there's no other way."

I scrub a hand down my face, closing my eyes. "This isn't a fling for me. I knew you weren't here permanently, and I tried to fight it, but I couldn't. We'll cross that bridge when we get there and figure out what to do. Right now, I want to enjoy the time you have here. I don't want it clouded with sadness, okay?" I'd rather focus on the time we have together than put our energy into her leaving.

"Okay," she whispers.

"You're coming over tomorrow. I'll cook dinner, and we'll spend time together. Bring a bag and spend the night. You won't have to work the next day." If all I have left are two weeks, then I'm going to be greedy with that time.

"I will." I'm relieved when she doesn't argue.

"What's going on with the coyotes? Can I see Midnight tomorrow?"

"Of course you can. He'll be happy to see you. Coyote attacks aren't uncommon, but it's not normal to have them back-to-back, which concerns us. It might be a pack, and that's harder to control. We set traps, so hopefully, we'll get the problem fixed without losing any more livestock."

"I hope so, too. I hate the thought of animals dying because of this. I mean, I know you raise them for food, so they're going to meet their death anyway, but at least it's for your benefit and career."

I laugh and head for my room, throwing away the beer bottle on the way. "Yeah, I get what you mean," I say around a yawn. The stress from the day is finally hitting me.

"Go to sleep. We'll talk tomorrow," Hallie says.

"I'll *see* you tomorrow," I emphasize on a promise.

"Yeah." She finally sounds a bit like herself, and I can relax.

This woman is a lot more than a fling if that's what she thinks. Hell, I'm pretty sure I crossed the line of like into uncharted territory that I swore I'd never dare explore again. But my heart beats faster when I think about her, and I want to do everything in my power to make her happy.

It'd be like me to fall for the woman who isn't permanent in town, but maybe that's exactly why. Hallie is different, not to mention she's so oblivious to her beauty and charm. She's got a heart of gold, one I want to protect. When I'm with her, I feel like a better man. I feel like myself without the baggage, work responsibilities, and guarded walls. She was made for me, and if that's the case, then everything I lived up until this point would've been worth it.

I only hope we'll have what it takes to make things work. I refuse to lose my Bunny Girl.

Chapter 25

HALLIE

I snuggle closer to Wilder, who tightens his hold around me, and I tuck my legs to my side. We've been watching TV after we had dinner, but I'm staring blankly at the screen while I soak up these moments. Although we spoke last night, and I felt better after, I'm still anxious about leaving. My heart is invested in this relationship. My soul feels intertwined with his. It's more than sex and a good time. I'm afraid that if I leave, I'll lose my person. Because although we've only been dating a few weeks, Wilder very much feels like my person.

I sigh as his fingers stroke my arm, laying my head on his shoulder. His woody cologne invades my senses, and I smile to myself. If I had to choose one word to describe Mason Creek, it'd be Wilder. He's the epitome of this place—rugged, kind, helpful, and charming.

I shift, stretching my legs out when they begin to cramp.

"You're antsy," Wilder comments.

I look over at him to find furrowed brows and a frown.

"I'm just trying to get comfy."

"Babe…" He tilts his head. "I thought we were okay."

I smile over at him, cupping his face. His eyes flutter closed as he leans into my touch.

"We're more than okay, Wilder. You and I aren't the problem."

His eyes snap open to stare at me. "I don't like that there is a problem." His brows pull together.

"We knew an obstacle stood in our way from the beginning."

He opens his mouth and closes it quickly, shaking his head.

"I don't want to talk about this tonight. I want to enjoy the time we have without this interfering in our happiness."

I nod and trail my hand from his cheek down his neck to his chest, feeling the steady beat of his heart against my palm. It soothes me, and I breathe in time with each thump. My head rests on his shoulder again, and I focus on this moment. Wilder's arm moves from my shoulder to my waist, hugging me so close I'm almost forced on top of him.

When his fingers move under my shirt and tickle my skin with featherlight touches, I shiver. Then, the tips of his fingers run along the waist of my jeans, tauntingly.

I glance up at him and find his eyes on me, dark with desire like ocean right before a storm. He's the tempest that has slammed into my life, leaving it turned upside down. Nothing will be the same after him.

His lips crash onto mine, needy and possessive. There's nothing gentle about his onslaught, tongue piercing through my lips in a desperate search for mine, tangling the same way I feel our souls are tangled. He inches his fingers under the backside of my jeans, squeezing my butt and tugging me onto him. I land half on him, one leg draped over his thighs, as we kiss fervently. My hands slide into his hair, pulling the roots as our lips fuse in a messy and raw kiss.

His erection presses into the inside of my inner thigh, and I moan, arching my body against his. Wilder's hand follows the curve of my backside until he runs a finger along my pussy.

"So wet for me," he mumbles into the kiss.

It's a more challenging angle, so his finger teases more than pleases, and I feel on the verge of losing my damn mind. I push back into his hand, hoping that will give him better reach, but he seems to be enjoying the teasing. A quiet chuckle sounds against my lips.

"Patience," he whispers, trailing kisses down my jaw.

"You're mean…" I moan when he nips my throat.

"I promise it's all for your own good." His other hand lifts my shirt, leaving a burning trail as he skims up my ribs.

"Hmmm…" is all I say.

It feels too good to argue. Instead, I reach for his crotch, rubbing my palm against his erection, and kiss his neck before seeking his lips again.

Lost in the kiss, I undo his jeans and reach my hand into his boxer briefs, stroking his dick. It twitches against my touch despite the tight constraints limiting me.

"Hallie," his gruff voice calls out.

Perfect MESS

I don't respond. Instead, I smooth my thumb over the tip of his head, spreading the pre-cum, which rewards me with a hiss. Wilder removes his hands, and I whimper at the loss of his touch, but in a quick movement, he's turned us, so I'm on my back, and he's over me, bunching my shirt under my tits, and his beard is tickling my neck as he kisses me.

Just as he brings down the cups of my bra and swirls his tongue around my puckered nipple, the shrill of his phone makes us both freeze. My heart thunders at the unexpected interruption, and Wilder drops his forehead on my chest.

"Fuck," he mumbles against my body.

"Answer it," I comb my hands through his hair and grab a fistful, lifting his head.

"Nope." He sucks my nipple into his mouth, teeth grazing my sensitive skin and causing my lower body to clench.

When it doesn't let up, I tap him with my thigh. "They won't stop calling until you answer. It could be important."

Wilder sits back and looks at me, running a hand through his disheveled hair. "What the hell could be so important right now?"

"I don't know, but check just in case." I scoot back, covering myself and leaning against the arm of the couch.

"Fine, but don't cover yourself that much." He points at me, heat blazing from his eyes.

"Okay," I wink, sneaking my hands into the back of my shirt and removing my bra, dangling it from my finger. "Better?"

Wilder growls, eyes glued to my chest before mumbling, "This better be important."

I laugh at his retreating form as he heads to grab his phone from the kitchen. He looks at me as he calls back whoever was trying to get a hold of him. I can't help but stare at him, taking in his undone jeans, wrinkled t-shirt, and messy hair. The look in his eyes is full of hunger, one my body is very familiar with.

"Hello?" He's silent a moment, eyebrows pulling together.

"What? Shit." He scrubs a hand down his face, and I sit up, more alert.

"Okay... Yeah... I'll be right there." His lips press into a straight line as he looks at me.

Wilder stalks toward me after hanging up, sitting beside me and cupping my face, dropping a hard kiss.

"That was Levi. He and my dad heard some noises and found a coyote in one of the traps we put yesterday. I'm gonna go help them, and I'll be back."

"Is it safe?" I eye him carefully.

"Yeah," he promises. "It's trapped, and we'll go armed for protection in case there are more nearby."

Hearing that doesn't calm my nerves. I saw Midnight earlier, and his wounds were deep.

"Be careful," I say slowly, staring into his eyes.

"I will." He brushes his lips against mine and squeezes my knee. "I'll be back. Don't move, and do not dare to put your bra back on. We're gonna finish what we started." The lust-filled promise runs through my veins, and I simply nod.

While Wilder is checking on the coyote with his dad and brother, I pace his living room, nervous that they'll get injured. I'm not familiar with wild animals and their behavior, but I'm positive coyotes are dangerous. Different scenarios race through my head while I bite my nails and the skin around them.

Talk about a bucket of ice water to ruin a heated moment. Although, Wilder didn't seem one bit worried about having to face a trapped coyote. This is his life, so much different than mine. The most contact with wild animals I've had until coming here is finding rats in the streets of New York searching for food in trashcans. And I stayed the hell away from those.

I sit back down and scroll through the channels in search of a distraction. When nothing holds my attention, I grab my phone and scroll through social media. I pause when I see a picture of Jeff with a woman. She's thin, with perfect makeup, long brown hair, and designer clothes. They're smiling widely at the camera in what looks like the apartment where we were supposed to live.

I read the caption, and my eyes widen. A mixture of ridiculous laughter and feeling sorry for this girl runs through me.

No one else I'd want to share this home with *kissy face emoji*

It seems he found a replacement when he didn't have a solid argument when he tried to get money from me for the rent. Some people are just meant to be douchecunts. Shaking my head, I hope the girl knows what she's gotten herself into, or maybe she's just like him.

Regardless, I'm relieved he's no longer my problem. I've spent too much time undoing the damage he did. Thanks to Wilder for opening my eyes and heart, for showing me I'm worthy just as I am. And thanks to myself for coming here to help Uncle Sal. This trip was more for me, to learn my strengths, my capabilities, and to know what it feels like to belong in a community. I had no idea what I was missing out on.

I unfollow Jeff, something I should've done a long time ago, and breathe easy. I may not be one-hundred-percent content with what I see in the mirror yet, but the road to self-love is long and winding. Each day gets better. I get better. I'm finding more and more things I love about myself instead of nit-picking and judging.

Sitting back on the couch, I wait for Wilder to return. The past few weeks flash in my mind. A smile covers my face at the memories I've made here. They've been healing. And if I'm being honest with myself, I don't want this to end.

Grabbing my phone again, I do some research. Would it be possible to stay here? I'm halfway through my search when the door opens. The phone fumbles in my hands, and I set it on the coffee table as Wilder returns.

"What happened?" I stand and face him, the couch separating us.

"We got it." He moves around the couch.

"Got it…?" My question lingers.

He presses his lips together, hands moving to my hips. "We had to shoot it."

"Oh. That makes sense, though. If you let it free, you'd risk it returning." I hold on to his arms, his muscles hard beneath my touch.

"Exactly. The other traps were empty, so either this coyote was running around on its own, or the others stayed hidden."

"I hope it was just the one." My hands smooth up and down his biceps.

"Me too." He lowers his head, skimming his nose along my jaw. "You kept the bra off." His breath tickles my neck.

"Yeah," I sigh, tilting my head to the other side to give him better access.

"You want my lips there?" He brushes his lips along my neck.

"Mmhhm…" I close my eyes.

"I wanna taste you everywhere." His husky voice makes me shiver.

"I'd like that," I whisper.

"Yeah?" He leans back to look at me.

Heat creeps up my cheeks, but I nod through the embarrassment of voicing what I want. Wordlessly, Wilder holds my hand and guides me through the kitchen and up the stairs. When we reach his room, he skims his hands up and down my body, following my curves.

"Gorgeous," he says with conviction. "All mine." His fingers inch under my shirt and take it with them until I'm standing before him naked from the waist up.

Wilder drops his head, skimming his lips along my clavicle and down to my breasts, taking a nipple between his teeth and tugging lightly before doing the same to the other. Goosebumps crawl up my skin. I throw my head back on a moan when he sucks my nipple harder and palms my other breast, tweaking it with calloused fingers.

"Shit," I groan, running my palms down his biceps.

When Wilder kisses further down, I squirm. He's been vocal about what he wants, and my body is tense with anticipation. Excitement and the suspense of coming pleasure make my body rock.

He turns us around, his tongue swirling down my stomach, and pushes me down, so I'm sitting on the bed. In the process, he kneels before me, hooded eyes glancing up at me. I rake my hands through his hair, scratching his scalp, and his eyes close on a loud exhale.

It doesn't take long for Wilder to undress me, gliding my jeans and underwear down my legs. I sit before him, completely nude now and highly aroused. His wide palms slide under my ass, lifting me, and I slide back on the bed, holding myself up with my elbows, not wanting to miss one second of the show he's putting on.

"I can see your wetness. Fuck, I can't wait to taste you." He spreads my legs, kissing up the inside of my thigh. "I bet you're sweet. Delectable…" He brushes his lips along my other thigh.

Fire licks my body, lust and need and desire all rolled into one.

"*Pleaaase…*" I beg him to stop teasing me. I grab his hair, pulling him where I want him.

"So needy. So ready for me." Wilder chuckles and drops a kiss right above my pussy.

I groan and fall back, frustrated. He takes advantage of my irritation and swipes his tongue up my pussy before sucking my clit in his mouth. My hips buck, and I yelp in surprise before clamping my thighs around his head.

"I was right. You're fucking delicious. My favorite treat." He doesn't miss a beat, returning to my core, sucking, nipping, licking, and fucking me with his tongue while I rip his hair in my fingers and thrash uncontrollably.

I can't remember the last time a man put me before himself. Wilder is a giver, and what a freaking gift that is.

He pushes a finger into my core while flicking his tongue over my swollen clit. The sensations that arise are colorful and explosive. My body arches and tightens, my hips lifting to meet his hungry mouth as if I were the starved animal. It's too much and not enough. He's never enough.

An amplitude of sensations hit me at once, and I'm free falling into an abyss of pleasure, crying out his name as I crash quickly. My orgasm rushes through me, leaving my body limp and heart racing. Wilder kisses up my body, positioning himself over me. His lips meld with mine, giving me a taste of myself.

I wrap my arms around him as he blindly searches the bedside table. When he's ready, he thrusts into me, and I moan his name.

"God," I cry out, arching my hips to meet his thrust.

"So tight...so perfect for me," he says through a clenched jaw. "Need you always."

We get lost in each other, fucking hard and fast. Desperate and messy. We hold on to each other, knowing that the uncertainty of the future is looming closer than we'd like.

Chapter 26

HALLIE

"Like this?" I hold up the pitchfork in the air and look at Wilder, who's on the other side of the stall.

"That's perfect." A big grin covers his face while he's also spreading hay.

Pride swells inside of me. Not so long ago, I would've been staring at the pitchfork with discomfort and stood on the outside, watching someone else work. Not because I thought I was too good for this kind of work but because I thought I'd screw it up, make a fool of myself, or let my insecurities push me back into my shell. When Wilder asked me if I wanted to help him, I didn't hesitate to agree since the butcher shop is closed today.

With Uncle Sal out of his boot, he's more self-sufficient at home, making it possible to spend the night with Wilder again.

I drop the bunch of hay collected on the pitchfork and begin to spread it evenly on the ground. Midnight's pained bellows ring around the barn, and it breaks my heart. Although his wounds are better, he seems to be stressed. I wonder if animals experience fears the way we do. Maybe Midnight is fearful the coyote will attack again.

Or maybe his leg just hurts, and I'm overthinking again.

When his bellows don't stop, I rest against the pitchfork and look at Wilder. He's in major work mode, raking hay around the stall with his arms flexing and tensing as he does manual labor. It's sexy as hell, and I get distracted from my own purpose of stopping.

"Tired?" he asks, eyes still focused on the ground, but his lips quirk.

"No," I glare at him.

"Oh, I know… You were taking a moment to admire my rugged sexiness while I work." He glances up at me, humor lighting his eyes.

I press my lips together and tilt my head, looking at him with raised eyebrows. Although I have been admiring his rugged sexiness, that's not the reason for my stopping. Wilder chuckles, leaning his pitchfork against the wall, and stalking toward me.

"Is that it?" He waggles his eyebrows, his hands moving to my hips and around to my butts.

"No," I shake my head firmly.

"Darn…" He frowns teasingly and scratches his chin. "Then you were—"

My phone rings in my back pocket, interrupting the moment.

"Go ahead and answer. I'll finish here." He drops a kiss on my lips and steps back, eyes sweeping up and down my body as I fish my phone out of my pocket.

"You look sexy working here with me." The deep voice in his comment makes me shiver as I look at my screen.

I'm expecting to see my mom or maybe Uncle Sal's name. What I find is an unfamiliar number with a New York area code. I almost don't answer in case it's Jeff being a dick, but then I remembered his new girlfriend and grab the call before it goes to voicemail.

"Hello?" I step out of the stall but stay near.

"Hello, may I speak with Hallie Hughes?" A woman asks with a professional tone.

"This is she. How can I help you?" I step a bit further from the stall, curious about who's calling.

"Hi, this is Mrs. Sanders from Big Apple Media. We received your resume and job application for our finance department, and I'd love to have you come in for an interview."

Everything halts. Blood rushes to my ears in time with the wild thumping of my heart. In the distance, I hear Midnight's bellows getting louder as if his pain were mine. I applied for this job months ago. Since I never heard from them, I assumed they'd gone with someone else.

"It's not for the original job you applied for, but it's in the same department, and I think you'd be a great candidate for it."

Mrs. Sanders continues talking, but I'm only half-listening to her. I look up and see Wilder staring at me. His brows are pulled in as he narrows his eyes, trying to decipher what's going on.

If ever there was a sign, I guess this would be it. What are the odds that I'd hear from a company I applied to months ago, just a few weeks before having to return to New York?

But staring at the man before me shatters me. I wish I wouldn't have the option.

I lift my finger at him, letting him know I'll be a minute, and turn toward the outside of the barn.

"I'm actually out of the state at the moment. Would it be okay to check flight schedules and confirm the interview date?"

"Of course. You can call me back as soon as you know, and we'll schedule a day. I have most of this week open for interviews, so it won't be a problem."

This week. I'd have to fly out immediately. Forget the spring festival. Forget helping Uncle Sal while he's in therapy. Forget my heart. I'll leave it here with Wilder. No one else will ever be able to care for it the way he has.

I blink away tears and promise I'll call her as soon as I have a return date.

My eyes sting as I look around the area. Nature runs for miles, from open fields to rolling hills that lead to looming mountains.

I wrap my arms around myself, and my lip quivers. I'm going to miss this place. This phone call makes it real. My life is in New York, not here. No matter how much I've fallen in love with it...and the people—one in particular.

"Hey." I close my eyes to trap the tears, grateful my back is to him. "What's wrong?" His strong hands grip my arms, moving them up and down in comfort.

I shake my head, not ready to face him.

"Hallie…" His lips are by my ear, breath tickling my neck. "Who was that?" There's an edge to his voice.

I gasp for air, my chest rising with my inhale before I turn to face him. I stare at his chest, unable to look him in the eye as I deliver the final blow.

"That was from a job I applied to a while ago. They want to interview me for a position in their finance department."

His face morphs from surprise to understanding. "Oh, wow…that's fantastic. Congrats, babe." His voice doesn't hold the normal pitch of someone who's excited. "I'm really proud of you." The ends of his lips lift, but his eyes cast down.

This is so damn hard.

I reach for his hands, lacing our fingers and squeezing. No words come out, so I look into his eyes, getting lost in the sky blue orbs. I hope he can read my mind and heart, know what he means to me.

"I said I'd have to let them know when I can see them since I'm out of the state."

His eyes widen. "You're going, though."

"I feel like I have to, but…" I shrug. I roll my eyes toward the sky, willing the tears to stay at bay. "I don't want to leave you," my voice cracks regardless.

"You owe it to yourself to see this through. You've worked so hard for it, and the opportunity is there. I won't stand in the way."

"But…"

He shakes his head, dropping my hands and crossing his arms. The loss is immediate. I miss his warm, calloused touch. The safety I feel when he's holding me in any way.

"I won't stand in the way," he repeats. "After everything you've been through, all the shit that douche put you through, you need this. You *deserve* this." He's closed off, stubborn mind set, and his jaw ticks.

"What if I don't want that anymore?" I challenge his decision regardless. Stubborn for stubborn, we're pretty even.

"Nope, not letting you do that. If you miss this opportunity, you'll grow to resent me. I don't want that. I'd rather have short-term memories that I'll always cherish than longer-term ones full of resentment. Because that's what will happen down the road, you'll blame me for holding you back. You'll wonder how life would've turned out if you tried to succeed instead of putting your dreams on hold."

He drops his arms, shaking his head as he stares straight ahead toward the mountains. His shoulders are tense, and I want to walk up to him, wrap my arms around him, and make him feel better. But he's put this distance between us. Though it's invisible, I feel it in my bones.

I step back, fidgeting with my fingers. I guess he always was aware that we're stamped with an expiration date, accepted it. I'm the one that ignored it. I gave him my heart, knowing I'd never get it back.

"I'm gonna go." I look away to hide the tears in my eyes.

"I'll take you." The fact that he doesn't fight me or ask me to stay splinters more pieces of my heart.

"No," I shake my head firmly.

"Hallie, how are you gonna get home?" He sighs.

"I'll walk. I could use the time to clear my head." I turn from the barn, wiping my cheek from the roll of tears.

A strong arm grips my arm and turns me around. "I'll take you." His jaw is set.

"I said I could go on my own," I rip my arm away. He doesn't need to be a gentleman right now. Not when he's pushing me away.

I trek toward the entrance of the barn and follow the road. Tears stream freely, blurring my vision. I'm such a fool. Such a fool for thinking this would turn out differently. I was always meant to leave.

Crunching tires on gravel make my feet falter. I make sure I'm on the outside of the road so the car can pass. Instead, it stays behind me. Great, I *am* going to die in this place. Thoughts of murderers cross my mind.

Don't turn around. Don't turn around.

I breathe heavily from the nerves and walking under the sunshine. All I have with me is my phone. In my attempt to leave Wilder's place in a hurry, I didn't think to go back to his cabin and grab my purse. I clutch my phone in case I need to call someone and focus on the ground below me.

When the truck speeds up, I sigh. Until it slows down right beside me, forcing me to make contact with the person. My eyebrows jump when I see Wilder.

"What the hell are you doing?"

"If you're gonna be stubborn and not accept a ride, then I'll follow you in case you wanna jump in." He's leaning toward the lowered window on the passenger side with his eyes turned to the road in front of him.

What a ridiculously romantic gesture from the man who just rejected me.

I look at him for a beat longer, but when the tears reappear, I face forward and continue walking.

"Hallie." After a couple of minutes, he calls my name.

I look at him, unable to deny him my attention. "We're six miles from town. Get in." He stops his truck, but I continue walking.

The old metal slams loudly, and Wilder is in my face, holding it, stilling me. I fight against him, gripping his forearms, but he doesn't relent.

"Listen to me, damn it. I'm not doing this to hurt you. We knew we'd eventually meet at this point in the road. Two weeks from now or two days, it was inevitable. We come from two different worlds."

My lips quiver and my nose is tingling with impending tears.

"You have to do this for yourself." His hands curl around my jaw. "You need to prove how amazing you are, show these people what they've been missing out on. I've already had the opportunity to witness it." His eyes cast down.

"If you think I'll forget you, you're wrong. If you think it's easy to let you go, then you have no idea what I feel for you. But I have to. It's your time to shine." He crushes his body to mine, hugging me tightly. I claw at his back, inhaling the mixture of sunshine and pine on him, inhaling home.

My tears soak his shirt as I quietly sob. Wilder whispers encouraging words and smooths a hand up and down my back.

"You're gonna kick ass, and I'm gonna be so damn proud of you. I already am. And I'll always be here." He kisses the crown of my head.

But he won't always be here. Eventually, he'll move on, find someone to share his heart and home with. Now that he's opened himself up, it'll be a matter of time before someone sneaks her way into his life, showing him he's capable of being happy again. And I'll be left with memories of a short-lived romance that taught me more about myself and love than I ever imagined possible.

When I look up at him, his eyes shimmer. "Sorry for wetting your shirt."

"I don't care about that." He strokes my cheek, leaning down to kiss me. "Let me take you home, please."

I nod against him, dropping my resolve. Chances are I'll be gone in a day or two. I can accept this favor from him one last time. The car ride is deathly silent. The roar of the engine vibrating through the air is the only sound. As we pass through town, I look at the place I've come to call home for the last couple of months.

Heaviness makes me feel sluggish. Sadness numbs me, but it's better than feeling the excruciating pain of leaving Wilder behind.

When he pulls into Sal's house, I feel like I'm half asleep. Robotically, I open the door and step down. I look at Wilder, who's still inside the cab gripping the steering wheel. Our eyes collide, and a swell of emotions pushes through us. He scrubs a hand down his face, slowly opening the door and stepping out.

Face-to-face, he holds me gently and kisses me lazily, as if memorizing the taste of me. His tongue slides along my own, and I press my body to his. Wilder slows the kiss, transitioning it to a few pecks before lifting his head.

"I want you to know that I'll never forget you."

This is the hardest goodbye. I have no control over the tears trailing down my cheek. They're too many for Wilder to dry.

"I..." I shake my head.

"Shhh... Go on, Bunny Girl. Call me after your interview and tell me how it went."

I nod, unsure I'll be able to keep that promise but not wanting to disappoint him. This is goodbye. Regardless of not having a flight yet, it's clear this is our dead end.

Instead of expressing everything I feel, I give a fake smile and turn away from the only man who's ever made me felt truly loved. The last piece of my heart shatters, leaving a void in my chest that I don't think will ever be replaced.

Chapter 27

WILDER

I chug my third coffee in the span of two hours and scrub a hand down my face. I've been sleeping like shit for two days since Hallie got that damn phone call. We were supposed to have more time. I was going to be able to smooth into a goodbye, not get blindsided by one. It was a slap to the face, a wake-up call that regardless of how much I lied to myself, she and I were always meant to be temporary.

"Man, I've been looking for you." Levi stomps into my parents' kitchen, where I'm refilling my fourth cup of coffee. His eyes narrow.

"I took a short coffee break." I shrug, lifting the mug to my lips.

"Bullshit. This is what? The sixth coffee break this morning?" He crosses his arms and raises an eyebrow.

"Third." Technically it's the truth, but in this third break, I'm having two cups of coffee.

"Wilder, we need your help. The traps are untouched, and another sheep is missing. I swear those damn coyotes are smarter than us." He runs his palm down the center of his face, expelling a frustrated breath.

"I'll go now," I clip.

He eyes me suspiciously, his hand still covering his mouth.

"I know you're going through a rough time, but we have a job to do, and you're our leader."

I blow out a breath and nod. "I know, I know. Sorry." I drain what's left of the coffee down the sink and rinse the mug, placing it in the dishwasher before heading back outside.

I wish I had the liberty of taking a personal day. People joke about mental health days, but I don't have that freedom. I can't stay home because my mind's a mess and my heart's broken. This job comes with great responsibility, and I have to be an example to our ranch hands.

Levi and I meet the ranch hands by the barn, all of them talking about the coyotes.

"About time you showed up," Caleb jokes, and I look at him unamused. He chuckles, ignoring my reaction, and clapping my shoulder. He's lucky he's the best worker on this ranch and a friend. I'm not in the mood for smart-asses.

After a quick update about the traps and the missing sheep, Levi and I get on our horses to check the perimeter while the ranch hands all get to their daily work. We can't all waste a day trying to figure out what's going on. There are numerous chores to complete on the daily.

As I ride throughout the land, I reminisce about Hallie's wonder when we rode the tractor. She was amazed by the area, asking questions and taking it all in.

I wish I had more time to show her more of this place. It seemed like enough time. It was definitely enough time to fall in love with her, but it wasn't enough in the grand scheme of things. I want more, selfishly wanting to covet her time and heart—all of her.

I sigh, following Levi in the direction of the trap. For years I've held my emotions back. I've hidden from any possibility of caring about someone. Despite the pain I feel from Hallie leaving, I don't regret it. Knowing her, even for a period of time, is worth it. I'm a better man because of it.

"Look here." Levi points to the ground and dismounts.

I follow him, observing the footprints he's signaling.

"You see the prints here? Well, as soon as it got to the trap, it sidestepped it. I don't fucking get it." He runs a hand through his hair. "I swear I thought the traps would do the trick, especially when we caught that coyote."

"Me too." I wander around the area, looking for any clues. I glance up at the pen where the sheep are. "What if we put electrical fencing around the pen?"

"That costs a lot of money, and it won't get rid of the coyotes, just prevent them from entering this pen. Our cattle roam, and we can't risk losing calves."

He's got a point. Electrical fencing will help, but it won't solve the problem. We need to catch the coyote and kill them. Clearly, the one we caught wasn't a solo traveler.

"Let's set up more traps. We'll put a few in this area, so if it tries to avoid it, another one will catch it. Hopefully." I scan the area, finding a spot to add some more.

"Yeah, we'll have to try that. If not, we're gonna have to hide out here and wait for it to show up and shoot the bastard stealing our livestock." Levi shakes his head. "It'd give us some hunting practice," he jokes, but his forehead wrinkles with frustration.

"We'll get it done." I clap his shoulders.

Levi and I return to the barn to grab some more traps and spend the morning marking new ones down and making sure they're set. Using sheep wool, we hope to lure them to the trap with the scent instead of them getting distracted by the live sheep nearby.

By the time we're done, I'm ready for a nap.

"I'm starving," my brother says as he dismounts by the barn and removes the saddle from his horse.

"I'm tired." As if to emphasize my point, a wide yawn takes over.

"You haven't heard from Hallie?"

"Nope." I look away from him, removing the saddle and brushing Bro. I don't want to think about Hallie's silence and what it means.

I made sure she knew I wanted to keep in contact after she left on many occasions. Maybe she didn't believe it. Maybe I need to prove it to her. I've been tempted to call her since I dropped her off at Sal's house, but I didn't want to cause her more confusion and pain.

"Why'd you let her go? If you love a woman, you fight for her." Levi stares at me as if I were insane. It sounds simple from the outside, but relationships aren't black and white. Ours was definitely far from that.

"You don't know her like I do. You don't know what she's been through. She needs this." I refuse to be the reason she misses a great opportunity.

Losing her hurts, but her staying and resenting me through the years would be unbearable. To know I would be the cause of her giving up her dreams, finally proving she's got what it takes to be admired for a job in her career choice. I wouldn't be able to stand it. I wouldn't be able to stand her waking up one morning, blaming me for being miserable, and watching her go.

Levi grumbles something about me being an idiot. It's best that I ignore him. It wouldn't do any good to take my anger out on him.

Instead of having lunch with my family like usual on work days, I head home and prepare a sandwich. My phone taunts me from the kitchen counter, and I swipe it forcefully, unlocking it.

I stare at Hallie's name for a few beats, finger dangling over the call option. Blowing out a breath, I drop the phone again. It'd do us no good. Holding on to what we have would be more damaging since we can't be together.

Long-distance relationships are hard, even when you know that eventually, the distance will end. I should know, considering Lisa and I did it. That turned out to be a mess. Instead of returning to me, she chose a different path without me.

Hallie has no plans to return to Mason Creek. It would hurt us to stay together since we don't have a future. My life is here, and hers is in New York. *I knew this, and yet, I went for her.*

I smile to myself. I had no choice when it came to Hallie. She lured me in. Her charm wrapped me up, and I wanted to hold on.

Looking at my phone longingly, I shove the rest of my sandwich in my mouth and head to the barn. Midnight's looking out of his stall, and I walk straight to him, reaching out to pet him.

"Hey, buddy." I've never grown attached to my cattle. They serve a purpose in our business, and that's that. But since Hallie met Midnight, I haven't been able to see him as just a steer. He seems to have become an unknowing confidant.

"Do you miss her? I miss her, too. I promised her I'd take care of you, though. I may not be a ray of sunshine like she is, but I'll grow on you." I run a hand down his face, and he quietly moos.

Blinking away tears, I stare into his dark eyes. "I miss her so damn much. She hasn't been gone long, but I feel like I'm missing her in reverse. It's as if she's been gone for years and I'm still here wanting her. Huh…this is therapeutic. No wonder Hallie would talk to you." I pet the side of his neck.

Midnight stays still, allowing me to vomit all these emotions on him without flinching. "Eventually, I'll go back to the way life was before her. I was surviving then—working, going for drinks with friends, working. My life revolved around this ranch. It was my escape so I wouldn't have to look at every other aspect of my life I wasn't living."

A throat clears from behind me, and I lift my eyebrows when I see Sal standing at the barn's entrance.

"Sorry to interrupt." He limps toward me. His leg is healed, but clearly, he's still got weeks, if not months, to go to fully recuperate.

"No interruption." I hope to hell he didn't hear my talking to this steer. "How can I help you?" I slip my hands into my pockets, unsure as to why he'd be here. We don't have an appointment to talk about livestock.

"I wanted to drop this off for you." He holds out an envelope. "It's from Hallie. She asked me to give it to you."

I blow out heavily, taking the envelope from him.

"Thanks." I lift it. "I take it she left already."

"I dropped her off at the airport this morning," he nods, rocking back on his heels. Awkwardness settles between us.

I squeeze the envelope, likely wrinkling the letter inside. A few seconds tick by, and Sal claps his hands.

"Well, I'll leave you to it." I sense he wants to say more, but he's holding himself back.

"Thanks." I don't ask for an update when he hears from her. I don't ask for anything.

He turns to walk away and pauses. Looking me straight in the eye, he says, "I know this is a difficult situation, but for what it's worth, she cared a lot about you. I wish things could've worked out differently." He frowns, shaking his head. Seems like I'm not the only one who's going to miss her.

"Me too," I nod. "Thanks for bringing this by."

"No problem. I'm back at work, so I'll be in touch to stock up on inventory." He lifts his chin toward Midnight.

"That one's not for sale."

Sal smiles knowingly and leaves. I watch him go to the sound of Midnight's heavy breathing and then stare at the envelope in my hand.

Wilder is written across the center in pretty script. I've never seen her handwriting before, but it suits her. Instead of reading it here, I saddle up Bro and take a ride down to the river. I don't want interruptions while I read her parting words.

The sun shines down on my back as the wind rushes past me. Bro picks up speed, racing freely through the fields. Riding has always made me feel better, helped me gain clarity. When we enter the forested area, I slow him down. My eyes attempt to take this place in for the first time like Hallie did, but it's difficult when you were raised here. No matter what, I can't imagine living anywhere else. I wonder if I'd have sacrificed this for her had she asked.

That's the thing though, we both knew what was important to each other, and that is a fault as much as it is a gift. It's not every day you meet someone who cares for you unconditionally and wholly and selflessly. The same way I wouldn't stand in Hallie's way, I know she wouldn't take this away from me.

Finding a spot to sit, I climb off Bro and lead him to the river so he can drink water while I sit and read. My heart thunders at the words I'll find. Is this our final goodbye? What she couldn't say in person?

It takes me a few minutes to gather the courage to rip open the envelope. When I pull out the paper, I close my eyes. It's full of words. Words we should've been able to say to each other in person. Words we should've been able to kiss away.

I skim the letter without reading, taking in her penmanship. The more she wrote, the messier her handwriting got.

There's a smudge in the center from tears, and I run my fingers over it.

Leaning back against a tree trunk, I begin reading.

Dear Wilder,

I'm not sure where to begin with this. I've never been good with words. Well, that's not true. I've never been good with confrontation, always better at writing what I feel. It's easier not to have to look someone in the eye and allow them to see your vulnerabilities.

But you've already seen all of mine. It should be easier than this. But it's not.

Thank you for all you did for me in the short time we knew each other. Our meeting may have been unconventional, but I'm glad we met on the side of the road like that. Or should I say, re-met? You may not remember me from when I'd visit Uncle Sal as a girl, but I always had a crush on you. It's silly now that I think about it. lol Ugh, I don't know why I wrote that, but I told myself I wouldn't rewrite this letter. I'd let out what comes to me for you to read. I hope I don't regret that. (I almost wrote lol again).

You gave me something no one ever has. No amount of gratitude will be enough. You taught me to believe in myself, to accept myself as I am. You cared for me, showed me gentle intimacy.

I'd say you never judged me, but well, we both know what you thought when you saw me on the side of the road and then again at the butcher shop the first time. Not to mention my city boots.

You never judged me where it counts, though. And I'll never forget that. I'll never forget you. You're in my heart, permanent and prominent. I didn't think a guy like you existed. He didn't exist in my world, but then I entered yours and was shown an array of differences, a life worth exploring.

I'm probably rambling now. I definitely won't re-read this in case I change my mind about giving it to you.

I hope you know how important these couple of months were to me. Even before we started dating, when you'd help me at the shop, make sure Paul took care of slaughtering the animals. You slowly eased into my life in a way that I'll never get rid of. Not that I'd want to.

Because of you, I felt brave enough to be myself. Your courage became mine. Your love became mine. I felt it in my bones, deep in my soul. We may have never told each other, but know that I loved you, do love you. Maybe this isn't a very courageous way of saying it, so scratch the bravery comment above.

Just know that my leaving has nothing to do with you. You're right that I owe this to myself in more ways than getting a job. I have to witness face-first what you already know about me. But I can't believe in myself through you. I can learn to believe in myself because of you, but I need to experience it, and this job interview is one way.

This letter is much longer than I imagined. I have so much I want to say and not enough words to say it. Thank you for sharing your heart with me. Thank you for caring. Thank you for showing me not all guys are douche-cunts. But most importantly, thank you for letting me love you.

Love,
Hallie (Bunny Girl)

I rub my eyes, moisture building in them, and crumple the letter in my fist as I lean my head back on the trunk. Her voice was in my head the entire time. Sweet, soft, nervous. I don't know that I'll ever get over her.

Unable to stop myself, I send her a good luck text message and close my eyes again. Flashes of our time together move through my eyes like an old movie reel. I just hope they won't fade with time.

Bro's deafening neigh snaps my eyes open. When I look at him, I'm frozen with fear. He's been taken down by a coyote who's got his teeth on his neck. Bro looks at me with pain and sorrow.

"Hey!" I look around for something, wishing I had my gun with me. The coyote turns to me, eyeing me like a competitive predator, and snarls.

Fuck. *Fuck, fuck, fuck.*

Grabbing a rock, I throw it at the coyote in the hope that it'll save my horse, but by the amount of blood on the ground, I don't think that's possible. The wild animal turns on me, and in a flash, I'm on the ground, crying out in excruciating pain.

Chapter 28

HALLIE

As soon as I saw the skyscrapers from the airplane window, my chest felt tight. I'd spent the entire trip convincing myself that returning to New York was the right decision. When I step out of the airport, hit by the smells and sounds of a busy city, my doubt increases, but then I see my parents' smiling faces by the car, and I can't help but grin in return.

They're both waving wildly, embarrassing me, but I've missed them, so it doesn't bother me. I hurry toward them, dragging my suitcase behind me. I wrap my arms around my mom, sucking in her comfort. When my dad hugs me, I swallow back tears.

"We're so happy you're home," my mom says from the passenger side once we're driving out of the airport.

My cheek is pressed against the window, watching the scenery. Anyone from out of town would be in awe of the brownstone townhomes, the row houses in Brooklyn, and the magnificent bridges that connect all of us here. For me, it's all mundane and redundant, even the magnificent skyscrapers that seem to create a maze for the clouds.

I close my eyes, mostly to trap the tears threatening to make an appearance and focus on my breathing.

"I think she's asleep," I hear my dad whisper to my mom.

Pretending to be asleep leads to exhaustion actually winning over, and next thing I know, I'm being woken up by my mom. Shaking out the grogginess, I blink my eyes and look out the door.

"Hey," she smiles sweetly. "We're home."

Home. I don't know where that is anymore. I bite my lower lip to stop it from quivering and blink my eyes rapidly.

Nodding, I step out of the car and stretch, noting we're halfway down the street from our townhome. *Ah, life in New York.* I guess it beats parking two streets down. My parents own a car though we hardly use it except moments like this. I'm grateful I didn't have to take the subway home. I need space, not be crammed in a tiny metal car and pushed by people in a rush.

It's so different from Mason Creek. I wonder how my mom got accustomed to life in a big city. I've only been gone a couple of months, and I already feel more out of place than I did before. Maybe that's just it; I never felt like I belonged here despite it being my birthplace.

I try to grab my suitcase from my dad, but he tugs on the handle and refuses to let me take it. I smile and shake my head at his stubbornness as we enter our house. No doubt I got that trait from him.

"I'm going to take a shower and unpack." I grab my bag and head for the stairs.

"Take your time. We'll make lunch," my mom calls out. I hear faint whispering as I climb to the second floor but can't make out what they're saying.

Shaking it off, I enter my room. The tears are no longer controllable as I sit on the edge of the bed and bury my face in my hands.

I hate this. I hate being here. I hate that I had to leave Wilder.

I've tried to rationalize my leaving since he told me to go, but it's been unsuccessful. Everything reminds me of Wilder, even what shouldn't because it's the opposite of him. Like the guy a few rows ahead of me on the airplane in a fancy suit that refused to stand so the person next to him could take his seat. Instead, he just turned his legs as if he couldn't be bothered. I kept thinking how Wilder would never be that stuck-up.

I miss him, and it's only been two days since I've seen him. It was unbearable to say another goodbye, so after he dropped me off at Uncle Sal's house, I didn't call him again. It's over. What's the point in digging our wounds?

My phone beeps and I grab it thinking it's Joy making sure I arrived okay. I see two messages. One is from her, so I reply quickly, letting her know I'm home. The other makes my fingers pause before opening it.

Wilder.

All it says is "Good luck." I wonder if Uncle Sal already gave him the letter I left. I reply with a simple "Thank you" and take a shower.

It takes me a while to go back downstairs. I had to make sure my face wasn't blotchy from all the crying I did in the shower, so unpacking will have to wait. I don't want to worry my parents, although I'm not sure it's possible to hide my overall mood. A gray cloud hangs over me for all to see. Once again, I'm Eeyore.

My dad hands me a beer. "Let's sit." We take a seat on the couch while my mom finishes preparing sandwiches for lunch.

"Tell me about this company you're interviewing with tomorrow."

"Um…" I scan my brain for some information. "They're a media company, do work for communications. A position opened in their finance department."

"That's great. And they're in the city?" He takes a drink of his beer, his green eyes crinkling around the edges.

"Yeah. I need to look up the address, but they're here."

"It's going to be great, you'll see." He smiles encouragingly, deepening the lines around his mouth and eyes.

I simply nod, unsure about the entire thing. I've changed in the last two months. I don't know if my dreams are the same. I don't even know if finance ever truly was my dream or something that made sense—a need to fit in somewhere. I never considered this until I spent time in Mason Creek and became part of a real community.

"And don't worry about Jeff. We got all that cleared up."

I nod, taking a sip of my beer.

"I'm not worried. It seems he found a replacement." I grimace.

My dad's eyes narrow, his nostrils flaring.

"What?" His voice booms.

I lean back, staring at him with wide eyes.

"Calm down." I hold my palm up. "It's okay. I'm okay. I'm glad he got someone else to busy himself with so he'll stop bothering me."

"That guy..." his lips thin. "I wish I would've told you to dump him. I knew he was bad news."

If he only knew... But then, maybe my connection with Wilder wouldn't have been as strong. *No*. I think regardless of how we got there, Wilder and I would've experienced what we did. However, my past with Jeff, my experiences in that toxic relationship definitely carved a path in the way Wilder treated me.

Would he have cared so much if he didn't feel the need to prove to me that I am worthy?

I drain those insecurities away with the rest of my beer and place the empty bottle on the coffee table. I refuse to cry in front of my parents.

"Here we go." My mom's interruption couldn't come at a better time.

"Thanks."

We have an informal lunch sitting in the living room. I tell them all I did while I was in Mason Creek, even though we spoke often.

"Uncle Sal is all better now. You know, I think he and Patty are serious," I gossip.

My mom laughs. "I think in a way they always were."

"Really?" That surprises me. It seems as if their relationship is newer, from their adult life, not before.

"Yeah," she nods. "Their relationship seems to work for them."

"It does," I agree with a smile.

After seeing them interact, it makes sense, although I wonder why they don't live together. Not that it's any of my business.

As I'm unpacking, a knocks echoes in the silence of my room.

"Come in." I finish folding a shirt and stack it with the rest on my bed.

"Hi, sweetie. Do you need help?" My mom looks around at the current mess in my room.

"I'm okay. With the jet lag, I'm wide awake, so I might as well take advantage."

My mom sits on the bed and folds a pair of jeans anyway.

"How are you really?" She examines in the way only a mother can.

"I'm good," I lie, my voice rising a bit.

She arches an eyebrow, not buying it.

"Sit." She pats the spot next to her.

I oblige, shifting to look at her. "I spoke to Sal." She holds my hand.

"And?" I raise my eyebrows, my heart thundering.

Her thumb brushes over my hand as she smiles softly. "He told me about Wilder."

My heart stops, a knot forming in my throat. I should've known he'd tell her.

When I don't say anything, she continues to speak. "It seems you really like him. From what Sal told me, the feeling was mutual." I guess Mason Creek gossip made it to New York City.

I nod, fighting the tears. "But we always knew I'd return here." I wave my free hand around my room.

"I guess the interview was bad timing…" she attempts to joke.

"You have no idea." I shake my head. "But maybe it was necessary?" The question in my voice makes me sound unsure.

"Yeah," my mom squeezes my hand. "Do you want to tell me about Wilder?"

I've always had a great relationship with my parents, and I've confided in my mom on many occasions, but I'm not ready for this.

"Maybe another day? When I'm not still so raw from it?"

"Of course." She moves to stand, but I stop her.

"Can I ask you something?"

"Always," she smiles brightly.

"How did you move on from Mason Creek? I mean, I know you went away for college because you wanted to see more of the world, but why didn't you return afterward?" I tilt my head.

I wondered this when I was younger, but it isn't until now after I've experienced Mason Creek in all its glory, that I question how my mom never made a life there.

"I did it for love. I knew that as long as I had your father, I'd be happy. He was my home, not the place where I grew up." Her response is so confident, with no hesitation.

"Don't you miss it? It's such a wonderful town. The people are great."

She smiles sadly, tilting her head. "I do, but I'm happy here. I love the life we've built. I'll always carry my hometown with me, but you and your father are my home now."

"Many people asked about you. They wondered if you'd visit." I toy with the hem of my t-shirt.

"Are Hattie and Hazel still around? They used to make the best ice cream." Her face splits into a smile.

"They are. They're so funny, such opposites of each other and huge gossips." I widen my eyes.

"Yes," my mom laughs. "They *were* always bickering. Competing with each other about who's ice cream flavor was best."

"Still are. That hasn't changed." I smile as I think about them. I never got to try their ice cream before I left. I was hoping to do that at the spring festival.

We're quiet for a moment. My mom studies me carefully.

"You had a good time, right?"

"I did. I loved reconnecting with Joy and Aunt Ruth. They miss you, too. Becky says hi." I update her on our family.

"I spoke with her," my mom nods.

"Good." Another stretch of silence fills my room as we sit there.

"At what time is your interview?" My mom finally breaks it.

"At eleven. I'll leave here at nine-thirty to make sure I get there on time. I looked up the address, and it isn't super far, but you know I like to be punctual."

"I do." My mom pulls me in for a hug, and I hear a soft sniffle. My arms wrap around her, and I bury my face in her neck to soak up more of her peace and comfort.

"You'll do great," she nods. "I'm positive things will work out as they should." This time when she stands, I don't stop her.

We say goodnight, and I'm left in my room, staring at piles of clothes. I put away what's already folded and leave the rest for tomorrow. Then, I grab the mirror Wilder gave me what feels like years ago and stare at my reflection, the words he wrote covering parts of my face.

With deep, even breaths, I repeat the mantras I've been practicing while looking at myself in the mirror in preparation for the interview tomorrow. More than knowledge, I need to be emotionally prepared for this big change. The whole point is to prove to myself that I'm more than a twenty-six-year-old living in her parents' house.

If I had to give up the man I love, it better be worth it. This job has big shoes to fill, and I'm going to be as critical of them as they will be of me because the question no longer is if I'm good enough for them but if they're good enough for me.

Chapter 29

HALLIE

I hike my bag higher on my shoulder and walk through the city. The smell of this place infiltrates my senses, making me miss Mason Creek even more. Not even Central Park provides the peace the small town I left behind does. I've been wandering through it for over an hour now, and it's nothing like Montana. Thankfully, I was wise enough to throw a pair of sneakers in my bag so my feet wouldn't kill me from wandering in heels.

I never heard back from Wilder after I wrote to him. Not that I left an opening for him to do so. In the span of a few days, we became nonexistent.

I was with him for a fraction of the time I was with Jeff, and this break-up hurts more. Neither one of us wanted it, and Wilder is incomparable to my douche of an ex. They're night and day, happy dreams versus nightmares.

I run a hand through my hair and re-read my mom's text message asking how the interview went. She wrote to me an hour ago, but I haven't had the heart to tell her.

I bombed the interview—big time. Like, a huge explosion that I wouldn't be able to clean up in a million years. It was for the best, though. Leave it to me to have an epiphany in the middle of a serious moment. If I find myself wishing they won't hire me, then that's a clear sign of my inner feelings.

When the interviewer asked me why I'd like to work for their company, it gave me pause. I scrambled my brain for a reason and kept coming up with the same response. It spit from my mouth before I could at least filter it.

I didn't want to. I had no attachment to this interview or company from the beginning. Hell, I could barely remember who they were until I looked them up before going to bed last night. I was so desperate for a job, I sent hundreds of resumes in the span of months, so I couldn't keep track of them all.

Her face was shocked when I told her that I didn't want to work for them. I apologized profusely, trying to explain the situation, but she didn't care about my personal life. Not that she owed it to me.

As soon as I walked out of that building, the sun shining down on me, I took a left and wandered. Numbness took over as I walked the crowded streets, bumping into people with a whispered apology. Everything I thought I wanted was no longer my dream.

Now, I'm swallowed by trees and greenery in search of something, *anything*, but it doesn't fool me. As soon as I exit Central Park, I'll be transported back into the chaos of a cosmopolitan city, even more lost than a first-time tourist trying to understand our subway system. You'd think in a place like this, with the different backgrounds, growing population, and varying tastes, I'd find myself. Find a place where I fit in.

I wonder what Wilder would say about the interview. Would he think I left for nothing? That it was all in vain?

I'm not even back in square one. I'm standing on square negative a million. All because I'm not being honest with myself. All because I'm avoiding the truth I already know.

Mentally exhausted, I leave Central Park and trek home. I'm looking down, lost in thought, when I bump into someone. I give another mumbled apology, but the steely voice that responds makes my spine straighten. I know he works in this district, but what are the odds I'd actually run into him?

I look into angry brown eyes that stare at me with distaste and curled lip. "Watch where you're going."

I narrow my eyes at a man I once thought I loved. How very wrong I was. Jeff was someone I used to feel better about myself, but look at how that turned out.

I take in his tailored suit covering his skinny body, perfectly combed hair, and clean-shaven face. His entire look is too smooth and primped for my liking, even more so now.

"Maybe you should be careful about where you're walking." It's a childish retaliation, but months of anger swirl inside of me until they've formed a disastrous tornado.

He eyes me up and down, pausing at my white Converse before taking in my pencil skirt and tucked white shirt. Instead of cowering, I stand with my hands on my hips.

"I see you're still as classy as ever," he arches a brow. "Still haven't hit the gym, huh?"

My heart thunders, but unfortunately, I'm not surprised by his words.

"I see you still have your douche card."

I turn to walk, but he grips my arm. I yank it away and clench my teeth.

"Let. Me. Go," I seethe.

"You think you're better than me now because you got your daddy to pay a lawyer to throw the case. You're just a brat. Always were and always will be."

I tilt my head and smile. His nostrils flare in annoyance, so my grin grows.

Shaking my head as if he were a child, I say, "You can't ruin my life anymore. You no longer have that power. You lost it a long time ago." I've never felt the true meaning of words as much as I do these. They rattle my core with truth.

I turn to walk away while he's still steeping but pause and turn to him one last time. "By the way, I met a real man, and he fucked me good and proper. Something you never could do."

With that, I walk away from him, leaving behind not only the man but the ghost of him that tormented me for far too long. Freedom travels through me. It felt good to tell that jackass what I really felt. Seeing his face morph from anger to shock was priceless. Maybe I shouldn't have put my intimacy with Wilder out there like that, but it came out, and I couldn't stop it.

I walk home feeling a bit lighter. At least that's one problem out of the way. It's healing to face the assholes in your life and tell them what you think. No longer the compliant, quiet, insecure girl.

By the time I arrive, I'm starving, and my feet hurt. I let my mom know I'm home, so she doesn't worry about my unanswered text message and drop my bag on the couch before dragging my bare feet to the kitchen to make a sandwich.

I keep replaying the interview in my mind, and the common thread to everything unraveling is Mason Creek. I want to be there. More than that, I feel a tie to the place and the people. Yes, Wilder's a big part of the reason, but it's about more than a guy.

All the times I thought about staying, I always found an excuse not to. I thought I needed to come back to New York and make a life here. As if I had something to prove. A day in, and I'm sure that the only person I have to prove anything to is myself, that I can succeed anywhere if it's where my heart wants to be. What my mom said last night resonates with me. Home isn't a place; it's being with the people we love.

"Hi, sweetie," my mom's voice rings through the downstairs and out the opened back door where I'm sitting in a chair, reading a book.

Our small fenced-in patio is mostly concrete slabs with a few potted plants for color, but my mom and I usually struggle to keep our plants alive each winter, so we're slowly giving up on trying.

It may be more claustrophobic than where I spent the last couple of months, but any time I'm outdoors, I feel better. I'm allowed to think, and the sun peeks through and shines on me.

Although, nothing is better or more therapeutic than talking to Midnight. I hope he's healing okay.

"Hi," I call out, resting my book on my lap.

"How was the interview?" My mom beams as she sits on the chair beside me.

I bring my feet up and bend my knees, resting my chin on them and tilting my head toward her. I glance up through my lashes, and my lips press together in a frown.

"I'm sure it wasn't that bad." She pats my leg reassuringly. Her smile softens. "You're smart, talented, and a hard worker. They'll be lucky to have you on their team."

How do I tell her what happened without disappointing her? Without disappointing my dad when he hears the news? They were both so excited about the prospect of me finding a job.

Scratching the back of my head where the sun heats it, I shift, dropping my legs again, and the book slides off them and lands with a thud on the ground. I leave it where it is and look at my mom.

"I don't want you to be disappointed." Her eyebrows lift, and I think I should've started another way.

"You could never disappoint us. Your father and I are so proud of you."

My eyes fall shut, and I nod. "You know I always have a delayed reaction to things." She nods. "Well, it took me going to the interview to realize I really didn't want that job. The interviewer asked why I wanted to work for them, and I just spit out that I didn't want to before I had a chance to stop myself. We were both surprised by my response, but... Well, actually, I kinda wasn't. I apologized profusely and left, embarrassed but liberated." I rush out the words, talking a mile a minute.

My mom stares at me blankly.

"I'm so sorry, Mom." I reach for her hands, eyes cast down.

I don't need to look at myself to know my eyebrows are pulled in tight. It's the same face I'd give her when I was a child and broke something in the house.

My nose tingles with incoming tears, but I swallow them down.

"Why are you apologizing?" Her gentle gaze locks with mine, and she pats my hand.

"Because it was a good opportunity, and I turned it down." I lean back against the wooden chair, the horizontal slabs digging into my tense back.

"Can I be honest?"

I nod, breathing deeply.

"I half expected this to happen. The only reason I thought the outcome might be different is because you're stubborn like your father." She arches an eyebrow, and I snort. My mom's just as stubborn, but she's in denial.

"Why did you?"

"You haven't been yourself. I noticed as soon as we picked you up from the airport. After we spoke last night, I had a feeling…" She shrugs.

"Feeling?" I lift my brows and nod my head to urge her on, brushing my hair behind my ear.

"It seems to me you're being guided by your heart."

"Well, my heart's gotten me into trouble in the past," I deadpan.

"No," she shakes her head. "I don't think it was your heart that stayed with Jeff for so long. I think that was your head rationalizing." She taps my temple.

"I ran into him," I smirk.

"Jeff?" Her eyes widen.

I nod, unable to hold my chuckle.

"It was wonderful. I told him off, and now I feel so much better." A giggle bursts out of me, and I cover my mouth.

"I'd like to say a few words to him, but I'm glad you were the one to do it." She reaches over and hugs me.

"Thanks, Mom."

"So tell me, what *do* you want to do?" she whispers against the side of my hair.

"I don't know."

"Yes, you do." She leans back, holding my upper arms. Her eyes stare into mine as if luring the truth out of me.

I close my eyes, tears building behind my lids. If I verbalize it, it will be true, and I'm scared. It seems, though, as if mother's intuition can't be fooled.

"I miss it. I've only been gone two days, and I miss the smells, the view, the people." My lip trembles as my heart breaks all over again. I've been so focused on today's interview that I haven't given myself a chance to really think about Mason Creek.

"I know you do."

"I keep telling myself I'll get over it with time, it's just the first few days, but I don't know. I think I'll regret it. I don't like living in the city. It's always felt suffocating, and in Mason Creek, I was able to breathe freely, fill my lungs with air and feel life."

She looks at me sadly and rubs my forehead like when I was younger. I thought it would be harder to tell her how I felt. Somehow, it seems like she understands.

"Sweetie, I know. Your father and I talked about this last night, the possibility of you wanting to go back. You have to do what's right for you. If you visualize a life in Mason Creek, then chase after it. All we've ever wanted is for you to be happy."

The tears are freely falling now, no longer attempting to keep them at bay. My mom's match mine, both of us sniffling out of tune. I chuckle and nod.

"I love that place. I came back because I didn't see a future there when it came to a career. Sal is already working, and while the butcher shop is successful, it's not enough to pay me the kind of salary I'd need to live. Besides, I want to find my place independently. I learned a ton working at the butcher shop, but I need to stand on my own two feet. I'm not sure what I'd do in Mason

Creek with a degree in finance." I look at her, desperate to find the answers in her.

"You'll find something. You can always become a financial advisor and have clients all over. Technology is so advanced now that the possibilities are endless. Think about it. Most of the clients you'd have working for a company here would likely live elsewhere."

She's got a point. I need to stop looking at the tiny details and take a step back, look at the big picture that curates endless possibilities. It's not like I have a super niche career. Finance can open many doors.

"Do you think Uncle Sal will let me stay with him for a bit until I get settled? I'd hate to disrupt his life again."

"I think he'd love it. He misses you, too. I keep getting messages from him asking how you're doing."

"Would you and Dad come visit?"

"As often as we can," she nods.

"I love you, Mom," my voice is watery.

"I love you, too, sweetheart. All we've ever wanted is the best for you."

I wrap my arms around her, seeking comfort and confidence. This feels right. I'm finally on the correct path for me. I just hope that when I arrive, Wilder will think the same. Regardless, Mason Creek is where I belong, with or without a boyfriend.

Chapter 30

HALLIE

"You promise you'll come to visit?" I hold my mom's hands and look between her and my dad in the middle of the airport drop-off area.

I didn't hesitate to book a flight yesterday and repack what I had put away from my trip plus more of my personal belongings in a bigger suitcase. If I wait too long, I'll talk myself out of going back to Mason Creek, and I'll always regret it.

"We promise," my dad says, putting his arm around my mom's shoulder.

This feels so final. I'm terrified of this decision, yet peace has settled in my bones since I made it. It's an odd combination—my heart and mind competing for my attention. I refuse to let my anxiety win.

My mom wipes her cheek and nods. "We'll look at our work schedules and plan a trip soon. It's been too long since we've visited, and I miss Sal and Aunt Ruth and Becky."

"I'll hold you to that," I smile sadly. "I'm going to miss you guys so much." I wrap my arms around both of them in a group hug.

My dad kisses the top of my head while my mom silently cries. My own tears escape, knowing my life is about to change.

"We'll talk every day," I assure my mom.

"We will, honey. Now go, before you miss your flight. Let us know when you land in Dallas for your layover." She wipes my tears, hers still falling.

I nod and kiss them both on the cheek before heading into the airport. I look at them before disappearing behind the doors and find my dad comforting my mom while she cries into his side.

I want that. I want the kind of love they've shown me is possible. I only hope I can find that with Wilder.

The only person who knows I'm returning to Mason Creek is Uncle Sal since I needed to make sure it's okay that I stay there. Joy is going to be so surprised, and I'm glad to be able to keep my promise to be present at the spring festival. Nerves rattle me as I think about Wilder's reaction, but I hold on to hope that it's positive.

The airport is packed with people coming and going, but the security check flows smoothly. Soon, I'm sitting by the gate waiting to board. My hands tremble as I spin my phone around.

When it rings mid-spin, I fumble with it. Seeing Joy's name, I answer and hope I can keep my return a surprise.

"Hey." I lean back in my seat, keeping my carry-on tucked between my legs.

"Hallie? Oh, thank God." Her greeting sounds panicked and breathy.

"What's going on?" I sit straighter, looking around the airport.

"It's Wilder… I wasn't sure if I should call you or not, but I think you'd want to know." She speaks rapidly.

My heart pounds as fear prickles my skin. "What happened?" I whisper.

"He was attacked by a coyote yesterday. Levi found him."

"What?" I gasp. Heat rises inside of me as fear takes over. Devastation wraps me in a blanket. My heart shatters.

"Is…is he okay?" I stutter through my overwhelming emotions. If she says he's not or if it's fatal… I don't know that I'll overcome it.

"I'm not sure. Everyone is speculating, and you know how that is. Who do you believe? I heard about the attack but nothing more. I'm trying to get ahold of my brother to see if he knows anything else. I'll keep you updated."

"I may not answer right away, but leave me a voicemail. I'm actually at the airport. I'll be in Mason Creek tonight."

"What?" she screeches. "And you didn't tell me! Oh, my goodness."

"I wanted to surprise you all, but now I feel like I won't get there fast enough."

"Shit, I gotta go. Customers just walked in. I'll call, and we'll talk tonight." The last part is a squeal, and I'm sure she's trying to hide her excitement due to the tragic news she just delivered.

"I get in late, so we'll talk in the morning, okay?"

"Perfect!" This time she doesn't hide her elation.

I hang up and call Uncle Sal. Maybe he knows more than Joy does. When he doesn't answer, and they start boarding my plane, I sigh in frustration and stash my phone in my purse, heading to the line. I tap my toe as I wait my turn. Then, I find my seat, stow my carry-on, and play with the seatbelt until the person taking the seat next to me arrives, and I move so they can slide in.

My fingers tap the top of my book incessantly. I can't focus on reading. I'm stuck in limbo, with different scenarios playing out. A coyote attack could be deadly. I assume so. If Wilder was alone… If he couldn't defend himself… *Damn it.*

I close my eyes and attempt to sleep. I talk to Wilder in my mind, letting him know I'm on my way to him. I need him to be okay. I need to have a chance to talk to him, tell him I love him in person. Alive. Maybe if I wouldn't have left… *No.* I shake that thought away. I can't carry the blame.

The four-hour flight to Dallas is interminable. I still can't get ahold of Sal in my short layover, but I do talk to my mom and tell her what happened. She promises she'll try to talk to Sal, but it's pointless. I'm boarding another flight soon and will be in the air. I may as well wait until I see him at the airport.

Needless to say, I get no rest like I had hoped and arrive in Montana beyond exhausted and jacked up on anxiety. Uncle Sal is waiting for me by arrivals, and I rush to him, dragging both my big suitcase and my carry-on.

"How is he?" Wild eyes stare up at him while my body shakes.

"He's stable." He nods, bringing an arm around me in a comforting hug. "I haven't been able to get much information, but I was able to get that tidbit."

"I'll go see him tomorrow if I can borrow your car." It's way too late to go tonight, especially that we still have about an hour's drive to Mason Creek.

"Of course." He nods, taking my bigger suitcase and leading the way to his truck.

"Want me to drive? How's your leg? You shouldn't overdo it." I go into caretaker mode.

Uncle Sal chuckles. "I'll drive. My leg's doing better, and the doc gave me the go-ahead to make the longer trip. You relax."

I relent, knowing he's right. If I get behind the wheel right now, there's no telling what will happen. I'm too nervous and anxious.

"I was thinking," he starts as he pulls out of the airport. "I've still gotta go to therapy, which will take time away from the butcher shop. I originally thought about cutting back hours while I'm there since I can't be at two places at once. Unless…" He eyes me with a hopeful smile, and tears blur my vision.

"You want me to help you?"

"I'd love it. Your mom told me you want to find your own way, and I respect that, but I could use the help until you do."

"Deal." I nod, so grateful for his support. "Will it still be okay to go see Wilder tomorrow morning, or do you need me to open?"

"It's okay. Therapy is twice a week, although if I have your help, I can increase the days and finish sooner."

"Don't overwork yourself," I warn with a pointed finger, causing him to laugh.

"I'm glad you're back. Any chance your mom will follow?" He eyes me quickly before focusing back on the road.

"I don't think so. They're happy in New York, but I made them promise they'd visit as often as work allowed. I think we'll be seeing them in a couple of months, maybe sooner." I lean back, resting my head on the seat and releasing all the tension. Knowing that Wilder is stable gives me hope. I cross my fingers that's the truth and not a Mason Creek rumor.

It's taken every ounce of patience to not show up at Wilder's door at six in the morning. I barely slept, anticipating seeing him and what state he'll be in. Instead, I made coffee and drank an entire pot to kill some time. Now I'm jacked up on caffeine, nervous beyond belief, and scared that he won't be as stable as Uncle Sal heard.

Finally, I drop Uncle Sal off at the butcher shop and drive to Roman Wilde Ranch. My palms are sweaty against the worn leather steering wheel. Each mile that gets me closer to his house makes my heart pound harder.

I drive through the entrance, dirt lifting on either side of the truck. I can't fully remember which direction to take to Wilder's house, so when the main house appears, I stop. Levi looks up from the barn trying to figure out who showed up at his ranch by covering the sun from his face.

I wave him over, hoping he can see me through the windshield. A wide smile takes over his face as he jogs toward the truck. He doesn't seem like someone whose brother is on his deathbed, which is a relief.

"Look who's back." He leans into my opened window, resting his arms on the door.

"Hey, yeah, uh… How are you? I wanted to see Wilder. I heard what happened. Is he okay? I can't remember how exactly to get to his house." I'm rambling and talking a mile a minute.

"Thank fuck," he mumbles. "He's okay," he assures me.

"Are you sure?" My voice trembles.

"Promise. Go on and see him. Make his sad ass happy again, *please*," he practically begs.

If Levi's attitude is anything to go by, Wilder really is okay. His brother wouldn't joke if it were serious.

With the right directions, I follow the path that will lead me to Wilder. *My home.* From what Levi said, Wilder should be happy to see me. I hope. He's become such an integral part of my life that losing him when we do have a choice would be devastating, but mostly I want him to be healthy and happy.

My palms continue to stick to the steering wheel as I curve along with the terrain. No real road leads me to his house, except washed away tire marks. When his house pops up, nausea hits me. *I'm going to puke.*

My heart beats so hard it feels like it's going to rip through my skin and land on his porch, along with my vomit. I was so confident about this yesterday. Now, I'm shaking.

I sit in the car, staring out the window at his house for an interminable amount of time, stabilizing my harsh breathing and swallowing past the lump in my throat. I want to be able to speak when I see him.

This is what I want, and I need to fight for it. If I don't try, I'll never know if Wilder and I have a future or if this is where our road ends.

I release a long exhale, dry my palms on my jeans, and grab my purse. When I knock on the door, I eagerly wait for him to answer. Instead of opening the door, I hear him call out, "Come in."

Surprised, or maybe he's that injured he can't stand, I open the door and take tentative steps. Wilder looks over his shoulder from the couch, and his eyes widen. My steps halt as we stare at each other. Every concern and doubt melts away. It's replaced by overwhelming emotions and love for this man.

"You're here. Why are you here?" He scrubs his eyes, blinking a few times as he stares at me again.

"Hi." I smile.

"Come in. Sit down. I thought it was Levi or my mom checking in on me." He shifts on the couch, sitting taller as I make my way around it but grimaces.

"Stay. Don't move."

When I come face-to-face with him, I cover my mouth, eyes watering. I'm able to see what the couch wouldn't allow me to. His right arm is bandaged, as is his torso.

"Wilder," I whisper.

"It looks worse than it is," he promises with a smile. "Come on." He pats the seat next to him.

I'm careful to sit on the other side of his injuries even though I want to hug him tightly.

"What are you doing here? Did you come because of this?" He waves his hand at his body with his eyebrows pulled in.

"No, I heard about your injury when I was already on my way."

This makes the valleys between his eyebrows deepen.

"I don't get it. How was the interview?"

"Well…" I chuckle. "I told them I didn't want to work for them."

"What?" He pushes forward, and his face screws in pain.

"Okay, you need to stop moving." I place my hand on his bare shoulder to stop him from trying to sit up. "You're worrying me."

"I'm okay. I promise. Just some bite wounds. I've still got a lot of years ahead of me."

"I was so scared when Joy told me." I bite my lower lip, vision blurring. "She didn't know anything except that you were attacked. I was afraid I'd get here, and you'd be…" I can't finish that thought.

"Shh…" He pulls me in gently and kisses the top of my head. "I got lucky. Levi wasn't too far away and heard Bro's pained cries. He showed up as I was pushing the coyote off me and killed it."

"It could've killed you," I whisper, blinking up at him.

"If he'd bit me somewhere else, yeah," he nods somberly. "That fucker got a tight grip, so I could barely push him off me, but I was able to put force into it. I kept thinking about you." He brushes away my hair, placing it behind my ear and trailing my face.

"I wasn't ready to lose you that permanently." His smile is caring with a hint of sadness.

"I'm so glad you're okay." I shake my head, lacing my fingers with his. "It took me leaving to realize where I belong. That job wouldn't have made me happy even if I lied to myself. I want to be here. I don't know if you want this to go further than a temporary relationship, but regardless of that, I'm staying."

"Come 'ere, babe." I scoot closer, careful not to hurt him, and let him hold me into his side, digging my face in the crook of his neck and inhaling all that is Wilder James. "I want more than temporary. I want forever, permanent, tattoo yourself on me." I laugh against his skin.

"That's absurd." I look up at him.

"God, I missed you." His breath tickles my chin.

"I missed you, too. It was a few days, but I'm sure this is what I want. You're who I want." I lean forward slowly, pausing a few inches from his lips. "Is this okay?"

"You damn well better kiss me." His hand squeezes my waist. A shiver runs through me.

I smile, brushing my lips against his, keeping it PG considering he's recovering.

"I love you," he murmurs against my lips.

Everything is right once again.

"I love you, too." I smile softly.

"I read your letter. That's what I was doing right before I got attacked, actually."

"What?" My eyes bug out.

"It wasn't your fault. I was irresponsible to go out with Bro knowing coyotes were around our land. I should've taken my gun." He shakes his head, lips formed in a straight line.

I run my finger over them, releasing the tension, and he kisses the pad of my thumb.

His eyes burn into mine. "You gave it all up for me?"

"No." I shake my head, arching a brow. "I made a choice that was better for me. You, this town, my family and friends here, you're what I need." I tilt my head. "If you didn't want me anymore, I'd still stay."

"You gotta stop with that. I want you. So damn much, and I think I've proven that throughout the time we've known each other."

"You have," I swallow thickly.

My fingers trail his face, following the contours of his features. No more words need to be spoken as we look at each other, silently promising to love one another unconditionally.

My mom was right—home is a person. And Wilder's heart and soul are my home now.

Chapter 31

HALLIE

"You're here!" Joy squeals, leaving the customer at the counter half-attended to tackle me in a hug. I laugh, holding onto her, so I don't fall. The bag from the diner holding lunch dangles from my arm.

"I am." My smile splits my mouth as I look at my cousin, bopping on her toes.

"I can't even tell you how excited I am, and you're *staying*!"

"Shh…" Quieting her is in vain. Nothing is calming her down.

The customer, who I recognize from the butcher shop, looks at us with a smile, waiting patiently. I expect the entire town to be talking about my return soon.

"I actually need to go. I came to grab lunch and wanted to pick up a sweet treat. Can we get together tonight?" I lift the bag.

"Of course. Have you seen…" Her eyebrows lift, but she doesn't say his name.

"Yeah, I was just there. Lunch is actually for him, and I thought he might like dessert, something sweet to lighten his mood a bit."

She arches a brow and stares at me. "You mean, you aren't dessert?"

"Joy!" I shove her shoulder, laughing incredulously. "No." I shake my head, feeling heat creep up my face.

"I'm joking. So, he's okay?" She scrunches her nose, walking back around the counter.

"Yeah, thankfully." I clasp my hands in front of me and stand behind the customer, waiting my turn.

"I'm glad. I'm sure he was ecstatic to see you."

"Mhmm…" My lips press together, face heating further. I love Joy, but sometimes she forgets she's talking in front of an audience.

Thankfully, the customer leaves with a small smile, and I hope she won't run off and tell the entire town that I'm Wilder's dessert.

"What would you like?" She leans forward on the counter, wearing a huge grin and her body shaking with excitement.

"Actually, do you know what Wilder would like?" I don't think he's picky, but if there's something he loves, I'd rather choose that.

"He likes anything," Joy shrugs, closing one eye. "You know what? He loves the huckleberry bear claw."

"Awesome, I'll take two."

I grab my wallet while she packs the bear claws. I'm antsy to get back to Wilder's house. Despite telling me he's okay, I could read the pain all over his face when I was there. It feels amazing to be back, though. To sit with Wilder and just talk, take care of him, and watch TV.

"It's on the house," Joy waves away my money.

"Uh, no. Not this time." I shake my head, ready to argue.

"It's a get well soon gift for Wilder." Joy crosses her arms.

"This is your business. I need to pay you." I push the bills forward on the counter, and she pushes them back.

"Gosh, you're stubborn." She rolls her eyes. "I'm not taking your money. You can buy my secret pastry at the spring festival."

When I don't take my money, she lifts an eyebrow. "I can do this dance all day. You're the one with a sexy as fuck boyfriend waiting for you."

"Ugh, *you're* stubborn." I put my money away.

"It runs in the family," Joy laughs. "Besides, this is what we do here. We take care of our own."

Her words hit me with an onslaught of emotions. Tears build, and I'm consumed in happiness, knowing this is the kind of life that awaits me.

"I'll text you later about tonight. Coffee's on me." I smile triumphantly.

"You're impossible." She waves me off.

I head back to the truck and return to the ranch, this time knowing where I'm going. Instead of nerves, excitement rolls through me.

A woman's voice flows through the house as I walk in. I pause, not wanting to interrupt. As I tip-toe back out of the house, Wilder calls my name.

"Is that you?" I squeeze my eyes shut and cringe. I didn't see a car outside, so I didn't think he had a visitor.

"Hey." I enter the living room with the bags. Wilder sits on the couch, looking at me over his shoulder with a wide grin that illuminates his face. Beside him sits his mother. I've met Mrs. James a few times. Always superficial meetings, but she's been sweet.

"Hi, Hallie," she waves me over. "Wilder was just telling me you're back in town."

"I am," I nod, placing the bags on the counter and meeting them by the sofa. I rock back on my heels, and my eyes ping pong between them.

"I can go so you can finish talking." My hands move awkwardly in the direction of the door. I fight the urge to roll my eyes at myself and drop my arms by my side.

"Please don't. I just wanted to check in on him and make sure he was listening to doctor's orders about resting." Mrs. James smiles lovingly at Wilder in a way that reminds me a lot of how my mom looks at me when she's worried.

A pang hits my chest. It will be difficult living so far away from my parents. It'll be a first, though it's a step in the direction I want for my life. I finally have clarity. When my watery eyes collide with Wilder's smiling ones, I know I'll be okay as long as I'm by his side.

Wilder winks and extends his arm out. "Come sit."

I take his hand as I sit on his good side. My fingers nervously stroke his as his mom smiles at us. She doesn't comment on our relationship, but the way she's watching us is full of curious approval. It's as if she's itching to ask how this all occurred while enjoying the sight of us together. I'm guessing Wilder hasn't been completely forthcoming about our relationship, maybe since it was never meant to last, but enough rumors have been circulating town.

"I brought plenty of lunch if you want to join us," I tell her. When I saw the specials at Wren's Cafe, I grabbed two, which is more than enough food for Wilder and me.

"Oh, my!" She jumps to her feet with wide eyes. "I just remembered I left dinner's roast in the oven." She rushes around chaotically.

"I'll call Dad and tell him to check on it," Wilder says, grabbing his phone.

Mrs. James sighs, nodding. "Please do. Darn it, I got so distracted."

Wilder talks to his dad while Mrs. James looks at me. "I'm so sorry for the outburst. You two enjoy lunch. We already ate. You're more than welcome to join us for dinner."

"Oh, thank you. I promised Joy I'd see her tonight to catch up, and she's so excited I'd hate to disappoint her." I frown apologetically.

"That's okay. I have a feeling we'll have plenty of chances for dinners." She smiles sweetly, kissing Wilder's cheek. "If you need anything, call me."

Her eyes glance to mine. "He's stubborn, so make sure he does as I say."

Laughing, I nod. "I will."

The door shutting echoes behind us, and I turn to Wilder. "Want me to bring lunch here so you won't have to move?"

"I can sit at the counter." I reach for his hand to help him stand, making sure he puts as little force into it as possible.

"So you're going to see Joy tonight?" Wilder asks while I heat up our food and plate it.

"Yeah," I nod, serving us each a glass of water. "I went into the bakery for dessert. She had no idea I was coming until she called to tell me what happened to you. I promised we'd hang out, and I'd catch her up." I set his plate in front of him, dropping a kiss on his cheek.

"Thanks, babe." He squeezes my hip as I walk around him and sit beside him.

"You're welcome. Now, eat so you can take your medicine."

"Yes, ma'am," he salutes me and begins eating.

We're quiet for a few beats as we begin eating, but then Wilder breaks the silence with a whispered awe.

"I still can't believe you're here to stay. I don't think I've fully wrapped my head around it."

"I know. It wasn't the original plan, but life changes our directions."

"I'm glad it did." He takes a bite of his mashed potatoes, eyeing me.

I lift my eyebrows, waiting for him to say something, but he continues to eat silently, eyes never leaving me.

"What?" I finally ask. "Do I have food on my face or something?"

He laughs boastfully before cringing. "No."

Wilder turns toward me. "I'm just thinking."

"About…?" Thinking usually leads to things I don't like.

"Us." My eyes widen, and he quickly adds. "About how I'm going to get you in my bed tonight if you're going out with Joy."

A throaty laugh escapes me. "You're such a guy. Shall I remind you that you're injured?" I lift my brows, jutting my chin toward his bandaged body.

"Dirty mind... I just wanna sleep with you."

"Mhmm..."

"You should move in with me."

"What?" I choke on my sip of water, spraying it all over him. "Oh, my God! I'm so sorry." Embarrassment heats my face and causes my entire body to prickle.

Wilder laughs, wiping his face and chest with his napkin. "It's okay. If I had to have anyone's spit on me, I'd choose yours."

"*God*," I hide my face in my hands, forgetting about the reason I sputtered water in the first place.

"What do you say, Bunny Girl?" His voice is soft, and I peek up at him through my fingers.

"It's too soon. I just got back." When he frowns, I add, "I want to get there with you, but I want to stand on my own before. If not, I'm going from one crutch to another. I want to find a job here first. Figure out what I'm going to do. I want to be your equal, not someone you feel the need to take care of." I reach for his hand, kissing his palm.

"I love you with all my heart, so don't take this as a rejection."

"I know it isn't," he smiles. "I'm just selfish and want you all to myself."

"You do have me all to yourself." I cup the side of his face. "That's a promise I can keep."

He nods, turning his face to brush his lips against my palm, tickling my skin. I missed him. I missed the opportunities we wouldn't have had I stayed gone.

"You're beautiful, strong, and all mine. I respect your need to find your place in this town, but know this—I won't be very patient. I'll want you in this home sooner rather than later."

I smirk because that's the Wilder I know. The bossy, stubborn man I fell for, but underneath all that is the kindest, most gentle soul I've ever met. And I'm so damn lucky to call him mine, too.

"I should warn you, though, if you're looking for a live-in nurse," I point to his bandaged body. "I get queasy at the sight of blood."

Wilder's deep laughter is music to my ears. "Don't I know it."

He tugs me closer, puckering his lips. I close the few inches of distance and kiss him lazily. There's no place I would rather be than with this man.

Chapter 32

WILDER

"This is amazing!" Hallie looks around Town Square in awe. "I'm just…wow. I knew the spring festival would be great, but this takes it to a different level of awesome."

I chuckle as I hold her hand, weaving through the crowd, careful not to bump into anyone, so my injuries don't suffer. Thankfully, I'm okay and survived the coyote attack, but I've never been more scared in my life. The thought of never seeing Hallie again was the motivation I needed to put all my force into pushing the coyote away.

It was a miracle Levi showed up right when he did and killed it before I was attacked again. Unfortunately, Bro didn't make it. We cared for him as much as we could, but I had to say goodbye to the best horse a few days ago when we put him down. The injuries were far too great.

"It is amazing." I tighten my hold on her hand and smile over at her.

The town is full of booths for local businesses, games for the kids, and a stage is set for live music by our very own Tucker Simms.

Hallie will have an extra surprise today, and I can't wait to see her face when she sees it. I've been biting my tongue, but I'm excited for her to know.

"This looks amazing," she squeals in front of Joy's booth.

"Thanks!" Joy beams. "You got here right on time. It's slowed down."

"Tell me what your secret pastry is." Hallie bounces on her toes, and I laugh at their shared enthusiasm.

"Ready? It's extra special for you. I had to do some research, but…" Joy draws out, letting the anticipation grow. "It's a huckleberry cream-filled cronut! I know cronuts are popular in New York, and I wanted to tie in something related to you. You totally inspired this without even knowing it."

Hallie blinks rapidly, smiling at Joy before looking up at me. I brush her cheek before kissing her forehead.

"They're tossed in cinnamon sugar, then topped with a glaze and candied nuts since I've heard those are sold on the streets of New York."

"Wow…" Hallie whispers. "Seriously?"

"Yeah," Joy nods. "I was kinda sad when you told me you wouldn't be here for the festival because I so wanted you to try this, but you're here!" Another squeal and I laugh louder.

I'm not exactly sure what that is, but I take the donut-shaped pastry Joy hands each of us.

"Try it," she urges us.

Hallie smiles at me before taking a bite, crispy dough crunching loudly. She covers her mouth with her hand, and her eyes widen.

"This is delicious."

"You like it, then?" Joy eyes her hopefully.

She finishes swallowing, nodding constantly. "It's amazing. It tastes like home but different at the same time. You should sell these at the bakery afterward. I'm sure people are going to love it. Try it." She waves a hand at me.

Chuckling, I take a bite of this cronut thing and groan.

"So good," I say around a mouthful.

"I'm so excited," Joy claps. "So far, people have loved it."

Hallie and I continue wandering around the festival while we finish our cronuts. People in town ask how I'm doing when we pass them by, sharing how happy they are to know I'm okay. Brayden smirks when he sees us and comes over to meet us.

"Hey." He eyes our cronuts. "What's that?" He lifts his chin toward the little that's left of our dessert.

"A cronut. Joy's selling them," I smirk.

His smile fades, and his eyes narrow. Hallie giggles at his reaction and hides her face behind the pastry.

"Get me one," Brayden says, sticking his hands in his pocket. "I'll give you money."

"If you want one, you gotta get it yourself." I shrug, finishing off mine.

"Jackass. I'm good, then. She'd probably know it's for me and poison it." He shakes his head. "No offense, Hallie. I know she's your cousin and all…"

"None taken." She bites her smile, eyes narrowing.

"I'm gonna get ice cream from Hattie and Hazel. Wanna come? I think the churning contest is starting soon. Grady was getting dragged into participating by Jillybean. She wants to win the year-round free ice cream. Since he lost at the last festival, he feels guilty."

I laugh, wrapping my arm around Hallie. We head to meet up with my cousin and find Levi is already talking to him. When the contest begins, Jillybean pushes Grady onto a spot by the old-fashioned churn.

Charlee, Grady's wife, stands with us carrying their newborn and keeping Jillybean close by, all of them cheering Grady on. I look at Hallie, imagining what life with her will be like. One day, I may be the one up there trying to win ice cream for our son or daughter.

She's been back a week and a half, and I'm already making plans. I've got all these ideas for our future. I never thought this moody rancher would fall head over heels for a city girl, but she's proven that judging someone upon first seeing them is a sorry mistake. Had I kept my judgments about her based on that first meeting with the dead bunny, I wouldn't be where I am right now. I wouldn't have risen above the past and found a love so deep that nothing could break it.

She leans into me, resting her head on my shoulder, and sighs. A relaxed smile brightens her face. We can be surrounded by the entire town, but all I see is her. She's my truth, my love, my perfect mess.

A throat clears behind us, and she lifts her head, looking back.

With wide eyes and a loud gasp, she screams, "Oh, my God!" and jumps into her mom's arms. I stand back, watching her greet her parents while everyone near us looks on with curiosity.

"What in the world are you doing here?" She hugs her dad next. Sal smiles triumphantly at being able to pull this off without Hallie finding out.

"When you left, we decided to put in vacation time at work to come visit and spend some more time with you. We were both approved, so we planned to come." Her mom smiles at her adoringly before looking up at me. "You must be Wilder."

"Yes, ma'am." I stretch my arm out to shake her hand. "It's nice to meet you."

"It's great meeting you. I've heard so much about you, and it's nice to finally see you in person."

I shake her dad's hand, and Hallie goes into action. "These are my parents, Anna and Graham. I'm so shocked."

"I hope it was a good surprise," I chuckle, kissing the top of her head.

"You knew?" Her wide eyes swing to mine.

"Yeah. Sal told me what was going on."

"Is that why you insisted I stay at your place last night?"

"Guilty," I grin.

"When did you get here then?" She turns to her parents.

"Last night. We took the same flight you did, so we didn't land until eleven."

"Wow... I still can't believe it." She looks between her parents and then at Sal. I can tell she's on the verge of tears by the way she keeps sniffling.

I pull her to my side. "Why don't you go see Joy and find Ruth?" I suggest.

"We'd love to," her mom says.

"Go, babe." I tap her lower back.

"Are you sure?" Her doe eyes look at me.

"Positive, go be with your family." I watch her go, knowing how important it is for her to find her place and carve her own path.

"She's the real deal, huh?" Brayden says beside me.

"She is," I nod, not taking my eyes off her until the crowd swallows her up, the churning contest long forgotten.

"Is she gonna continue to work at the butcher shop?"

I turn to look at him. "Just until Sal's done with physical therapy. She's looking for something else."

"Like what?" His stance is wide, hands in his pockets, as his eyebrows furrow. Mason Creek doesn't exactly have a ton of work opportunities, so I understand his confused expression.

"Not sure yet. Her degree's in finance. Her mom gave her the idea of working on her own, becoming a financial advisor so she can work with people locally and through the internet."

"Finance?" Brayden asks. "Hmm… Would she be interested in a position at the bank?"

"Really?" I look at my best friend with raised eyebrows. I didn't know he was hiring.

"Yeah. I need someone at the bank who can not only guide locals with their finances but the businesses in the area ever since Caroline moved. I get a ton of questions and appointments from people here needing financial advice, but I can only help so many with all my other responsibilities. I'd like to have a life outside of work."

"I think she'd love that. We'll talk to her after the festival. Sound good?" I clap his shoulder. "Thanks, buddy."

"Of course."

When Tucker starts playing, I go in search of Hallie by Joy's booth.

"Dance with me?" I hold my hand out.

"I'd love to." The way she smiles at me wins me over once again. It's the shy, sweet smile that shows off that dimple on her cheek.

Wrapping my good arm around her, we sway to the music.

"Thank you," she whispers.

"For what?" I lift my head to look at her. "I didn't have anything to do with your parents. That was all them and Sal."

Hallie shakes her head. "For everything. For loving me, supporting me." She blinks away tears.

"You don't need to thank me. I'm lucky I found you." I kiss her temple. "By the way, I spoke to Brayden, and he's looking for someone to help at the bank. I told him we'd talk to him after the festival."

"To help as in a job?" Her eyebrows lift.

"Yeah," I chuckle. "He gets a ton of requests for advice, but he can't do all that and run the bank since he's understaffed. You think you'd be up for it?"

"Are you kidding me?" Her voice rises. "Of course I'd be up for it. That's amazing." She smiles, shaking her head. A soft chuckle escapes her, and I look at her with furrowed brows.

"What's so funny?"

"All this time, I could've had a job here. The irony."

"You know what I think? We needed to take the road we did. It made us both realize how deep our love ran. *You* needed to go back to New York and come to terms with what you wanted outside of me influencing your thoughts." I hold her waist tightly, singing the words in her ear.

"You're right," she nods. "I think me returning, being there after experiencing Mason Creek was necessary. Almost losing you, so I could truly appreciate this. Not that I didn't before, but I see it differently now. As equals." She nods slowly, resting her head on my shoulder.

"Move in with me," I ask again. I'm hoping that having the prospect of a job and having a few days of settling back in would've changed her mind.

"Okay," she whispers without even looking at me.

"Uh... What?" I tap the back of her head, so she looks at me.

"I said okay. I'll move in. I've spent half the nights there already in the past ten days or whatever since I've been back."

I tighten my hold on her waist and lift her feet off the ground, spinning her around. Injuries be damned. Hallie giggles in the middle of town, surrounded by neighbors. I kiss her hard, so fucking grateful she's in my life.

"I love you, Bunny Girl," I say against her lips.

Her fingers sweep against my cheek and down my nose. "I love you, too."

When I almost rammed into her car the first time she came to Mason Creek, I never would've imagined I'd be standing here with her. I vow to always make sure she feels loved, knows how special she is, and loves herself. I'll spend the rest of my days showing her how worthy she is and supporting her. I know she'd do the same for me.

Thank you for reading Wilder and Hallie's story! I hope you loved it. If you're inclined to, I'd love if you left a review on Amazon and Goodreads.

Learn more about my books at
www.authorfabiolafrancisco.com.

Next in Mason Creek Series
Perfect Excuse by A.D. Justice
Buy now on Amazon
Available through Kindle Unlimited

As if going through a divorce in a small town isn't bad enough, a custody dispute landed us in couples therapy. Before we can file to dissolve our marriage, we have to come to an agreement regarding... our pet bird.

Welcome to Mason Creek, Montana!

If you don't already know, Mason Creek is a 12 book series by 12 Bestselling Authors, all linked together by one fictional small town.

Check them all out on Kindle Unlimited!

Thank you for visiting Mason Creek, Montana. Welcome to Everton, Wyoming!

If you enjoy small town romance, then you'll love my other books on Amazon!

Love in Everton Series: Welcome to Everton—a small town hidden in the Wyoming mountains where cowboys rule, rumors run, and love wins.

Carlisle Cellars Series: Meet the Carlisles, a prominent family that is royalty in their small town. Three siblings, a family business, and emotional twists that will lead them through a series of life changes. The books include hate-to-lovers, second chance, and single dad romance.

Acknowledgments

First and foremost, thank you for taking this ride with us to Mason Creek. I'm so excited to share this small town with you.

Thank you to CA Harms, our fierce leader, for putting this amazing group together and inviting me to be a part of this magnificent town. I'm so grateful and honored to be a part of this group of talented writers. To all the Mason Creek authors, thank you for your support and being a kick-ass group of authors to work with. Mason Creek will always be out home.

Thank you to Sarah Paige from Opium House Creative for the gorgeous cover, Bex from The Polished Author for taking your time to make this story perfect, and Lydia and Megan at HEA Book Tours for putting this series out in the world.

Ally, I can't thank you enough for all your help. You keep me sane and grounded. Besides, you made me love all the single daddies.

Veronica, thank you for your friendship and always cheering me on.

Christy and Rachel, I'm so grateful for your friendship. It's priceless to know that I can count on you and turn to you despite distances, time zones, and life chaos. #soapythighs

Brit and Cary, thank you ladies for always being there to listen to me ramble and for providing feedback when I need to put things into perspective.

Savannah, thank you for believing in my work and helping me get my stories out in the world.

Fabiola's Fab Reads, you're the best group a girl could ask for. Thank you for being a part of my writing career and sharing everything from your fave reads to your life updates.

A huge thanks to my review team and master list for stepping up each time I have book news to share, reading and reviewing my work, and being there for me. It means the world to me that you love to share my work.

To all the reviewers, bloggers, authors, and bookstagrammers that have shared my work and supported me, thank you. I couldn't do this without you. It takes a tribe, and you're part of mine.

About the Author

Fabiola Francisco loves the simplicity—and kick—of scotch on the rocks. She follows Hemingway's philosophy—write drunk, edit sober. She writes women's fiction and contemporary romance, dipping her pen into new adult and young adult. Her moods guide her writing, taking her anywhere from sassy and sexy romances to dark and emotion-filled love stories.

Writing has always been a part of her life, penning her own life struggles as a form of therapy through poetry. She still stays true to her first love, poems, while weaving longer stories with strong heroines and honest heroes. She aims to get readers thinking about life and love while experiencing her characters 'journeys.

She is continuously creating stories as she daydreams. Her other loves are country music, exploring the outdoors, and reading.